XB

Please return/renew this item by the last date shown

**Herefordshire
Libraries**

**Herefordshire
Council**

MAKING NICE

Non-Fiction

The Theatre of Politics
The Subversive Family
The British Constitution Now
Communism (ed.)
Mind the Gap
Cold Cream
Full Circle
The New Few
The Tears of the Rajas
English Voices
Prime Movers
Kiss Myself Goodbye

Fiction

Tales of History and Imagination
Umbrella
Jem (and Sam)
The Condor's Head

A Chronicle of Modern Twilight
The Man Who Rode Ampersand
The Selkirk Strip
Of Love and Asthma
The Liquidator
Fairness
Heads You Win

Very Like a Whale
The Clique

MAKING NICE

Ferdinand Mount

BLOOMSBURY CONTINUUM
LONDON · OXFORD · NEW YORK · NEW DELHI · SYDNEY

BLOOMSBURY CONTINUUM
Bloomsbury Publishing Plc
50 Bedford Square, London, WC1B 3DP, UK
29 Earlsfort Terrace, Dublin 2, Ireland

BLOOMSBURY, BLOOMSBURY CONTINUUM and the Diana logo are
trademarks of Bloomsbury Publishing Plc

First published in Great Britain 2021

A catalogue record for this book is available from the British Library

Library of Congress Cataloguing-in-Publication data has been applied for

ISBN: HB: 978-1-4729-9287-1; TPB: 978-1-4729-9438-7;
eBook: 978-1-4729-9286-4; ePDF: 978-1-4729-9285-7

2 4 6 8 10 9 7 5 3 1

Typeset by Deanta Global Publishing Services, Chennai, India
Printed and bound in Great Britain by CPI Group (UK) Ltd, Croydon CR0 4YY

MIX
Paper from
responsible sources
FSC® C020471

To find out more about our authors and books visit www.bloomsbury.com
and sign up for our newsletters

'A Special Adviser works in a supporting role to the British government. With media, political or policy expertise, their duty is to assist and advise government ministers. They are often referred to as "SpAds" or "Spads".'

Wikipedia

'Into the street the Piper stept,
Smiling first a little smile,
As if he knew what magic slept
In his quiet pipe the while.'

Robert Browning, *The Pied Piper of Hamelin*

Contents

I

Champing

The rain had come in hard and late in the afternoon – as usual not forecast, you could never be sure of what would blow in next from the Irish Sea. We had pitched our tents close to the old stone wall at the top of the field, Flo and Lucy's in the corner, and ours just below them. They had hardly got the cards out to play piquet – I had managed to teach them the game, they didn't mind it being so old-fashioned – before it began to pelt, heavy sleety drops driven by the westerly gale. Then out of nowhere came the sound of a bugle, mournful, carried on the wind as though bringing news from some far-off battlefield.

I poked my head out of the tent and there in the middle of the field was the stumpy figure of Ivor blowing away at a tarnished old instrument with a red-and-white tassel dangling from it. Ivor was the campsite manager, or, as he styled himself, 'the Champion'. 'You're champing, see,' he said, gesturing at the forbidding bulk of St Dingle's Church the far side of the fence, 'so what you need is a Champion.' I hadn't even heard the word 'champing' before, until Jane was put on to it by Nella, an outdoorsy type in her oncology department. 'There are these redundant churches and they let them out to campers and you can bed down in the aisles. Of course, if it's a lovely starry night you sleep out in the field, but it's great to have the fallback and the rates are very reasonable.'

'Everybody in,' Ivor called, blowing the spit out of the bugle, 'and remember to take your tents down or they'll finish up in Bullslaughter Bay.'

'I didn't know you were a musician, Ivor, to add to your other talents.'

'I learned it in the TA. I play with Nerys's church choir.'

'In St Dingle's?'

'No, no, she's been deconsecrated for years, and we wouldn't get a licence because of the leaks. You're here strictly at your own risk.'

We shuffled across the already sodden field through the kissing gate into the church porch, about twenty or twenty-five of us, the site only half full this late in the season. It was deathly damp inside, the gloom scarcely reduced by the single hurricane lamp perched on the font. The churchly hush was broken by the splatter of raindrops falling in unseen corners of the gaunt Victorian pile (1866, architect J. P. Philipps of Carmarthen; encaustic tiles in memory of Ava, Lady Kidwelly, whose husband paid for the church; east window: St Dingle rescues three fishermen, in memory of the Hon. Trevor Kidwelly, k. at Jutland. St Dingle appears to be a purely mythical saint).

'There must be room for three hundred. How could they have ever hoped to fill it? We only saw about three cottages on the way here.' Jane shivered as she looked up at the damp-stained beams. I could see her thinking, what a ridiculous waste. It's not that she's indifferent to God, she hates Him – or she would if He existed. I was surprised in fact that she had agreed to go champing, but it was perhaps a sort of revenge to put these bare ruined choirs to some practical use after so many centuries of enforced delusion. In her position, I can't say I blame her. If I had to hand out death sentences to so many patients, I might be sceptical about Thy goodness and loving-kindness to all men. She is handsome, Jane. I love the way she looks, with such a classical profile, that alabaster skin and those grey-blue eyes – rather how I imagine the goddess Athena looking. But there is something severe about her, I can't deny it. She is not the first person I would choose to tell me that from now on it's palliative care only.

Flo had got the Primus stove going and Lucy was pricking the sausages, while I uncorked the Chilean Merlot. The half-dozen other parties were now encamped in little groups around the church. I waved at a young man with spiky hair whom I had queued behind for the toilets.

'It might be really nice to be a refugee in one of those camps like on TV,' Lucy said thoughtfully.

'Don't be silly, Lucy,' her elder sister snapped back.

'No, but having nothing and being with lots of other families in the same situation, it would be like a real community.'

'They haven't chosen to be in that situation. We could be nice and warm at home if we wanted to.'

But I could see what Lucy meant. It was peculiar, after all, that being in a camp could be the worst thing in the world or one of the most exhilarating experiences there was, according to some people anyway.

The light was fading in the church now, despite the two extra lamps Ivor brought in and placed on the lectern and the ledge of the pulpit. Their lights flickered across the stained-glass windows as the colour drained from them in the gathering blackness.

Nerys, as raven-haired as her husband but taller and with a beaky distinction that he lacked, had set up a tea urn and soon the steam was hissing down the aisle. 'It's our kind of champers,' Ivor said as he passed out the plastic mugs. 'Nothing's too good for our guests. Would you like a little music to go with it?'

'Music, Ivor, how lovely.'

They stood side by side on the chancel steps, Nerys leaning rather rakishly on the lectern, as Ivor in his scarlet fleece began to play the tune of 'Calon Lân' on his bugle. After he had finished the verse, Nerys began to sing unaccompanied. She had one of those contralto voices that takes you by surprise like nothing else.

Nid wy'n gefyn bywyd moethus,
Aur y byd na'l berlau mân:
Gofyn wyf am galon hapus,
Calon onest, calon lân.

'What's it mean?' I whispered to Jane, who was née Prys Thomas and has the Welsh.

'Oh, something like, I don't ask for a life of luxury, or gold or pearls, all I want is a pure heart, just a heart that's honest and pure.'

'My sentiments exactly,' I said. 'Funny, though, isn't it, that the Welsh don't seem to have their own word for honest?'

'Do shut up, Dickie,' she said and elbowed me in the ribs, which wasn't her style at all.

The applause echoed round the church and we demanded an encore – I don't remember what it was, another Welsh song anyway. Then we all went back to our supper.

But I was left with a feeling of utter sadness, one of those sudden dejections that startles you as Nerys's voice had. The church seemed so abandoned, not just by the Christian faith, but by all human hope. I wondered what a service of deconsecration was like, because I felt I was in the middle of one, a huge ongoing impalpable ceremony that was draining the sacred not only from this church but from everything on the whole planet.

The dejection didn't really lift even after supper when we played our usual family game of racing demon by the light of our own torches.

'Cheer up, Dad, it's only a game. We just happen to be quicker at it, that's all. *No*, Lucy, I was first.'

They were fifteen, almost sixteen, and fourteen now, but they still squabbled as they had when they were six and five, still pinched, needled and sly-kicked. Jane hated all that sort of thing, but then she had been an only child and didn't understand about sisters. She hadn't got on with her mother either. Mrs Prys Thomas had been embittered by her life married to a popular GP in a gloomy house looking slap into the hill in a small market town in mid-Wales. I felt that it might have been possible to tunnel through to her earlier on, but by the time I came along the tunnel had pretty much fallen in. There had been one time, though, when Jane had forgotten her birthday and sent me out at the last minute to get a present for her because she was tied up at the hospital, and all I could find was a blue-and-white enamel mug inscribed To The Best Mum In The World, and Jane was amazed to get a phone call in her office from her mother sobbing so hard she could scarcely get out her thank-you. After she died, nearly ten years ago now, the enamel mug became a precious memento for Jane, if you can have a memento of a relationship you wished you had had but hadn't. She had brought the mug with her on the champing holiday and now she held it carefully in both hands as Nerys poured her a coffee. Oddly, Nerys bore a slight resemblance to Mrs Prys Thomas, who had been a handsome woman and so a slight resemblance to Jane too. But how easily Nerys chatted, while I could see Jane struggling with the small talk, as she did in all human relations, even with Flo and Lucy, though she loved them both with a deep silent passion.

It had been a long day. We had driven the 250 miles from London without stopping, and the girls were already half asleep as they snuggled down in their sleeping bags. I vaguely hoped that drowsiness might throw a comfort blanket over my dejection, but it only muffled it so that my unhappiness seemed to come from somewhere a long way off but was no less ominous, more so if anything. The flickering hurricane lamps ought to have cast a cheering glow, but they only threw huge unfriendly shadows on the damp walls.

All the same, I must have fallen asleep in the end, because I woke to see first light coming in through the east window, bathing St Dingle's cloak in a rosy glow. I lifted my head to sniff the dank church air, and as I wriggled my shoulders out of my sleeping bag, I saw a slight figure standing with his back to me, in front of where the altar would have stood, a young man by the look of him. He was wearing some sort of hooded smock, pale grey or beige in the early light, and moss-green leggings down to his slender ankles. The hoodie and the shrunken shanks made you think of a cowled monk doing penance on a medieval rood screen.

The young man bowed to the non-existent altar several times, three or four times, I think. Then he stretched out his arms with the palms of his hands towards the altar, and brought them high above his head, where he held them still for a few seconds, like a diver about to jump, before bringing them down again, in a gesture of what seemed like deep reverence. Then he took a few steps back and prostrated himself slowly to the altar space. It was only as he lay there flat out on the brown-and-blue encaustic tiles that I realised he was the young man with spiky hair whom I had queued behind for the toilet. Even on that brief glimpse he was the last person I would have expected to go through such a ritual, least of all in a place that wasn't holy any more. What sort of ritual was it anyway? Not, I thought, the kind of ritual that priests had once practised here. Was it some sort of Eastern mystical exercise (weren't there a dozen different variants of yoga?).

The dawn was flooding in over St Dingle now, and gradually the champers began to struggle out of their cocoons and slope off to the toilets and the showers which Ivor had rigged up in the old vestry.

'Hullo again,' I said, as Spiky Hair skipped down the aisle towards me.

'Hi,' he said. 'I'm Ethel, short for Ethelbert,' stretching out his hand and shaking mine in a vigorous and prolonged grip as if he was doing it for the cameras.

'Ethel,' I echoed reflectively. 'I suppose they could have shortened it to Bert instead.'

'Oh, that would have been dead common,' he said, putting on a dead-common voice. His normal voice was warm with a metallic undertone which lent it authority without being in the least off-putting.

'Still, I can see that Ethelbert would have been a bit of a mouthful.'

'That was my father's weird idea. He was an Anglo-Saxon nut, thought everything went pear-shaped after the Norman Conquest. He was rector here when I was a boy, so it's great to be able to come back and actually kip in the old place.'

'Yes, that must be a very poignant experience,' and I couldn't resist adding, 'I saw you earlier, up at the altar.'

'Did you?' He wasn't at all embarrassed. 'It's a little ritual I devised myself, a blend of East and West really. Dad would turn in his grave if he saw it. He didn't like show-offs, so it was bad luck he got landed with me.' He spread out his arms in a MC's gesture of welcome to his audience. At first glance, you thought he had a merry, beaky sort of face, like a parrot's because of the spiky quiff, but his eyes were as stony as an Assyrian effigy's, of basalt or porphyry. When he smiled, which he did a lot, his smile didn't look put on exactly, more as though it was only a preliminary to some more demanding type of conversation.

'Jane, this is Ethel.'

'Hullo, Ethel,' she said without any hint of surprise.

'Your husband has been watching my morning ritual.'

'Has he? He is rather nosy. He's a journalist, you know.'

This isn't quite how I like to present myself, but it gives a fair idea of what Jane thinks of my trade.

'Dickie Pentecost,' I said, realising that I hadn't introduced myself.

'Not D. K. Pentecost?' He fixed his basalt eyes on me. 'I read all your stuff.'

It is not out of modesty, false or otherwise, that I must record that in twenty-odd years in the game this was the first time that anyone had ever recognised my name. That is partly because my pieces often appear under the byline 'from our diplomatic correspondent', but also because not many people read my paper and even fewer read that bit of it.

'Originally Pentecostas, am I right? Left Smyrna in 1922 – not you of course obviously but your dad perhaps?'

'Yes, how on earth –'

'It must have been a terrible business, that burning out the Greeks and the thousands of refugees on the quayside with nothing more than what they stood up in.' I was amazed to hear Ethel recount these appalling events which my father had never quite recovered from, which gave him nightmares all his life and which he buried under the carapace of the most English Englishman you ever saw (in which respect I am very like him). Nobody else in this country seemed to have heard of the Greek expulsions at the end of a war which they also hadn't heard of. Yet the facts seemed to come effortlessly to our new friend. He trotted them out as though doing his special subject on *Mastermind*.

The girls came up behind us, still shrouding themselves in their sleeping bags to keep out the chilly damp.

'Flo, Lucy, this is Ethel. He seems to know everything about our family.'

'*Ethel*, really?' Flo giggled and Lucy giggled along with her.

The boy – I suppose he must have been twenty-two or twenty-three – nodded and looked at the girls gravely, as though daring them to contradict him – no, perhaps not gravely, that makes him sound solemn which he didn't seem to be at all. It was just that there was no expression in those grey basalt eyes. You could no more guess his real mood than you could the mood of an Assyrian effigy.

'Do you like being called Ethel?' Lucy, always the more direct of the two, asked when she had recovered from her giggles.

'It's my name, I didn't choose it.'

'You could have changed it. There's a girl in my class who was called Susan and she changed it to Natasha.'

'What would you like me to change it to?'

'Well, I like Freddy. I know two Freddys and they're really nice.'

'I might not be such a nice Freddy.'

'Then we could call you Nasty Freddy so you wouldn't get mixed up with the others.'

'Girls, I think it's time for breakfast.'

I could see that Jane was becoming uneasy. Lucy had a way of getting stuck into a conversation and not letting go. Sometimes she seemed so obsessive that Jane wondered whether she might be at the lower end of the autism spectrum, but I thought her way of engaging had a certain enchanting quality and that if she was not exactly like other girls, there was nothing wrong with that. All the same, I did become anxious myself when her little kittenish features began to stiffen into a stary, almost doll-like face.

'Well then, goodbye, Flo, goodbye, Lucy, have a lucky day. I think the sun's going to stay out for you.'

'Goodbye, Nasty Freddy.'

He strolled off towards the vestry, his sandals slapping on the tiles, but not before he had managed to give separate smiles to each of us.

Later on, we walked along the cliff towards Dingle Point, hoping to hear the croak of the chough or catch the last of the guillemots before they headed off over the sea for the summer. As Ethel had predicted, the sun kept dancing along the milky blue sea, and we had to shade our eyes to look for the seabirds.

But the first thing we saw was Ethel in his canvas smock – in the noon light it was a creamy oatmeal colour – his sticking-up hair gleaming in the sun. He was bent over a camera on a tripod, which he was angling towards the highest crag in front of us.

'There, do you see, on the top rock, the one with the orange gash on its side? It's a peregrine – the fastest living creature on the planet.'

'Really? Faster than a cheetah or an antelope?'

'Or a dolphin?'

'Much faster. It's been timed at 217 mph when it's stooping. It sounds like a jet engine when it goes past you.'

'Stooping doesn't sound like going very fast.'

'Stooping means diving down on its prey.' He mimicked the falcon's dive with his hands so violently that Lucy jumped back. 'If it hit you, it would probably kill you.'

They both stared at him, bewitched by the information he was unloading. He didn't put on the excited tone that nature broadcasters adopt to hold the viewer's interest. On the contrary, it was his offhand delivery that had them enraptured. He invited the girls to have a look through his telescopic sights and they wanted to know how many times it was magnified and he told them, plus other technical details which weren't their normal kind of thing. As he moved the tripod a few yards along the path to get a better angle, they danced beside him, shouting 'Ethel, Ethel'. I could see the peregrine now, perched in a cleft just below the top of the crag. How small it looked. Never grew larger than nineteen inches, Ethel said. They had been nearly wiped out by the pesticides in the birds they fed on, but since the pesticides were banned, they had made quite a comeback.

An odd feeling towards him came over me, not of warmth exactly, in fact there was something irritating about the calm way he dispensed information as though he had a special licence not to be interrupted. It was more as if we had known him a long time, as though he had always been part of our lives. Yet how strange he looked in the bright midday light, with his beaky face and sticking-up cider-coloured hair and his mouth half-open even when he wasn't talking, as though about to answer a question you hadn't yet put.

'When can we see Ethel again?'
'Can we see him tonight?'
'I think he said he was off to somewhere in Snowdonia this afternoon.'

I had questions too. Where had he come from? Was he on his own? Did he have a campervan, or what? He didn't pass on any personal details in the way that people you met camping usually did. I continued to think of him as I had first seen him properly, performing his devotions in front of the altar that wasn't an altar as the dawn came in over St Dingle's shoulder: a pilgrim loner, unattached, going who knew where. Pilgrim, peregrine, weren't they the same word, wanderers on the face of the earth, outsiders looking down from a great height?

As we clambered over the stile into the next field, I paused with my legs on both sides and looked back. There he was, in the middle distance now, pedalling away from us on one of those old-style tradesman's bikes with an iron carrier, with his tripod sticking up out of the flapping canvas bag, the cowl of his cream-coloured hoodie blowing behind him.

I could see how disappointed the girls were to see him go. In fact, they went on missing him for the rest of our stay. I had pre-planned quite a few excursions – a boat trip to Gerald's Island, the shell collecting on the limestone beach (not as good as the Jurassic coast but still marvellous if you had never stumbled on an ammonite before). Flo and Lucy certainly seemed to enjoy them, but I couldn't help feeling there would have been more spark to them if Ethel had been there. Jane said, 'Don't be ridiculous, they only met him for five minutes.' But she didn't sound convinced. Anyway she was fussing about having lost her mother's blue-and-white enamel mug, the one inscribed To The Best Mum In The World. I said she might have left it on the beach, and we could leave a message with the lifeguards, but nothing turned up. It was strange that the one thing she really treasured should have gone missing, and she was not one to drop things or forget where she had put them.

The final evening of our stay, Ivor had promised us another music show, this time with a mystery guest star.

'Who is it, Ivor?'

'Wouldn't be a mystery if I told you, would it?

This time, after the farewell fish pie generously provided by Nerys, Ivor sat down at the piano by the font, and Nerys sang us a medley of old favourites, 'Down by the Salley Gardens', 'Blow the Wind Southerly' and, by request, 'Calon Lân' again. Then Ivor stood up from the piano stool and spread his hands to still the applause.

'And now by special invitation …'

There was a flash and a bang and an explosion of sparkles by the font, and there was Ethel in a swirly cloak with stars on it and a curly hat like an empty beech nut. In his hand, he had a gleaming flute, and without a word of introduction he launched into a bewitching solo, full of trills and dying falls and seductive slides, melancholy but somehow cheerful too like all the best sad tunes. I had no idea what it was, I didn't really want to know either, it would break the spell.

'You see,' Lucy whispered to me, 'I knew he'd come back.'

But had he ever gone away? Had he been lurking all the time somewhere on the campsite or down in the village, waiting to make this dramatic entrance on the last night? Just as we hadn't a clue where he was sleeping when he appeared to be champing with the rest of us, so now his status seemed even more shadowy. Was he perhaps a regular helper at St Dingle's, a friend of the project who came every summer? Was he even the manager, in effect Ivor's controller? Well, we weren't going to have a chance to find out, because he played one more tune and then, before we had finished clapping, boom, the church lights went out, and when they came back on again, in about twenty seconds, he was gone, this time for good.

2

Smiley Face

'I know you're still on holiday, but would you mind popping into the office any time tomorrow? – MM.' Never good news; that kind of summons, especially when it came from Maurice Mackintosh, or Tosh as he was unaffectionately known. Tosh added a grim sanctimony to the unlovely mien of the average managing editor, somehow conveying that he operated on a higher moral plane than the rest of us, coming as he did from a long line of Scots Presbyterians, although he had in fact been raised in Dorking where his father was the leading turf accountant. He gave off the air of being teetotal, although we knew he kept a half-bottle of Bell's in his top right-hand drawer.

'You know I don't like to fuck about, Dickie.'

'No, Tosh.'

He drew his purple lips from his teeth in his strange trademark snarl, designed I think to show friendliness, a mannerism much imitated in the office, though never with the full alarming effect of the original.

'We are, as you know, Dickie, reshaping our editorial capacity. We have to be facing outward to the digital age. The old-fashioned "usual channels" just don't cut it any more. I mean, who needs diplomatic briefings on Chatham House Terms when it's all out on social media and the Foreign Secretary himself is tweeting like a bloody blue tit?'

I nodded assent to this incisive analysis. In truth, I had been having my own doubts every time we trooped in for the 11 a.m. briefing from the head of the News Department who could only repeat in more muffled, and decidedly less picturesque, terms what his lord and master had spewed out on Twitter over breakfast. *Par exemple*: 'The Foreign Secretary has taken note of the latest *démarche* from the President but is not yet minded to pursue the easing of sanctions in the present climate.' It being two hours earlier that the FS had tapped out to the world his 140 characters to the effect that if Assad thought he was going to screw us this time, he had another thing coming.

My mind had already begun to drift, which it tends to as a defence mechanism against bad news, so I only switched back on halfway through Tosh's denouement.

'... so going forward, we cannot visualise an appropriate space for a diplomatic correspondent in our new configuration. We had of course given careful thought to how we might deploy your talents in some other department, but you know, Dickie, we just couldn't conceptualise a new role for you which would make proper use of what you bring to the table, because, quite frankly and there's no sense wrapping this one up, Dickie, what you have is what a modern forward-facing paper like ours doesn't need any more.'

He leaned forward and unleashed the snarl, though he seemed a little off-put by what I knew must be the vacant look on my face.

'I hope I have made myself clear, Dickie. It's only fair to let you know our thinking in depth.'

'You have, Tosh, crystal clear.'

'It's six months redundo, of course, which I'm sure you will agree is pretty reasonable in the circumstances, and, oh, if you wouldn't mind clearing your desk by close of play, because we've got a new troubleshooter from IT coming in tomorrow.'

There were a couple of capacious orange bags labelled Office Waste Only already sitting by my desk. HR thought of everything. I toyed briefly with the idea of sitting inside one of the bags myself and asking Front Desk to come up and collect me. My larky old mate Simon Redditch, the security correspondent, would have been up for a gag like that, but my spirit was broken.

'This is terrible news, the worst.' At that moment, spot on cue, Redditch sidled up to my desk. In the nicest possible way, he was the Office Vulture. He was always first on any scene of carnage: a stand-up row with the News Editor, a girl on the Diary in tears because the Diary Editor had dumped her and she was pregnant, there he would be, hovering by the glass partition, spectacles twinkling, a smile of sympathy and, it had to be admitted, relish breaking out on his face, which wasn't reddish at all but had a Balkan pallor – he was né Redič with an accent on the c, from Zagreb or Bratislava, I forget which. He had this liquid, sibilant voice which you couldn't forget – 'my Balkan brogue', he called it – and it gave you the feeling that he was letting you in on an exclusive, even when he was only telling you the weather forecast. We're both greasy foreigners, he liked to say to me, to which I would reply, speak for yourself, I'm public-school-educated. A rather minor public school, he would riposte. Si was the paper's specialist in spooks and international skulduggery, but this never seemed to affect his sunny nature.

'It's all part of management's latest mass purge, I suppose.'

'If only,' he twinkled back. 'This one is strictly personal, I'm afraid.'

'You mean I'm the only one?'

'Yup. Tosh has been looking for an opening to let you go, and the reconfiguration of the features desk was perfect.'

He gave his imitation of the Tosh snarl, which as I say didn't come close to the malevolence of the real thing.

'But I'm always so extra polite to him, because I know how prickly he is.'

'That's just it. He thinks you're condescending. I'm not sure he didn't use the word "effete". Part of the long-haired public-school brigade, though not of course long-haired in your case.' He gazed fondly at the frizzy tonsure that girdled my scalp, in his words like a monk with a perm. 'If I were you,' he added ruminatively, 'I'd go and grab a nice billet in PR, that's the only place they value talent these days. This place has totally had it.' He surveyed the row of our colleagues staring glumly at their screens. Coming through the glass doors beyond them, I could see a couple of men in overalls pushing ahead of them some hefty new office furniture still in its wrapping.

'The shape of the future, no doubt,' Si gestured. 'Ah well, I must go and file and my piece on the latest mole in the Washington Embassy, before they tell us it's all cobblers.'

There wasn't really much to put in the bags – office diaries for the past five years, a few photographs from old conferences, me arm in arm with the Turkish Minister of Information (now in jail), me in front of the Colosseum with a pretty girl from Agence France-Presse who thought I was flirting with her but it was only my fractured French, a sheaf of other people's business cards which I'd never followed up, a small hip flask in the shape of a rugger ball, oh, and the MS of the first chapter of my little book on the EU in the twenty-first century, the first chapter being all there was. I filled the bag with this stuff. I only needed one bag, though it was quite heavy to lug downstairs, not to mention the weight of the inexpressible melancholy I was also carrying.

It was not unusual of course for someone to be sacked out of the blue, and on his or her own, but these days there was safety in numbers, for the company at least. To make it lawyer-proof, management could argue that this redundancy was a necessary part of a larger restructuring and so did not need to explain exactly how you had disappointed them. Simon was probably right about Tosh's motives. Personal malevolence was never to be underestimated in office politics or anywhere else.

As I stood under leaden skies at the corner of Victoria Street waiting for the Uber, the deep sadness of the unwanted flooded over me. I became conscious of the contrast between my quite new midnight-blue suit with knotted blue silk tie (polished shoes too) and the grubby orange bag rustling at my calf. I fancied that anyone passing by could guess my situation in a flash, with a shiver of gratitude that they weren't yet in the same boat. I wished I'd sent a courier for the bag, but then I am economical by nature and this did not seem like a moment to splash out.

I had thought of preparing Jane for the bad news before I left the office, but it would be terrible if I broke down and someone in the next pod overheard, while texting seemed too abrupt and going into the gents to make the call too furtive. Still, I was dreading the ordeal, as I lugged the bag out of the taxi up the steps where it got tangled with the prickly shrub whose name I could never remember. As I did so, I noticed an old-fashioned tradesman's bike propped against the railings.

To my surprise I heard a man's voice, a light tenor, in the sitting room and then a girl laughing, I wasn't sure whether it was Flo or Lucy, and then unmistakably it was Jane, with her clear, precise way of talking which always sounded like someone giving you instructions and quite often was.

'Oh, it's you. You *are* early.'

'Yes, well …'

'Isn't it wonderful, darling? *Look.*'

I scarcely took in what she was saying because I was still goggling at the sight of Ethel standing there with that weird grin of his, puckish you might think at first but not really puckish because of those stony basalt eyes which seemed not to move with the rest of his face. It was chilly-damp outside, early-November weather, and the leaves tawny yellow on the sodden pavements (and not too warm in our sitting room either, we were economical about the heating too), but Ethel was still in his champing outfit, the creamy oatmeal hoodie and the mossy leggings, which must be his kit for all the year round. Perhaps like Puck, in the sense that Puck could circle the globe in, was it thirty, forty minutes, and would never have time to change his clothes, would be indifferent to climate shifts that made mortals sweat or shiver, probably didn't sweat or shiver at all himself and in his line of business had to be just as indifferent to shifts of emotion too.

My startled gaze swerved in response to Jane's command, and I took a look at what she was holding in her long white fingers, viz., the precious blue-and-white enamel mug her mother had left her, which she had lost when we were champing.

'Ethel found it in the brambles where our tent had been, apparently.'

'You're a genius, Ethel,' I said, 'and it's lovely to see you again. But how on earth did you find us?'

'Oh, it wasn't a problem, the address was in Ivor's register. Sorry to drop in without warning, but I couldn't wait to get it back to you, because I knew how much it meant.'

I hadn't remembered telling the story of the cup when Ethel was around, but perhaps Jane had told him when I was out shopping in the village.

'So what's your news then, Dickie? It's so great to see you all.'

If I had thought about it at all, which I hadn't because I was in such a state, Ethel would have been the last person I would have wanted to confide my humiliation to, but somehow it seemed inevitable that he should be the first.

'They've just given me the boot,' I said. 'My finely honed skill set is apparently surplus to requirements.'

'Oh *no*, it's not true.' I can't quite describe the way Jane shrieked out the words, so unlike the calm, measured way she spoke, not just in normal circumstances but in any circs I could recall in our life together. You might call it operatic, in the sense that if you don't like opera you think the soprano's lament is absurdly overdone. But this was genuine, I knew that, and she threw herself into my arms, which again wasn't like her at all. She was no longer the imperturbable oncologist, rather the patient's hysterical wife. Even in that moment, I remember thinking how peculiar it was that it should take my misfortune to uncover the depth of her love.

When she had stopped sobbing, I told them the story of my interview with Tosh, and also about how Simon had said it was because of a personal grudge.

'That's really bad.' Ethel came forward and clasped my hands in his pale slender fingers. There was something priestly about the gesture, and I thought of his ritual prostrations in front of the non-altar at St Dingle's. We stayed clasped like that for a few seconds, and I have to confess that the clasp was unexpectedly comforting.

Then, as if that wasn't enough, I heard a sound that I thought I knew all too well – an obscure, convulsive noise halfway between a cough and a sob, which came and went with a couple of seconds in between. We have a cat, Hunter (named by Jane after the famous surgeon, nothing to do with his prowling after mice), and this was the noise of Hunter being sick, and I thought this was all I needed, except that then I realised it wasn't the cat, because there was Hunter curled up on the sofa in front of me. What it was turned out to be Lucy sobbing into her mother's mauve wool skirt, which was why her sobs were muffled, as they were also by her elder sister nuzzling up against her and rubbing her back up and down in that modern gesture of comfort which usually annoys me when I see other people doing it, but which seemed to me poignant when Flo did it. I thought how weird we must look, the five of us frozen in these postures of grief as in a baroque altarpiece of some much more profound scene of bereavement, the Crucifixion perhaps or the Pietà, when all I had been bereaved of was a not very good job on a not very good newspaper, neither of which would soon exist if present trends continued. We had not thought to mourn like this when Gwen Prys Thomas died, though the girls were only babies then. So far as I could remember, this was the first show of grief we had shared as a family, and the thought broke me up, not that I wasn't shattered already.

'Smiley face, Dad,' Flo said, turning from her massage to look at my crumpled features.

'Smiley face,' I repeated, stretching my lips into the rictus of a smile, which probably came out looking more like Tosh's snarl.

'Although,' Ethel said, releasing my hands and rubbing his own together as if to recharge the electrical energy he had expended on me, 'there's a lot to be said for giving your emotions some airtime.'

'Let it all hang out, you mean?'

'Yes,' Ethel continued, unfazed by my invisible quote marks of derision. 'Not just space for the grief but for the rage too. I'm assuming that you're really angry and not very deep down either. So the best thing is to write HR a really rude letter to start with, and then keep texting them, while you hire a lawyer to write a lawyer's letter, just one letter because they charge a bomb, and you'll get another 20 per cent on the comp, I guarantee. Dignified silence is the worst possible policy. That's just what HR trade on.'

'Who's HR?' Flo asked brightly.

'Human resources. They're the people who are supposed to look after you when you're sacked.'

He spoke very gently, not at all in a patronising way, and when she said, what a funny name for a department which sacked people, he said, yes it was, but it was meant to sound nice.

I went to make some tea, pondering how odd it was that Ethel seemed to have installed himself as my personal HR department. But then it was odd that he was here at all, and that he should have found the blue-and-white mug in the first place.

When I came back with the tea tray, Lucy had obviously not fully recovered, because she was sitting on the sofa with Ethel, and he had his arm round her and was talking to her the way people talk to horses to quieten them.

Then he started talking to Jane, saying how interested he was in the genetic origins of cancer and he'd love to come and pick her brains because he knew it was her special subject, though I don't know how he knew that. And Jane said, oh, that would be nice, obviously not thinking about it, because she was still so concerned about Lucy, who I could hear saying through her sobs how awful it was and how Dad would never get another job and Ethel saying, don't worry, people change jobs all the time and Dad would have half a dozen offers tomorrow. This wasn't true of course, but he made me half believe it.

'Thank you,' I said as he got up to take a cup of tea.

'Don't thank me. It's just so great to see you all again, I'm only sorry about the circumstances. Actually, as it happens, I might have one or two ideas.'

'Ideas about what?'

'About what you might do next. There's a whole lot of possibilities out there if you only know where to start looking.'

He gave me his beaky smile, and he suddenly looked much older, almost at will, as though switching to whatever the appropriate age setting for careers adviser might be. Was he nearer thirty than twenty, or older than that, even?

Then, quite quickly, but without any sort of hurry, he was gone, like a doctor whose house call is finished. As soon as he left the house, Lucy quietened down. But his absence left a void.

'When will we see Ethel again?'

'Soon, I'm sure.'

'But how can we see him if we haven't got his email or his mobile or anything?'

'Oh, he'll find us again.'

Anyway I wasn't going to run after him, even if I had known where to run. Besides, I had the farewell drinks to organise. The only place I could think of was the Foreign Legion, a club of noxious gloom up three flights of stairs in Notting Hill. The Legion had started out as a watering hole for overseas correspondents and real or pretend spooks, though in no time it had been colonised by the usual spillover from advertising and publishing, so that the tradecraft you tended to hear was more about the double-crossing of literary agents than the other sort.

On the floors below, there were rather smarter private dining rooms serviced by the restaurant on the ground floor with a chef who had once had a TV programme. As I trotted up the grubby stairs that same evening, I peered in at a half-open door, attracted by the laughter coming from one of the dining rooms. Inside, I could see an imposing bald man in a dinner jacket reading from some kind of script and around him several girls in slinky black dresses laughing their heads off and flashing a lot of lipstick. Then just visible in the corner, still in his oatmeal hoodie, I spotted Ethel, looking quizzical and good-humoured, but not actually laughing, somehow conveying in this brief glimpse that laughing was not part of his job description that evening. I knew the bald man, though, by reputation anyway. He was famous for his public badinage. I think it was he who said, 'I'm the poor man's Clive James and so is Clive James.' Anyway, Ethel wasn't laughing.

3

Hi-Vis

I got filthy drunk that night – well, you are expected
to at these dos – and fell asleep – passed out would be
a more accurate description – in the cab on the way
home (Jane had said that nothing on earth would drag
her to a party like that, if you could call it a party).
In the morning I felt wretched as I have never felt
wretched. And wretched was how I went on feeling for
the next few weeks, too drained to put out any feelers
for pastures new, unable to focus on where I was and
what I could possibly hope to do next. I went for long
walks round the Common, watched the herons flop
into their high nests and the derelicts on community
service in their hi-vis jackets sweeping up the leaves
and clearing sticks out of the little stream that led into
the pond – at least they had an occupation.

What I did manage to do was to get an employment
lawyer to write a sharp letter to HR. To my delight I got
a letter back within the week to say that on reflection
and in consideration of my years of valuable service,
the company had decided to increase my comp by
20 per cent, exactly the figure that Ethel had forecast.
That was something, quite a large something, £12,000
in fact. But at the same time, even this *bonne bouche*

brought home the finality of the pay-off. I thought of seamen in the old days, perhaps nowadays too, being paid off at the end of a voyage lasting months, even years, and there they suddenly were, ashore and adrift, trying to find their land legs on the slippery cobbles of the quayside. That was me.

But there was one thing to look forward to, something I had been looking forward to for weeks. Flo had always been agile, much stronger too than her slender limbs suggested, and she had always loved dancing, from nursery school onwards. In her teens she had become a dark and elegant girl with a proud neck and a classical profile, rather like one of Picasso's models, and like her mother and grandmother too. Flo went twice a week after school to the Beaumont Academy of Dance, housed in a grim warehouse north of Oxford Street and presided over by Madame Dubarry who had danced for Marie Rambert and in her seventies danced still with her pupils in a primrose leotard, her white curls tucked under a matching primrose bandeau. It was a struggle now to keep the Beau going. Pupil numbers kept dropping, and some of the parents had trouble paying the modest fees, which in any case were hardly enough to cover the ever-steepling rent, but Madame never looked like surrendering, her posture still as superb as when she had danced her first solo role in a production of *Giselle.*

What we were seeing at the Beau was what Madame called the *fête de Noël,* but known more irreverently as the Passing Out Parade, at which the little swans and sugar plum fairies danced their hearts out in front of parents and friends. Candles shimmered in the tall windows and the cavernous high-beamed ceiling made the dancers look even more fragile and faery. At the end of the show, Flo and her on–off friend Eloise did a double act, from a ballet I hadn't heard of called *Les Filles Perdues*. They were two sisters feeling their way through an imaginary forest, their pale hands parting the branches, their heads questing forwards as their slender legs skipped over fallen logs, represented by other girls reclining with their heads propped on their hands, and then they launched into a run of *jetés* across the stage until they finally broke out of the wood and finished with a joyous *pas de deux*, heads thrown back to revel in the sunlight, palms spread out to the sky. Behind them, the other girls and a few boys in woodcutter shorts swayed in time with the music, their twig-like arms waving in unison above their heads to show the forest moving in the wind.

'She has real quality, I think, your daughter.' Madame still had a touch of Merseyside in her voice (she was born Marion Barry from Birkenhead, Liverpool Irish and proud of it). 'Oh here she is. *Pas mal*, my dear. *Pas mal du tout*.'

Flo was still out of breath as she skipped up to us, her pale cheeks flushed with the dancing. My spirits soared as I held her, her bright eyes brimming with happiness.

'Is Ethel here? He said he'd try to come.'

'Ethel?'

'Yes, he texted me. It would have been so cool if he'd come. He said he couldn't wait to see me dance.'

'No, no, we haven't seen him,' I said.

'Well, I suppose it's kind of him to take an interest,' Jane said defensively, as though trying to convince herself, after Flo had run off to get changed. I wondered how he had got her mobile number. The whole thing made me think again, though there was not much logic in thinking it, that he must be much older than we had thought when we first met him, twice her age perhaps – though even to use that phrase was to imply that I thought he was after her, and I could see Jane was thinking the same thing, though she didn't say anything more. Instead, we got up out of our seats and mingled with a couple of the other parents we had got to know at pickup, both of us trying to still the slow thumping of our hearts.

'Should I say something?' Jane said just before we turned the lights out.

'What could you say? You don't *know*, it could be just a friendly gesture. In any case, it was a gesture that didn't actually happen, which suggests that it wasn't a very serious gesture in the first place.'

'And she'd be so scornful,' Jane said, half agreeing. 'All the same, don't you think I ought to warn her somehow?'

'About what exactly? About men in general, or about Ethel? Look, all he did was say how he'd like to see her dance.'

'But how did he get her mobile number?'

Somehow getting hold of Flo's number seemed worse than saying how he'd like to see her dance. Or rather, it was the two things together. But what to say and when to say it eluded us, so we said nothing, and prayed that we were imagining it all and that the whole thing would blow over.

'I don't think we've recruited anyone from your neck of the woods before.' The Financial Editor had rather fine features, but you wouldn't call them chiselled exactly, more as though he had been sculpted in butter. His voice had an urgent, confidential quality, which made you think he was giving you some heavy piece of advice, like a sports coach muttering to one of his team going out to bat or trotting onto the field from the subs bench, even though at the moment he was merely showing me into his office. 'As I'm sure you know, what we trade on here is Authority. You might say it's our USP. Our report won't necessarily have any sensational details in it – we aren't thinking about beating the so-called competition – but it will be multiply sourced from the sources that count. Of course it's possible to work up one's contacts over time, but I have to say that we appreciate someone who comes here with his or her contacts book pretty full already. And I have to ask whether someone with your background would be quite the right fit for us.' He could not have said more plainly that all these years I had been wasting what talents I might have on a shoddy rag, and what they were really looking for was a bright young thing fresh from the Lex Column.

Si Redditch had fixed me up with the interview, but he had warned me that the Financial Editor was notorious for his gravitas. I resolved in that instant that if there were to be any question of a job here, which there clearly wasn't, I would have to be drugged silly before I said Yes and then dragged there in irons. No, it was more than that. The whole interview had stirred from my depths a long-suppressed loathing of respectability, a revulsion against always doing the right thing. It was blazingly clear that whatever I was going to do next, it wouldn't be this or anything like it. Perhaps it would be nothing at all. Nothing at all sounded good to me. I thought with affection of Quinny Tearle who had thrown it all up, not that there was much to throw, and gone to live in somebody's lodge – more like a henhouse really – from which he dispensed racing tips online to a small and decreasing band of followers. Or Harry Warre-Jones who lived in a meticulous attic opposite the British Museum and who survived on the compensation he got from being run over and partially crippled by an American tourist driving on the wrong side of the road. When asked what he did, W-J would say he was cataloguing the museum's pre-Islamic tomb inscriptions but only till the pubs opened. Indolence in such guises now called to me too. I hankered for a parking permit in the land in which it seemed always afternoon. Jane, I thought with sudden brutality, could carry on with the day job. But like everything else in life, I reasoned, lotus-eating required a degree of practice, of training even. On recent visits to Quinny and W-J – both weirdly enjoyable – I had been struck by how carefully they spaced out their days and how curiously busy they seemed. Was I too capable of winding down for good, of enrolling in a life of serious idleness?

Probably not, but in the event I was never to find out because something happened three days after my interview with the butter-faced Financial Editor, which of course ended in zilch – 'I much enjoyed our meeting, but we' – ah, the dear old evasive we – 'have with regret come to the conclusion that …' and so on. And his butter features and confiding voice slipped out of my memory.

We hadn't been thinking much about Lucy, Jane and I. All our anxieties were tied to Flo, who was alternately snappy and taciturn, neither being at all like her. She could see that we were trying to keep an eye on her contacts while trying not to look as if we were. Not that we had a hope. Where would the Barretts of Wimpole Street have been if their daughter had owned a smartphone? But not wanting to look as if we were spying meant we really hadn't a clue where she was half the time, which made us fret twice as much.

Although she was so direct, most of the time Lucy was the quieter of the two, except when she got the giggles and couldn't stop and her face flushed and froze simultaneously, and you couldn't help worrying that something was wrong with her. Jane, oddly, was reluctant to take her to the doctor – after all she was a doctor herself. Instead, she trawled the medical literature, but couldn't find any illness which had symptoms like Lucy's, except something called Coltman syndrome which was extremely rare but probably linked to petit mal, the lesser form of epilepsy. But Jane was convinced she didn't have that because she didn't do the sudden staring into space.

Except that now she did. They were quite brief, these staring episodes, no more than ten or fifteen seconds. Mrs Skeaping, the Year Ten form teacher, was the first to notice them, which made us feel bad that we hadn't, but apparently the teacher is often the first to notice, I suppose because she is always on the lookout for any pupil not paying attention, and Mrs Skeaping was a stickler. Jane was especially upset that she hadn't noticed, because noticing things is her speciality as an oncologist. She once said she wished she were a sniffer dog, she'd be so much better at her job.

'Oh, it's curable of course,' she said in between her own convulsive sobs, then correcting herself with something like a return to professional calm, 'or at least controllable, two-thirds of children grow out of it before they turn twenty.'

'And the ones who don't?'

'They go on taking the drugs, there's dozens of drugs, you just have to find out by trial and error which one works best.'

She had her reassuring voice on, but I felt she was trying to reassure herself as well as me. I knew so little on the subject beyond what she told me and what I could call up online, but I soon gathered that this was one of those illnesses that tortured you with its subtle and violent variations, from relatively harmless, even comic episodes to terrifying lurches with frenetic jerks and blackouts, all of which could happen at any moment, with potential life-threatening consequences when swimming, say, or crossing the road.

The next thing that happened was that Jane announced without a moment's hesitation that she was giving up her job and staying at home to keep her eye on Lucy and to finish her abandoned thesis on hereditary influences in cancer.

'But surely, I don't want to sound callous, but Luce will still be at school all day.'

'I don't want to be the sort of mother who has to be called home from work when her daughter has an episode in the playground.'

There was no arguing with that, and I loved her for it and liked to think that I'd have done the same if I'd been in her position. And when I saw Lucy coming into the sitting room with her fair little face scrunched up with misery and terror, I knew this was the only answer.

So a month ago, we had been a healthy two-income family with an SUV in the garage and two foreign holidays a year. Now we were a no-income family with one sick daughter and the other having tantrums. The only thing that was clear on the narrowing horizon was that I had to find a job, and soon.

I walked out into the dank January air to pursue my endeavours on the park bench, already dialling up a couple of implausible contacts as I strode through the laurel bushes towards the pond. But when I sat down, instead of tapping in the last of the numbers that Si Redditch had thought of, I just switched off and tried to catch my breath, letting my gaze wander out over the ducks skittering on the broken ice and the Filipina bending down to put the brake on the old lady's wheelchair and the sycamores beyond the pond shivering in the cold light breeze.

'I thought I'd find you here.'

Ethel sat down beside me, as naturally as if he were keeping a long-arranged rendezvous.

'Oh, Ethel, what brings you here?' I said, trying to deny him the satisfaction of hearing any surprise in my voice.

'I heard about Lucy, and I wanted to come and see if there was any way I could help. It must be a ghastly shock, but you don't need to worry, I promise you. Depakote is the answer, reduces both severity and frequency in 70 per cent of cases, maybe more.'

'How did you hear? We've only just been told ourselves.'

He ignored my question and swept on. 'I didn't think there'd be much doubt about the general diagnosis, although I expect she'll need a brain scan to establish her exact place on the spectrum.'

As a concession to the cold, he had a high-collared anorak wrapped around him, like a parrot ruffling up his feathers to keep warm. Still wearing the mossy leggings, though.

'Well, that's a comfort if it's true,' I said, failing to keep the annoyance out of my voice, being further annoyed when one of the community service lags in his hi-vis jacket poked under our bench with his long broom to hoick out a plastic coffee cup.

'Oh, hi, Denis,' Ethel said cheerfully. 'You still doing the hours then?'

'Oh, Johnny, hi. Yes, only another fifteen to go. Nice to see you, to see you nice.' His stubbled face broke out into a toothy grin. 'How's it going in the office?'

'Great, Denis, fabulous in fact. We miss you.'

'You watch out, I'll be back stirring it up after my little holiday.'

'Counting the hours, Denis, counting the hours.'

Ethel got up and they exchanged fist bumps before Denis shoved his broom back on his cart and trudged off round the pond.

'Johnny?'

He looked at me in surprise. 'You didn't think I was really called Ethel, did you? I just tried it on for a laugh to see if anyone would swallow it, and now I'm lumbered with it because of you lot.'

'Not Ethelbert then? And your father who was vicar at St Dingle's for however many years?'

'Oh yes.' Ethel sighed, seeming to summon up the recollection from some distant synapse. 'Yes, I'd forgotten that. It would be nice to be a vicar's son, don't you think? Gives you so much to rebel against.'

'And that man – Denis – where had you met him before?'

'Denis? Nice guy. He was with us for quite a while. Got caught downloading paedo porn on the office computer. If he thinks he's coming back, he really has got another thing coming.' He paused and switched into softer mode. 'I'm sorry I called by when I did. It wasn't exactly great timing.'

'Well, it was nice to see you again. The girls were really pleased.'

'Great girls, lovely girls. But how about yourself? Got your next move sorted by now, I expect.'

'Not exactly. In fact, no, not at all.'

'Because if you're still looking for something, I do have a thought.'

He cocked his parrot head towards me, like a parrot who has just spotted a juicy berry.

'Really?' I said, unable to keep the *froideur* out of my voice. Any sort of salvation from this unreliable figure with his bony knees visible through his green leggings seemed the longest of shots.

'You see, we're just starting to expand our Reputation Management arm. We have several high-net worthies lined up with serious money; they're looking to move into the UK, not major players yet but with real potential. The thing is, they've got no public profile, they've had their noses stuck in their screens and they need to get out more and show their faces. At Making Nice – that's what we call ourselves – we can train them in the dark arts of presentation, but what we don't have currently and what we badly need is a director of public affairs to take them by the hand and introduce them around.'

'Oh, I'd be rubbish at that. I don't know anyone worth knowing.'

'But you know the right bells to press, who to call. Once you get into it, with your experience you'll find it's a doddle.'

I looked out over the pond. The mist was lifting from the water. Between the bare branches of the trees beyond there was the faintest glimmer of sun. And I thought of Lucy's pale face the night before, frozen and twisted and frightened. There wasn't really much choice.

'Well,' I said. 'That's very kind of you. I'll certainly think about it, but I'm still not sure exactly what –'

'You don't need to worry about the details,' Ethel said, patting my shoulder – how bony his grip was even through my anorak. 'Think about it and say Yes. Seventy-five K – how does that sound for starters?'

It was five grand more than I had been getting, but then he probably knew that already, the way he seemed to know most things.

Almost in the same moment he was standing up and saying goodbye, as light on his feet as a robin hopping off its perch.

I watched him go down the path, then on an impulse followed him at a discreet distance through the laurel bushes down to the park gates where the bike racks were. I had a fancy to wave him off on the old tradesman's bike, because putting aside the Ethel business – and it was we who had been idiotic to believe it – he had somehow touched me. Not just the job offer but the concern for Lucy. Perhaps he didn't really know much about the treatment of petit mal, had just looked it up on Wikipedia as we all did these days. But he had taken the trouble.

To my slight surprise he didn't stop at the bike rack but carried on through the war memorial gates. On the quiet street outside there was an old-style Merc convertible parked, scarlet with silver trimmings, hood down despite the weather and a woman in a big faux-leopardskin coat sitting in the passenger seat, with a floppy woollen hat on her head which hid her face. Ethel jumped in and drove off, turning to the woman and talking to her in an animated style as though debriefing her on our encounter.

'No,' Jane said, 'you mustn't take it just on my account because I'm taking time off. At your age you need to think carefully about your career choices.'

'At my age,' I said, 'there aren't that many choices – in fact, there isn't anything that can be described as a career.'

'But it sounds so dodgy. You know what Ethel's like.'

'We don't know what Ethel's like. For a start, it seems he isn't even called Ethel.'

'That's what I mean,' she said.

But to be honest, it was the dodginess that caught my fancy. I'd had enough of my old profession, with its prissy codes – lobby terms, not for attribution, Chatham House Rules and the whole dreary rigmarole designed to make us think we were worming out important secrets instead of being fed pap.

All the same, I was still cautious and methodical enough to go down to the park the next morning to make sure in my own mind that this was what I really wanted to do. I had just sat down on my usual bench when the community service guy from yesterday came round the corner wheeling his little cart.

'Hullo again,' I said.

'Thought I'd catch you here,' he said with a larky grin. 'I've got something for you.'

'Something for me?'

Denis unzipped his hi-vis jacket and took out what looked like a split-new smartphone. He tapped the screen and the phone began to ring.

'Here, you just press Call,' he said as he handed me the phone.

'Hi,' the voice said, 'we didn't have your mobile, but we thought Denis might track you down. Here are the details. We'd love to see you up here as soon as you can make it.'

I looked at the phone and jotted down the address – Making Nice, Osmotherley House, 327–31 Great Baldock Street, WC1 – then handed the phone back to Denis.

'No, you keep it,' he said with his chirpy grin, 'it's yours from now on, Johnny says, he needs to have you plugged in.'

Receiving a smartphone from a convicted paedo was obviously only the beginning. It would be dead-letter drops in hollow oak trees next. Yet rather than being afflicted by angst or annoyance, I was seized with a curious light-headed glee. You could say I was hooked, though hooked to what was harder to say.

'He's something else, that Johnny Evers,' Denis said. 'He could charm the knickers off a nun, but deep down he's straight up, if you know what I mean.'

'So he didn't have anything to do with you landing up here?'

'Ah, well, that was different. He didn't have any choice, did he really? Look at the Horlicks those archbishops make when they try to cover things up. He gave me a brilliant character reference, so I only got a CSO. Chap in the next case went down for three years. No, I was lucky. Ah, there's my supervisor, I'd better look as if I'm doing some work.'

Denis took his broom off the cart and began prodding at the leaves in the gutter. As he waved me goodbye, I thought this was one more proof of Ethel's wizardry. He had managed to get Denis convicted, branded for life in fact, yet retained his respect, even a soupçon of gratitude.

I walked on home to update Jane on my latest news. She met me at the door, white in the face.

'I think she's better now. She's having a lie-down on the sofa.'

'Lucy? What …'

'Didn't you get my text? When will you learn to keep your mobile on, or at least look at the bloody thing from time to time? Angela Frewin called me from the school. She had three seizures, one after the other, at least the teacher thought there were three of them, but they were hard to separate. Lucy just sat there staring into space with that awful blinking. The first time she had a jerking leg too, but not the others. What upsets the teachers is that she doesn't remember she's had them, though I did brief them about that. Angela says it makes them feel she's left them, gone into another world, she's such a stupid woman, Lucy looks so tired now, just utterly drained, poor thing.'

Which was how Jane looked too. I hugged her and followed her into the sitting room. Lucy was lying on the sofa cocooned in her Harry Potter rug. I bent down and kissed her pale forehead. People said we looked alike, taking after my English mother, but I didn't really see that. She has such a sweet, contemplative look, which nobody has ever accused me of.

It was clear to me at that moment that the new arrangement was going to last a while, probably until Lucy grew out of her fits, as two-thirds of children were supposed to. Jane might go back to work part-time if things improved, but that wasn't going to excuse me from getting back into gainful employment, and soon.

4

The Real Greek

Osmotherley House was a featureless thirties block off Tottenham Court Road – Portland stone of course, there's no dull like Portland stone dull.

'Making Nice? Third floor.' The lugubrious porter did not conceal his distaste at having to utter the firm's name. The usual clonking lift and worn carpet along the airless corridor.

But then I pressed the buzzer under the winking sign of a happy face saying 'Hi You're Here!' and the glass door opened and I was dazzled: the walls alternating sky blue, pink and daffodil yellow, bouncy sofas curved round low glass tables to form inviting conversation snugs, everywhere a light airy feel. All so restful too, with none of the busy clamour you'd expect in an office at the cutting edge.

'Great that you could make it up to Smothers. Always best to go straight to the scene of the crime, don't you think? And this is the Glow Worm.'

A strongly built woman rushed forward to shake my hand. Although I hadn't seen her face then, I felt sure that she had been Ethel's companion in the Merc. She had a slash of lipstick and panda-blacked eyes, with a merry look on her as though the extravagant make-up was a joke which she knew I'd enjoy.

'Gloria Wormsley, Ethel's partner, so glad you're joining us. Ethel's told us such huge things about you.'

'Ethel? I thought …'

'Oh, we all call him Ethel now. It suits him so well, don't you think? The website still says Johnny Evers, but even the clients are starting to go for Ethel.'

'If you're trying to give your business a softer face, why not start with your own name?' Ethel put in.

'Is that what you're about? Giving business a more acceptable face?' I said.

'Well, not just the face. The long-term aspiration is that the human thing will really soak in. Making Nice – great, but Being Nice – so much greater.'

'It all sounds very idealistic.'

Ethel made a moue of disapproval.

'That's not a word we use round here. What we're all about is still the bottom line. You make nice, you make moolah, lots more moolah. You see, Dickie, capitalism may be the only game left in town, but it's not a game people like playing much. So we're engineering a paradigm shift, the ambition is to transform the System into a game you can't help falling in love with.'

Beyond the sofa huddles there were carpeted steps leading down to a curved open area in front of the high windows. From where we stood, I could just see the upper bodies of young men and women in gym kit swaying to and fro, then making small jumps in response to the commands of a handsome Asian in a basketball vest.

'That's the Fit Pit. It's the only unbreakable rule we have in the office. No matter how busy you're pretending to be, you have to work out for twenty minutes every day.'

'You must excuse us for dropping you in at the deep end,' Gloria intervened, 'but we have someone here we're anxious for you to meet, because we think you'd be really good together.'

Ethel and the Glow Worm shepherded me through a door at the far end of the big room, which led to an ordinary-looking office. A thickset man with slicked-down black hair, a Berlusconi type but a few years younger, was sitting in the guest chair fiddling with some papers and giving off the unmistakable fumes of a rich man being kept waiting.

'Giorgios, so sorry to keep you, but we couldn't let you go before you touched base with Dickie Pentecost.'

'They tell me you are Greek too,' the man said, getting up and thrusting out an irritable hand, as though even this preliminary was more than could be expected of him.

'Yes, or rather my father was – he fled from Smyrna when he was a small boy.'

'So, you are really a Turk.' He laughed the sort of laugh which does not demand a response. 'I am the real Greek, like the restaurant.'

I smiled and said nothing, this not being the sort of conversation I fancied getting into.

'As I'm sure you know, Giorgios has just moved his business to the UK one hundred per cent, which we're all absolutely thrilled about, and so naturally he wants to raise his profile over here.'

'I want to make splash – not big splash but enough so people know Mr Demetrios is in town.'

'So we thought the arts, Greece our cultural motherland et cetera, and by an amazing coincidence you came along at just the right moment, though I have to say it was Ethel who had the light bulb moment.'

'Me?'

'The thing is, even philanthropy has to tell a story. Billionaire entrepreneur gives a million to Covent Garden or the Tate. So what? Happens all the time, that's what billionaires do. But billionaire rescues struggling ballet school for poor kids. Now that's something people will really talk about, and if it's got the man's name stuck on it, they'll remember it.'

'Exactly.' Ethel took up the story. 'I happened to be having a chat with Madame Dubarry, wonderful woman by the way, and she told me that they were going to have to close down soon, because her rent's gone up by 50K in the latest review and she hasn't a hope in hell of finding new premises anywhere central.'

'Is a total slum,' Demetrios interrupted, 'I say to this man, why you take me to slum? Why not Belgravia, Chelsea, even?'

'So I explain to Giorgios, very slowly, in words of one syllable, being a slum is the whole point. Kid from the back streets of Athens brings hope to kids from the back streets of London.'

'I am not from back streets. My father is dentist in Piraeus, very respected.'

'Anyway, eventually he gets the point. I asked Madame, did she mind changing the name of the school? What's in a name? she said. The dance is the thing. So, the Demetrios Academy of Dance, and you, Dickie, are going to be deputy chair of the trustees and recruit a glittering board for us.'

All the time Ethel was talking, I was thinking, what the hell is Ethel doing having these chats with Madame, and knowing in my gut perfectly well what.

'We have big launch for dance school. Royalty come, maybe even Princess Anne, she big fan of ballet.'

'I think Princess Anne's more interested in horses.'

'OK, you choose which fucking princess. I have major appointment in City. Ten minutes late already.'

We bustled out of the office and back along the airless corridor. In the lift, there were further discussions about which royal should be invited. Giorgios now favoured Prince Andrew, because he was named after his grandfather Prince Andrew of Greece. Ethel gently demurred. Outside it was raining. We looked up and down the street for Giorgios's chauffeur. Eventually, a midnight-blue Jag glided round the corner. Giorgios banged on the passenger window. The chauffeur leaped out to open the door.

'You think I pay you to play fucking games? I say twelve thirty, you gotta be here twelve thirty on the fucking dot.'

'I'm afraid Giorgios is a work in progress. He has a way to go on the Reputation Journey,' Ethel sighed as we waved goodbye.

Standing on the pavement in the wet chill, I was wondering what I had let myself in for, when a black boy on an electric scooter came to a sharp stop in front of us.

To my surprise, he and Ethel exchanged high fives.

'Morning, bruv.'

'Kaylee, how's it going?'

'Breezing along, bruv, just breezing.'

Ethel turned to me with a proprietorial smile.

'Kaylee's one of the Smothers Brothers. They do fantastic work for us. Looks like just another messenger service, but what they're really ace at is intelligence-gathering. We sit up here in Smothers and they bring us the word on the street from all over. You want to know what real people are thinking about gay marriage or renationalising the railways, the Brothers will tell you quicker and better than any polling organisation. They're a bit like Sherlock Holmes's Baker Street Irregulars, only motorised.'

Kaylee beamed as he listened to this job description, nodding vigorously as he extracted a large envelope from his scarlet satchel emblazoned with SB in hi-vis lettering.

'When we started, they used to get stopped by the police on sus – thought they were running drugs, and there were complications because one or two of them had been in trouble and several had only just come out of care.'

'But now we all have ID and we're well respected,' Kaylee added.

Ethel opened the envelope, scanned the contents briefly and scribbled a few words on the top page, then handed it back to Kaylee and sent him on his way with a mock-fierce fist bump. As the boy sped off, another scooter drew up, the rider saluting Kaylee and then Ethel as he skipped into Osmotherley House lugging his scooter behind him.

I was more impressed than I cared to admit. Standing there beside Kaylee with his wicked smile, still a little out of breath (he had just come from Chelsea Harbour, he told me), I had been surprised by cheerfulness. Mulishly, though, I ransacked my brain to think of a sceptical question.

'But do your clients really believe what the Smothers Brothers tell them? Or don't you reveal where your research findings come from?'

Ethel looked at me with an expression hard to categorise, amiable pity perhaps.

'Revealing our sources is the whole point. It is precisely because our stuff has been gathered by young black boys who may have been in care or have a police record of some description that clients think it must be the real deal. After all, it comes from genuine people talking to genuine people, not from some middle-class focus grouper who's selected her panel to confirm what she already thinks. And there's something else, Dickie. Redemption is the most powerful plotline there is – what else has half the human race been obsessed by for the past two thousand years? It's because these boys had such an abysmal start in life that it's great to be part of their story. You can't help believing what they tell you.'

'You don't think they ever make some of it up?'

'*Dickie.* I had no idea you were such a cynic. Believing what the Brothers tell you makes you feel better about yourself, and a client who goes away feeling better about himself is a satisfied client who will come back for more of the same. This isn't the ordinary sort of networking – what we offer is an amazing opportunity to plug in to the streets. There you are in a traffic jam in the back of your BMW getting annoyed by the back of the chauffeur's head and suddenly one of the Brothers cuts in past you, and you think, wow, we're all on the same team.'

The second Brother came out of the front door trailing his scooter with one hand and waving to Ethel with the other, and I couldn't help feeling a little captivated. I don't much care for transformation scenes in pantos or anywhere else, but there was a nonchalance, a gaiety, about the Brothers and about Osmotherley House as a whole which was hard to resist. The world was suddenly full of possibility. You could make it all up as you went along, and it didn't matter. I had quite forgotten now that Ethel was not a boy's name. It was an intoxicating thought that life could be lived in the imagination, perhaps the best bits.

'You will help Giorgios out, won't you? As you can see, he's not exactly lovable at first sight. And he's not exactly flavour of the month in the City either.'

'Why's that?'

'Well, for one thing, he's been doing rather well recently by shorting some of the best-loved names on the high street. M&S, Thomas Cook – you name it, Georgie has been selling the shares short. And they don't like it.'

'I didn't know the City was so sentimental.'

'They aren't, but they do like to be the only vultures at the feast.'

He turned to look at me with his enquiring parrot's gaze.

'You're looking pale, Dickie, very pale.'

'Well, it's a cold day, Ethel.' For some weird reason, I found myself using his name more often rather than less, now that I knew it wasn't his name.

'You need a break. You've had such a lot on your plate recently.'

'I must say a holiday would be nice. Jane certainly needs one, as you can imagine.'

'Just for starters, why don't you take the girls for a spring break at one of our country house hotels?'

'Your hotels?'

'The hotels that Making Nice is a consulting partner with. There are some really brilliant ones – the De Quincey Court on Exmoor is just about my favourite. I'm sure Corinna can fix you up with one of the executive suites with that amazing view of the Bristol Channel. Oh,' he added, seeing my quizzical look, 'entirely free of course. All we ask is that you jot down a few of your impressions, which the girls might rather enjoy doing.'

'Well, thank you very much,' I said. What else could I say?

'A freebie, Dad, how fantastic. You two will be breaking the habits of a lifetime.' Flo giggled, mocking our ingrained parsimony. It was true that we had both been rather particular about accepting hospitality unless it was strictly official, for a legitimate conference or something. But now all that priggery suddenly seemed absurd, just another symptom of a life misspent on the defensive. I was ready to raid the minibar with the rest of them.

As the limo the hotel had sent to meet us at the station nuzzled up the mile-long drive lined with ancient holm oaks and glimpses of misty hills beyond, I hummed along to Alfred Brendel playing Mozart's Ninth on the CD and thought that I could get used to this.

'How would you describe the partridge?' Flo asked, her fingers poised over her smartphone. As Ethel had predicted, she took instantly to the role of hotel inspector.

'Melting in the mouth.'

'That's a cliché, Dad.'

'You're not writing a novel.'

'That's what you think.'

When I got to read them, her descriptions of the panoramic view from our window, the William Morris curtains, the walks through the azalea wilderness and our clumsy twangings on the archery lawn did indeed have the rich abundance of detail last seen in novels of the high Victorian age. Lucy looked over her shoulder and stabbed her finger at passages which she thought over the top.

'Florence, that's so boring, everyone knows what a rose garden looks like.'

But Flo was undeterred. As we walked along the spectacular ups and downs of the coast path, she kept stopping to take pictures or jot down the outstanding features of the view, a distant honey-coloured spire, the regency villas on the cliff, the dark moorland swelling out of the valley. I said there was a love poem by Thomas Hardy about walking on cliffs like these and she made me look it up on Poetry.org and then pasted it into her travelogue. Meanwhile, Lucy hurdled the stony brooks and held Jane's hand in a way she hadn't done for years. I could see how much Jane liked to see Flo tapping away, eager to record every detail. This was her own kind of diligence. She herself was already beginning to look fresh and well again, almost rosy, though rosy was the last thing she ever was.

There was one walk in particular that we took in a frosty twilight on the final evening. We followed Corinna's instructions to go through the little green Gothicky gate in the walled garden and out onto a wooded path that curved up onto the narrow ridge. The lights of the village the other side of the bay were just coming on, and I had one of those rare floodings of happiness that you know at the time you will always remember. In the same moment, I felt sure that Lucy would be well, not immediately or for a few years yet, but in the end she would be well.

'It was a wonderful break, I can't thank you enough. Flo's written a report as long as the *Encyclopaedia Britannica* about it all.'

'Fantastic,' Ethel said. 'She must come in and talk to Ollie.'

'Ollie?'

'We call him the Head Groundsman, because he's in charge of cultivating the grass roots. He'll be over the moon to have a keen new recruit.'

'I'm sure she'd love to.'

Flo was excited about the prospect of showing her work, rather overexcited I thought. So I glanced over her shoulder to look at the finished article on screen. As I suspected, effusive would be an understatement.

'...this glorious pleasure dome nestling in an undiscovered fold of the Exmoor Hills was a constant inspiration to the Romantic poets who came to visit their friend Thomas De Quincey here and no doubt shared many a pipe of opium in the beautiful Orangery.'

'Steady on, Flo. The house wasn't named after De Quincey till thirty years after his death. We don't know that he ever actually visited it. As for the others —'

'Oh, come on, Dad, they were living only just over the hill, they *must* have come to stay.'

She wouldn't alter a word and went off to take the Tube to Osmotherley House with that set look to her sweet chin which I knew, from the same experience with Jane, meant there was no point in continuing the argument.

Two hours later, she clattered back into the hall, with a look of triumph on her face.

'See, Dad, Ollie says that mine is the best hotel report he's had yet, and he's not going to waste a word of it.

In fact, he loves it being so long, because it means they can slice it up and scatter bits of it for the other blades to put in their reports.'

'Blades?'

'Blades of grass obvs. Making Nice has got hundreds of them all over the country, so they can all send in totally different reports to TripAdvisor and the other hotel sites.'

'You mean, even if they haven't actually been to the hotel?'

'But *I*'ve been, Dad, so it's based on real-life experience. Ollie says we're only levelling up the playing field with the big hotel chains who can afford to spend zillions on promotion. And the trolls write such bad things. Often small hotels have to close because they tell such awful lies, so it's only fair for us to get the truth out there. It's called astroturfing, by the way. Isn't that cool? Ollie has got several other clients who need help and he wants me to take a friend and try them out for him. It's the best holiday job ever, thanks so much, Dad.'

She was so hyped up, almost jumping off the floor with delight, that I hadn't the heart to pursue my quibble. I thought to myself I can take it up with Ethel. But then I drew back from that option too. I had only just joined the company, after all, and I didn't really know anything about its methods. What Ollie was supposed to have said certainly raised uncomfortable questions, but this might not be the moment to ask them, and in any case Flo in her impulsive way might have got the wrong end of the stick. I would find out how it all worked as I went along. That's what I told myself anyway. And we had had a lovely time and I didn't want to spoil the memory of it.

5

Board Games

As it turned out, time was too short for me to whistle up suitable governors for the Demetrios Academy of Dance, except for my old friend and squash partner Ashleigh Goodacre, a lawyer with crinkly silver hair and a whistling way of talking which made him widely loved. So Ethel flicked through his own address book and then talked me through his picks.

'Well, numero uno has to be Biddy Tootal Ross. She's thick as a duvet but warm as one too, works her arse off for every charity you've ever heard of – dementia, Aids, distressed priests, victims of paedophilia, injured jockeys, you name it. Married to Craig, the younger Tootal Ross brother, known to their old colleagues as Total Loss, though in fact they're about the most profitable hedge fund around, very popular with Arab sheikhs and Belgian bankers. Malcolm and Craig are inseparable, they share a grouse moor in Wester Ross whence their penniless ancestors emigrated a century ago. Besotted Catholics, visit Lourdes twice a year as knights of Malta, and both of them married distant cousins of the Duke of Norfolk. Biddy's a real brick, looks like one too.

'Then I'm going for Ariane Rancourt, partly because she used to be a dancer before she married the sixth richest man in France. She can be hard to get hold of, because she spends a lot of time racing her microlights, which double as her workstation, so she's often dealing from several hundred feet up. She's picturesque, to say the least.

'Then we need a politician of sorts, who can ask questions in the House on our behalf, write to ministers et cetera. There's a guy we've just taken on our books who thinks he's going places, wants to raise his public profile. Hinterland, he said, I need some hinterland – he sounded a bit like Adolf demanding the Sudetenland. Well, the ballet is prime hinterland, it's always an intriguing passion to confess to. He's never been to the ballet in his life, but he saw immediately that it was just the thing for him. You won't like him at all, nobody does, but somehow he makes you ashamed of not liking him. He's called Bryce Wincott, also known as the Wingco, because his great thing is having been in the RAF, wanted to train as a gunner, but his eyesight wasn't good enough, so he stayed a penguin in the RAF Logistics Corps. Ended up as Chef First Class, which not a lot of people know, but I do.'

'And I've also roped in Piggyback Piers, so called because he's always last into any big thing and first out. He trades as Piers de Hooch Partners, but started life as Pete Potter from Canning Town. He used to be one of those barrow boys in brightly coloured jackets dealing on the floor. But he's made something of himself, has Piers. He's got this brilliant houseboat on Chelsea Reach, more like a superyacht really, and I once spent an unforgettable afternoon on it with him and his girlfriend Tish, drinking Krug and listening to Scarlatti.'

'I'm afraid my friend Ashleigh will seem very dull in such glamorous company.'

'Oh, we need all sorts, and you'll both add a touch of quiet distinction to the line-up.'

'And then there's you, of course,' I said.

'Oh no, I stay strictly in the wings. I'm the guy who only comes onstage to tell the audience that the soprano has got tonsillitis. Don't worry, I'll be around to keep an eye on things.'

I could not help worrying how Madame would take to this flashy crew. But she seemed quite unfazed when I called on her in her little attic at the Beau as I still called it. She came towards me with arms outstretched, skittering across the floor, a dancer's welcome.

'I am so grateful to you all, to Mr Demetrios of course, but also to you and Mr Evers' – for a moment I forgot who Mr Evers was – 'we would have been lost without you.' She made a fleeting gesture of imagined loss, yet she had such grace, such dignity that there was no melodrama about it. As the parent of her prize pupil, I had admired her at a distance but found her a little steely. Now I thought her captivating.

'Mr Demetrios has taken over the lease, which is such a load off my mind. Those rent reviews have given me sleepless nights for years, now I can dream only of the dance.'

I had not known about the lease and I was struck by the generosity of it. I wondered if this too had been Ethel's idea. Not so, as I found out when I went to prep Giorgios for our inaugural governors' meeting.

'Of course I buy out the fucking lease. It's my fucking school. You think I let that silly old moo keep the lease? What happens if she go belly up?'

This did not look like a promising beginning to my coaching session. We sat in the offices of Demetrios

Enterprises, a *piano nobile* in sight of Victoria Station. He paced around the huge glass table while I sat with my notebook propped on my knees.

'You see, I've put in a bit about Madame Dubarry's contribution to the dance. Then you say how grateful you are for the opportunity to offer some modest assistance for her to continue the work which has made her a legend in the world of ballet.'

'Me be grateful? She's the one who should be fucking grateful. You call five million modest assistance? Without Demetrios, her school goes down the toilet.'

Then seeing my anxious face, he came round to my side of the table and put his arms round me in a suffocating hug.

'Don't worry, Mr Pentecostas. We Greeks know how to say thank you. We are famous for our gratitude, even Greeks who are really Turks like you.'

He did another half-circuit prowl, then paused, flung out his arms and declaimed in a sonorous voice, not at all how he normally spoke:

'Today we are happy to welcome Madame Dubarry, the genius of dance. It is our privilege to play a small part in carrying on her work, which has brought happiness and fulfilment to so many kids who have never had a chance in life. I feel so humble that she has generously permitted me to attach my name to her Academy. You see, Dickie, I know how to learn my lines.'

I was astonished. I had emailed him my draft script the night before but had not dreamed that he would have looked at it properly, let alone have it off by heart or spoken so, well, mellifluously was the only word.

In the passage on the way to the meeting, I expressed my gratified surprise to Ethel.

'Oh, that is good news. I told him he had better get it word-perfect because it was already in the handout. These bullies like to be told what to do, you know, Dickie.'

The fresh-minted board of governors began to shuffle into the conference room. And there was Giorgios to greet them, with a double handshake for Biddy Tootal Ross and a pretty compliment on her work for distressed priests. My friend Ash Goodacre got a joke about him beating me at squash and congratulations on being elected to the Council of the Law Society. Ariane Rancourt, now rather wizened and leathery in her parachute silk dress, was told she must have looked just so when she danced for Massine. Never was there a more perfectly briefed host, down to his humble disclaimer that he was only there to listen and learn, it was enough for him to be allowed to give his name to the Academy. No question of him mentioning the millions he had pledged (no need to, it was all in the handout). Then he wheeled a chair away from the huge table into the corner of the room where he was going to sit and watch the proceedings, although there were at least three PAs present who could have wheeled it for him.

'Amazing,' I said to Ethel afterwards. 'He seemed to do it all so naturally as if nobody had prompted him at all.'

'A-starred, I agree,' Ethel said, 'he even did the business about wheeling the chair himself, although he probably hasn't moved a piece of office furniture in twenty years. But you see, Dickie, it's so much easier teaching manners to someone like Giorgios, who knows he hasn't got any, than to some smart-arse who thinks he's Beau Brummell.'

The meeting itself was a breeze. There were oohs and aahs at the video mock-up of the Beau, now Demetrios, after refurb: the gleaming dance floor, the burnished leather barre, the spectators' gallery with its fretted balustrade, the dear little vegan cafe. The finale of the meeting was a video of the excerpt from *Les Filles Perdues* that the Beau had given at the last passing-out parade. My fellow governors clapped rapturously and congratulated me on Flo's performance, which to me at least looked even more magical than it had on the night. And I could not stifle a tear for the shabby old Beau as it never would be again.

'Glorious, just glorious, Dickie.' Biddy Tootal Ross enfolded me as if I had known her for years. I instantly fell in love with her big round face and her eager questing look. In fact I loved them all. Even if it had not been my own idea, I adored being a founding part of this new venture. I handed out the leaflets giving details of the bursaries that were to be available to boys and girls of slender means as though it were my own largesse. As we trooped out of the room, Ethel patted each of us on the shoulder like the director waiting in the wings for his cast.

That day was the beginning of a golden interlude we would always remember, and we knew it at the time. Once a month, maybe a little more, we went on a freebie for Making Nice, the three of us, that is. Flo was sixteen now, and in the holidays and at weekends she was licensed to take a friend on a different assignment. In her absence, Lucy blossomed, though we still kept our fingers crossed. Her episodes seemed to come less often, and her old wicked way of talking came back to her. We walked along the beach at Holkham (we were staying in a converted windmill just inland), and she gave a running commentary on the ungainly naturists who crossed our path as they wobbled down to the sea. A fortnight later, we went up to the Hebrides, to a baronial keep on an island I had never heard of, just off Mull, and we bathed with the seals and argued whether it was dolphins or porpoises that we could see curvetting through the waves further out. I had not seen Jane so relaxed for years, or rather I had not realised how all those years in oncology had tensed her up. I worried that she might query this succession of paid-for holidays but she never murmured. Now and then we would get a text from Flo, giving news of some other blissful retreat that she was casing. The fillet steak was amazing in this gastropub on Dartmoor apparently, to which we riposted that the langoustines were pretty amazing where we were.

In between these jaunts, I clocked into Osmotherley House three days a week to get up to speed on Making Nice's latest clients.

'Dickie, I don't think you've met Julius Afu.'

A tall African in a gleaming silk suit put down his *Daily Telegraph* and rose from his egg-shaped chair to greet me with a smile that seemed to promise all the fun in the world.

'We met when Julius was doing his MBA at Fontainebleau,' Ethel added. 'We did martial arts together.'

Julius raised his eyes to the ceiling as if the idea was intrinsically absurd.

'He is of course technically Chief Afu.'

'My dear Ethel, do cut the crap.'

'You know of course how Julius was robbed at the last election and then thrown into exile.'

'My departure was purely voluntary – I could not stay and watch the thieves ruin my country.'

'We have high hopes for the next election. They made the mistake of promising to let in UN observers and we have a fantastic database from a local savings bank which went bust and we bought it from the administrators. Between you and me it was really more of a Ponzi scheme but two-thirds of the adult population signed up. You wouldn't believe the stuff we can harvest.'

'I'm a bit of an IT geek myself,' Julius chuckled. 'I can tell you the data is really awesome, even from the villages in the tribal trust lands, real backwoods, but we know what they eat for breakfast and who their favourite pop group is. You know, Mr Pentecost, there are more mobile phones than bananas in my country now.'

Ethel whistled us through a PowerPoint presentation on the screen. Next to laughing villagers and women carrying water jugs on their heads there were columns of percentages in bold blocky type.

'Water's going to be big in this election. We've got a great thing going with two of the top UK water companies. A penny in the pound on your water bill over here goes to provide clean water for Julius's people over there, builds the company's ethical profile and at the same time boosts his "I can deliver" factor.'

'My team thought up this great slogan: "Waterboarding isn't torture with us",' Julius said proudly.

'It *is* a great slogan, fantastic pitch,' Ethel said, 'but we decided in the end that it was just a little too strong.'

'Which water companies are you hooked up with?' I enquired.

'Well, at the moment, it's the South Midland and Superaqua.'

'Weren't they the ones who —'

'Had all the trouble with the bonuses and the leaky pipes. Yes, that's why they need us and why we need to start them off on a fresh tack. The art of reputation retrieval, Dickie, is to change the subject. Never trigger painful memories.'

Julius nodded vigorously. 'So we won't waste time responding to the vile lies they told about me. We just tell them "Afu is Africa's future, your future",' he said, making imaginary quote marks with his long delicate fingers.

'Is he really, you know...' I said, after Julius had shaken our hands warmly, folded his *Daily Telegraph* and said goodbye.

'Julius is one of the good guys,' Ethel said firmly. 'It is true that some of his associates are a little bit iffy, but that's Africa, and we can rely on him to have a clear-out after he's won the election.'

'And is it really possible to run the campaign from here?'

'Oh, we'll send a monitor squad out there for the last few weeks, but the prepping starts now and it starts here at Smothers. By the time the candidates are actually out on the stump, voters will have pretty much made up their minds. Have a look at these.'

Ethel tapped his phone and the wall-screen leapt into life, flipping image after image with African music surging from somewhere to hail each one. There was Julius in a smart suit presenting something to a group of overjoyed women: The Man Who Keeps On Giving. Then there he was again, looking serious with palms outstretched (rather like the pose in which I had seen Ethel in the dawn light at St Dingle's): The Man With Clean Hands. Then his slim unmistakable figure, now dressed in tribal robes, walking up a path to the rising sun, and turning and beckoning to the viewer with a half-smile.

'The question was, do we caption this one "Follow Me" or "Follow Him", or no caption at all and let the viewer do the work? We trialled it in the trust lands and no caption won by a street. Pictures first, Dickie, words are at best a necessary evil.'

'I presume you don't flash the images as fast as that when you're doing it for real.'

'Yes, we do. You mustn't let the picture linger and allow the viewer time to start arguing with the message in his head. The old admen used to waffle on about subliminal pitches, but they knew sod all about how the brain works. Our aim is to hit the threshold of consciousness at the exact nanosecond when your receptors are at their freshest.'

Ethel wore specs now for using his phone and he looked like an ordinary young lecturer, somehow rather diminished. But now he took them off and leaned forward in his retro Eames chair, staring at me with his cold basalt eyes and he had his old aura back in an instant.

'I expect you can see where this is leading, Dickie. It would be really great if you could head up our team out there for the last ten days before polling day. I know that Julius would feel really safe in your hands.'

'But I don't know nearly enough –'

'Oh, the techies will handle all the data mining and message seeding. You'll be there to inject legitimacy into the whole process – you'll have the UN guys eating out of your hands. Quite frankly, having a Brit as our campaign director is the ultimate cred boost.'

'Even a Brit who knows nothing about the country and even less about these dark arts?'

'All the better. Nobody will be able to question your integrity. We can pay five hundred a day on top of your normal salary, plus exes of course. Please say yes.'

Well, I'm one of those unadventurous people who usually says yes when somebody else is setting up the adventure, so I said yes.

'That's fantastic news. No cleft sticks required for messaging. As Julius says, mobile phone coverage out there is better than in parts of the UK.'

My flight, as it turned out, was already booked for the following morning, so clearly Ethel didn't have much doubt about my accepting. Even as we left the building, a Smothers Brother scooted up with a package for me from the chemist: Imodium, Jungle Formula and a couple of anti-tropical disease medicines which I didn't have time to read the labels of.

That afternoon, though, we were off to the last meeting of the Demetrios Academy governors before the holidays. The tall windows were flung open to let in the scented summer air. Parliament had just broken up for the recess and this was the first time that our resident MP could make it.

'Bryce Wincott,' he said, putting out a firm hand. I suppose he was not amazingly short, five foot six or so, but his shortness somehow impacted as much as a more obvious feature like a scar or a missing arm might have. He seemed to be reaching up to the height he thought he ought to be, like a frog with no back legs and a lifelong grievance. 'Some people call me the Wingco, because I have this background in the RAF.'

'Oh yes, I heard about that.'

'You did? Wonderful bunch of chaps, best training for life you could have. But I'm really looking forward to this afternoon. Politicians need to get a hinterland, I always say.'

'Absolutely.'

'I'm counting on you to talk me through the finer points.'

'I'm hardly an expert.'

'They tell me your daughter is one of the stars here.'

That I couldn't deny. Nor could I prevent him from sitting close to me, his powerful thigh pressing against mine on the little plastic seats in the school's cafe where we were meeting pro tem until the office was finished. He may not have known much about ballet, but he appeared to know everything there was to know about VAT receipts, building on-costs and planning permission. It was quite a relief when we broke for coffee. Through the glass partition that separated the little cafe from the dance floor, we saw the pupils come out to take their places for the display: a trio this time, Flo and Eloise and a boy who was also leaving, Darren, the best of the boys in the school, who planned to rechristen himself Ivan. He was lithe and springy, but as he flew across the stage from one girl to the other in his star-sprinkled sky-blue costume, there was a wonderful languor about him too, which you would have thought only a full-grown dancer capable of. Courting the girls alternately, he seemed almost as shy as they were and yet in full flight he planed with the confidence of a seabird. It was an odd light to watch dancing in, the dusty afternoon sunbeams pouring over the gleaming new floor, yet all the more enchanting.

'I always thought ballet dancers weren't allowed to have tits,' Wincott whispered in my ear.

I didn't know whether he was talking about Flo or Eloise, I was equally indignant whichever — no, more than indignant, profoundly sad that evolution had come so far and still produced Bryce Wincott.

But my indignation fled when Flo darted in to say hullo after she had changed. There seemed to be an extra sparkle to her as she threw herself into my arms.

'I'm in, Dad, I'm in,' she said. The Royal Ballet School had just begun to take a handful of students from lesser schools when they were fifteen or sixteen, and Flo, and it turned out Darren too, were the first to get in from the Beau.

'You see,' Madame said, coming up behind her, 'she's not so bad.'

6

On Safari

Even inside the 747 I could smell the woodsmoke from the fires lit along the riverbank. The aircraft was flying so low that I could pick out the families gathered under the corrugated-iron and cloth shelters. Several waved at us as we swooped on up the broad sluggish river and then off over the thorn scrub towards the boundary lights of the runway. My heart lifted as I trotted down the steps, gulping in the fragrant warm air. Why did arriving in Africa always do this to me?

'Mr Pentecost, sir? My name is Michael.'

A slender young black man in a crisp white shirt helped me off the last step, smiling at me as he took my arm and led me to an SUV in the VIP car park.

'I did my doctorate in business studies at Westminster Uni, just opposite Madame Tussauds. The other campuses called us the Waxworks.'

'Great to meet you, Michael,' I said. 'How's it all going?'

'Fantastic, just fantastic, Mr P. We booked all the best poster sites. Radio spots first-class too. We've already spent up to budget.'

'Haven't spent it all, I hope?'

'Oh no, sir, we've got plenty of firepower left for the final push. Look there, that's one of ours.'

By the side of the sandy road, flanked by two date palms, there was the poster of Julius in his smart suit handing out largesse to a crowd of overjoyed women. Underneath the billboard, several families were sheltering under flapping lean-tos.

'The Man Who Keeps On Giving. Isn't that wonderful, sir? Did you write that?'

'Dickie, please, call me Dickie. No, I wish I could claim it, Michael.'

'I'll drop you off at the Lugard. Everyone stays there. I'm sure you'll meet a lot of old friends.'

We drove out of the scrubby savannah into wooded parkland. Between the trees I could see creamy villas with verandas.

'This is a good area, Dickie. No bad guys allowed. The Lugard is just around the next corner.'

The hotel was a long low white building with balconies running across both floors, festooned with bougainvillea. Beyond the hotel on a tall pole the national flag drooped red and gold in the light breeze of late afternoon.

'Another recruit to the legion of the damned.' A thin man with a withered red face leaning over the balcony saluted me as I got out of the car and Michael took my bags in to Reception.

I looked up, but his face meant nothing to me.

'Chip McCue, Reuters. We met at that UN thing in KL.'

'Oh yes, of course, Chip, hi.'

'You can be forgiven, I haven't worn well. I blame the climate, my doctor blames this stuff.' He waggled the heavy crystal glass, and although he was several feet above me I could hear the chink of the ice cubes and I remembered other evenings on verandas like this.

He met me at the top of the white wooden balcony steps.

'And what brings you to the dear old Lugard?'

'I'm a consultant for the firm that's looking after Julius Afu's campaign. I'm totally new to the game, so I'm really here to see how it all works.'

'Julius Afu? Really? I wouldn't have thought that – well, no matter. This is Bill de Lillo, known to one and all as Billo.'

A tall man with a heavy jaw and a big shark smile put out his hand. He was wearing a linen safari jacket of a strange silvery colour, the sleeves turned back to reveal his muscular forearms. His fingers were long and elegant. His handshake crackled.

'I'm really with FAO, but we're so short-staffed here that I'm doubling up with WHO until their man shows up. So you're working for Julius. Interesting, interesting.'

'In London they rather fancy his chances.'

'Do they now? Didn't you use to be quite a journo? I suppose like the rest of us you've had to, what's the phrase, seek fresh challenges?'

We had landed in bright sunshine, but now the sun had gone off the balcony and behind the forest trees, and we were sitting in a dusky half-light.

'It's not a bad place, this, not bad at all. Plenty of sport to be had, of one kind and another.'

'Including wildebeest.' I can't now remember which of them said this, but they laughed together, as if this was an old joke they trotted out at regular intervals.

'Wildebeest? I didn't know they ranged as far north as this.'

They both laughed again – an unforced laugh this time, as if I had said something surprisingly funny.

'Billo may be able to help you in that department if you're interested. He knows how to open the right doors.'

Then abruptly Chip changed the subject to something Putin had said on that morning's news which I hadn't heard because I'd been in the air at the time, and I felt a vague discomfort. It's true, I've never been much good at this sort of male bonding. While wishing really to say nothing at all, I often managed to say something which set the other men on edge. This was perhaps another such occasion, though I couldn't see why exactly. And I suddenly wished I was back home with Jane and the girls. But after all the cocktails I slept a dreamless sleep and was woken by Reception to tell me that Michael was downstairs but he said not to hurry over my breakfast.

'Let me show you our HQ first. We're very proud of it. Most up-to-date communications centre in West Africa, thanks to Making Nice.'

We bounced through the small town – pleasant tree-lined avenues with cream and pink bungalows, now and then a church with a small bell tower and a big sign saying 'Come to Jesus! He's Here Right Now!'

'Very nice place, Michael.'

'Thank you, sir.'

'Dickie, please.'

'OK, Dickie. We could have had the office down in Elizabeth. But Lizzie's really UPP territory, and they might have given us some grief. Up here no one's going to disturb us.'

We stopped at the security gates of what looked like a small industrial estate on the edge of the bush. A guard raised the barrier and gave an impish salute to Michael.

It was obvious which the campaign office was, because of the big placard stretching half the length of the cement wall, saying 'AFU – HE'S THE MAN'.

Inside it was like a City trader's office: banks of computer screens, and pretty girls in bright dresses bent over the keyboards or carrying spreadsheets to the shirtsleeved men behind the console at the end. That quiet hum, as though the office was talking to itself.

Michael led me over to an anxious-looking man about my age, perhaps a little younger.

'This is Dr Amos Musa. He's our campaign treasurer. He's been with Julius since the start.'

'Yes, sir, through the good times and the bad times. He just can't seem to get rid of me. It's wonderful that you've come over to see our little show for yourself.'

'It's very impressive,' I said.

'Last week we processed three million-plus bits of data. You see, sir, Africa's always been the mining capital of the world, first gold, then diamonds, now it's data, and really deep data mining too. We know which church every voter goes to or doesn't go to, what he likes for breakfast, his shoe size, everything.'

'Fantastic,' I said. 'Ethel will be over the moon. By the way, this may not be the right time to mention it, but you're obviously the guy to talk to. All the arrangements for the transfer of the first tranche are in place, I hope? Ethel told me he was a little worried about the South African end.'

'Oh yes, sir, all absolutely in place. The nominee account in Joburg is open now, there won't be any problems.'

'That's great,' I said. 'I'm a child in these matters myself, I'm just passing on what he said.' It was the last thing that Ethel had impressed on me before I left for the airport and I didn't have time to get him to explain.

'Now I'd like to show you a little of our beautiful country,' Michael said, patting my shoulder to move me on.

We said goodbye to Dr Amos, who seemed less anxious now after delivering his upbeat spiel. Michael put on shades and a forage cap. He suddenly looked more formidable.

We drove through dense forest, of tall trees strangled by vines, flushing birds who skittered off making tinny bell-like noises. At the side of the road monkeys looked up at us in an affronted sort of way as we passed. Then the road grew rougher as we twisted out of the trees and into open uplands, red earth rolling into the distance dotted with thorn trees under a huge hazy blue sky. Now and then we bumped over rocky watercourses tumbling down from the distant hills. I had that feeling that Africa and nowhere else gives you, of somehow being in at the dawn of creation. I drifted into one of those reveries in which all your mistakes are forgiven and the world is on your side.

We came to a small settlement. Families squatting in front of their huts waved at us and I waved back. I felt like a district commissioner in the old days.

'There should be another one of our sites just after the next corner.'

As we rounded a clump of larger thorn trees, I saw it: a big poster, about ten foot by five, mounted on stout bamboos. It was the same one we had seen on the way from the airport, Julius handing out largesse to a crowd of ululating women: The Man Who Keeps On Giving – only here 'Giving' had been crossed out with a big X and 'Bribing' written instead, in even larger letters.

'The bastards,' Michael muttered, banging his hands on the steering wheel in disgust. 'They were supposed to keep a guard on each site. You see, Dickie, we're coming into the badlands here. This is strictly UPP territory, but we need to expand our core constituency so we thought it was worth the risk. There's another one five miles further on.'

The road climbed to a stony summit. You could see for miles in every direction. Right at the top there was another huge poster. We had also viewed this one back at Osmotherley House: Julius looking serious against a background of clear blue sky with his hands outspread: The Man With Clean Hands. This time the graffiti artist had simply added a question mark to the caption and had splashed red paint all over Julius's hands in a pattern of dripping blood.

'Oh fuck,' Michael said and took out his mobile, stabbing the keys to report the desecration. Whoever he was speaking to appeared to have a similar story to tell.

'No, *no*, and in Eastern Province too? And Lizzie? Oh fuck, fuck. They must have done it all last night. What happened to the guards? Paid to go off and get drunk, not all of them surely? God, I need a drink myself.'

We were coming into a larger place now, quite a sizeable town, and Michael swerved off the main road to park outside a big bottle shop which was doing great business, the customers spilling out into the road, one or two of them waving their bottles to greet us.

'Michael, man, love the wheels.'

'This is Dickie from England – he's running our campaign.'

I protested that of course I was doing no such thing, but they brushed my protests aside. 'Welcome, sir. Any friend of Julius is all right with us, that right?' Cries of Yes, more waving bottles.

Michael reported the desecration of the billboards. His friends took a robust view.

'Well, what you waiting for, man? You go right out there and mess up their posters back.'

'We're working on it,' Michael said, but I sensed that his morale was shot away. The posters must have looked so compelling against the skyline the night before.

'You Arsenal or Spurs, sir?'

'As a matter of fact, Arsenal.'

'You still think it right they played Thierry down the middle? He's a winger, man, always was.'

'Well, he did score a lot of goals as centre forward.'

'Right, right, but he scored more from the wing. Now take Wrighty, he was a genuine centre forward.'

Standing there under the open front of the bottle shop, looking at the banana trees and the women in their bright dresses working in the vegetable plots beyond, with the smell of beer and woodsmoke and that other sweet smell floating past my nostrils, a deep peace overcame me. I almost forgot about the desecration. Michael did not.

'We could sue the UPP for damage to property.'

'You crazy, man? That way everyone get to hear about what they did to those posters.'

'Lovely people,' I said as I tossed away my bottle and followed Michael out to the Range Rover.

'Half of them got Aids or a criminal record, some got both.' Michael's mood had not lightened. We drove on in silence out of the hills. In the distance I could see the smoky silver ribbon of the great river.

'You fancy a curry, Dickie? There's a Gujarati place down at the fish market, serves the best kadhi you ever tasted.'

'Sounds wonderful.'

The Range Rover ploughed its way along the crowded quayside. Out in the bay, several huge grey tankers were slumbering at anchor.

'Oil exports up 30 per cent this year. This country would be really motoring if only it had a decent government.'

Michael had suddenly got his own momentum back, and he strode on under the awning of the restaurant as if he owned it.

'Hi, Vijay, how's your kadhi today? We've been driving upcountry all morning and we're starving.'

'Oh, Michael, no kadhi today. Those UPP thugs came in last night and trashed the place, tipped over all the pans. There's nothing left except a few samosas and patras in the back store.'

The neat little man was having trouble holding back the tears.

'Vijay, how terrible, did they hurt you? And your wife, how's your wife?'

'No, no, they didn't touch us, just laughed and said, wait and see after the election if you still have a restaurant. But she's so frightened, Michael, she won't come downstairs.'

'Have the police been? The inspector's a good friend of mine.'

'Oh yes, Michael, don't worry about us. Stay and have a beer on the house and I'll get a few little things from the back for you.'

Michael put his arm round Vijay's trembling shoulders and said, 'That would be great,' and then to me, 'You see what we're up against?'

As my eyes got used to the gloom, I took in the smashed light fittings and the spilled aluminium pots and pans stacked in the corner and the disconsolate waiter mopping the floor with a withered broom.

'It's a big pitch with the UPP just now – against Indian shopkeepers and food joints taking business away from African stallholders, in fact against Indian immigrants full stop. The thing is, the Indian food tastes so much better. Anyway, our data tells us that Keep the Indians Out doesn't play too well with the demographic, in normal times that is, but if people get frightened, then they may begin to believe that the threat is real, although their common sense still tells them it isn't. In the jargon, it's called Rushkin's Override – you see they do teach you something in media studies.'

As we were sitting there eating our samosas in the smashed-up restaurant, Michael seemed to cheer up again, the light of battle coming back into his eyes, another sort of override perhaps. Vijay brought candles to relieve the gloom but the sour smell of stale curry everywhere was too oppressive for us to stay long. Michael said he wanted to get back to the office to coordinate an official complaint. He drove like a tiger out of the port and back into the hills. As we left the town, I recognised from some way off another of the Julius posters that I had seen being trialled on-screen at Smothers. The poster was the last one Ethel had shown me, I thought it the most atmospheric of the lot. It was the one of Julius by himself in tribal robes walking up the path towards the rising sun, and turning and beckoning with that half-smile. No words, they had decided in the end, just the big man urging you to follow him.

Except that the unknown graffitist had been at work here too, and on a far more elaborate scale. Julius was no longer alone. Into the otherwise empty foreground, mostly grass and rocks as I recalled, there were now inserted behind him in bright colours a throng of unmistakably Indian figures, women in saris, old men in dhotis, bearded patriarchs in turbans and a flock of little children. This crowd – teeming was the only word for it – was responding to his beckoning finger, to follow him to the sunlit uplands. It was drawn with all the panache of a local Banksy, and, without in any way altering the figure of Julius himself, managed to convey the impression that he was plotting to swamp the country with these Asian immigrants. What had seemed in the unimproved version like a benign smile on his lips and a friendly come-with-me beckon now had an undeniably furtive and even creepy feel. It was a masterpiece of perversion.

Michael jammed on the brakes, got out of the Range Rover and rushed at the billboard as if he was going to tear it down with his bare hands, but it was too high off the ground for his fingernails to do more than scratch feebly at the hems of the Indian women's saris.

He abandoned the vain struggle, pausing only to take a photo of this final atrocity on his iPhone, then jumped back into the car, scarcely waiting for me to join him, and hit the throttle with a thump.

As we came back into the town, we ran into a crowd of people milling about at the roadside, some of them gathered round an open truck listening to a speaker standing on the buckboard, his voice squawking over the amps. Other people were ambling away from the hubbub down the misty side roads where I could see stalls and clusters of goats and cattle. Michael blasted his horn non-stop, but we could still only move at walking pace.

At that moment I glimpsed down one of these side roads an immediately familiar figure, easily told apart from the dawdlers around him, being the only European, a lean figure well over six foot with silvery hair *en brosse*, with a shark's smile, and dressed in an elegant safari suit of the same silvery colour.

'Isn't that Bill de Lillo?' I said, pointing down the murky lane.

'You don't want go down there, that's a bad place,' Michael said without interest, changing down as we were brought to a standstill by another surge of strollers.

I had not realised how late it was. The sun had gone behind the trees and the Lugard was lapped in a misty twilight as Michael dropped me off, promising me to text about tomorrow's plans after he had sorted out the billboard business. I looked up at the balcony and a hand waved down at me out of the half-light.

'Busy day, old boy? You deserve a long cool one. I hear your man's in a spot of bother.' Chip McCue looked as if he had not budged since I had seen him the night before, one hand draped along the balustrade, the other cradling his glass.

'You mean the billboards?'

'Billboards? I don't know about the billboards.'

So I told him.

'Oh yes, that'll be Pieter the Painter. Brilliant artist, they were going to send him on a scholarship to the

Slade, but he preferred to stay down in the Cape making trouble. I didn't know he'd moved up here.'

'So he's working for the UPP?'

'I don't know about that, he's a supporter of buggeration wherever it rears its ugly head, and it sounds as if he's come to the right place. Says on the radio they're launching charges of bribery, corruption and whatever against Julius in the High Court.'

'But I was given to understand –'

'Oh, I expect the charges are mostly trumped up. That's the way they play it here. The other side throws the kitchen sink at you, and you throw it right back at them. Some of the mud sticks, and some of it doesn't. You look pale, old boy. Where is that gin wallah?'

Chip got to his feet to pull the bell-rope by the little bamboo bar at the end of the balcony. I noticed how agile he was. It came to me dimly that there was something assumed about his whole persona – the old colonial soak, the antique lingo – some sort of pose which concealed an altogether sharper, more watchful character, but then perhaps I had just had a long day and was imagining a complexity which wasn't really there.

'I thought I saw your friend Billo down in town.'

'Did you now? I wondered why he wasn't in the congregation tonight.'

'In a rather rough part of town, according to my guide.'

'Was it now? He gets around, does our Billo.'

Chip sat musing over his glass, rattling the cubes as if they contained some occult power of divination.

'I wouldn't worry too much about your man,' he said finally. 'It'll probably all come out in the wash.'

The trees were blacked out now, the sky above them a dark velvet blue, and the birds were beginning their evening calls, and were those frogs burbling some way off? The air was still and heavy and I felt an odd chill as though I was coming down with some virus, although I had felt fine all day. Those rows of computers and the busy girls carrying the spreadsheets seemed a distant memory.

We had fallen into a silence which neither of us seemed to have the energy to break, and I jumped when my phone beeped with a text (how bright the little screen looked in the gloaming).

What the text said was: *Return immediately. Speak to no one. Do not reply. Ethel.*

The message was absurdly melodramatic. Yet I could not think what to do except what he told me to do. So I made my dazed apologies to Chip and trotted down the balcony steps to see what was the earliest flight home that Reception could fix me up with.

I had texted from the airport that I had landed, and there was Ethel waiting for me on the front steps of Osmotherley House. He embraced me with a weird ferocity, one of those embraces that are either making sure it really is you or checking you over for concealed weapons. He knocked the breath out of me, not least because I don't think we had ever embraced before.

'No,' he said, 'we're not going into Smothers, we're going round the corner to the coffee shop first, because I don't want you talking to anyone until you're properly debriefed.'

I could see how angry he was, a kind of nervous anger which he couldn't control and which was so unlike his normal composure.

'So,' he said as soon as we had sat down in the Hacienda, 'the first thing you have to understand is that we never had a contract with Afu's people. Yes, you did go out there but purely as an observer, you had no executive role, and you never even met Afu.'

'Well, that's true, I didn't, not out there anyway, but –'

'But nothing. Get it into your head. There never was a contract, because they never paid us a cent up front or any other time, and I don't think they were ever going to. That nominee account was blocked from the start. And it's a merciful release, because Afu is utterly fucked. The latest polling from Campbell Segal has him running fifteen points behind.'

'But Dr Musa said all the indicators were positive.'

'Dr Musa is a total loser. We don't do business with losers.'

'What about the office with all those computers?'

'Recon stock. We flew the whole lot in from Abu Dhabi, the kit's worth virtually nothing. With luck, we'll get out of the whole thing at under 100K. Africa is a dark continent, Dickie, I should have known better. Fuck, fuck, fuck.'

I didn't think this was the moment to tell him about the billboards. But I didn't need to bring the subject up because he brought it up himself.

'You may remember those images of Afu that I flashed past you before you left.'

'Yes I do, of course.'

'Well, you understand that Afu's people sent them over to us for our comments, we did not make them ourselves. Pretty second-rate stuff I thought, though of course I was polite about them at the time.'

'Oh, really? I didn't –'

'My spies tell me they're scoring very poorly with the target sectors out there.'

'That may be because —' But before I could begin to describe the billboards' grisly fate, Ethel had moved on.

'You've had a rough old time, Dickie. You need to forget about the whole thing and go home and get some —'

At that moment, my mobile beeped. *Where are you? Why aren't you back? J.*

'Yes,' I said, 'I think I better had.'

7

Flo Flown

I had spoken to Jane from the airport, very briefly. She told me to hurry home but not in her usual affectionate welcoming way. In fact she had sounded odd, distanced, strangulated even, as though there was someone else in the room preventing her saying something she desperately needed to say, which was why I was anxious to get home as quickly as I could, and not stay to argue with Ethel, although I knew some of the things he had said couldn't possibly be true and he couldn't expect me to believe them but he needed to have the new narrative on the record.

I could see her face at the window as I got out of the cab. Even through the glass I could see how pale and haunted she looked.

'She's disappeared. Flo. Gone. I haven't a clue where she is. Haven't seen her since breakfast yesterday. Thought she might be staying with Maryanne but Maryanne hasn't seen or heard from her for weeks, which she says is weird because she normally texts her every day almost. I've been calling and calling but she never picks up.'

'Has Lucy any idea?'

'She says Flo has sort of stopped speaking to her. She thought at first it was because they had a row about her saying Maryanne was a show-off, but she doesn't really think it was that.'

'Why didn't you tell me at the airport?'

She paused in her distress and looked at me with a flicker of contempt.

'What the hell does it matter? You're here now.'

'No, I only –'

'If you must know, I thought someone might be listening in and it would give them a horrible sort of pleasure. That's how deranged I've been.'

'A kidnapper, you mean?'

'Don't use that word. Of course that's what I mean.'

'Look, she's been doing the hotels for Ethel in the holidays, this is probably just another one of those.'

'But she's always been with someone else and she lets me know exactly where she is and how long she'll be away for.'

As we wrangled on, I could hear in my head our strained, stricken voices being played back like a clip from a TV play about a missing girl, which was what all TV plays were about these days, as Jane and I constantly remarked to each other, and one of the things that someone was sure to say at some point was that it all felt like a bad dream, and now that it seemed to be happening to us a bad dream was exactly what it did feel like, so that although I was sick with fear and a racing heart, there was still somewhere in my head a fancy that this was happening to someone else, some other family, which was also one of the things that people said in these films, which didn't make it a bit better.

'You've rung Smothers of course.'

'I don't like that nickname, I think it's creepy,' Jane said, with a touch of her usual asperity. 'Yes of course I have. They haven't seen her for a week at least, and they haven't got any gigs lined up for her. I don't like that word "gigs" either. In fact, I did call Madame in case she might know something because Flo's been doing some extra classes to get her ready for the Royal, but the voice message said she was on holiday in the Auvergne.'

The phone rang. It was the police. They had no fresh reports of any missing persons, but Flo's details were now logged in, and there would be a police liaison officer coming round.

For some reason, the police liaison officer was the last straw. Jane sat down and broke into a sea of sobbing. Until then, she had been standing up, pale and austere and erect, as if she was back on duty in her hospital, geeing herself up for a painful interview with a desperate patient, except that now she was the one on the receiving end.

At this moment, the door opened and Lucy came in wearing a T-shirt which said GANGSTA and the psychedelic pink leggings which I thought didn't suit her, or anyone for that matter. She kissed me and took my hand. I looked at her anxiously, fearful that Flo being missing might set off one of her episodes.

She laughed, which was the last thing I expected, that queer gurgly laugh which wasn't like any other girl's except her sister's.

'Dad, I can see you thinking, is she going to have another one of her turns, but you ought to know by now it doesn't work like that. It's usually something silly that starts it, like we've run out of Coco Pops.'

Sometimes she seemed like a child of five, sometimes she could have been twenty-five, whereas Flo always behaved like exactly the age she was. Anyway, luckily this was one of her grown-up moments. She sat down beside Jane and put her arms round her and said something in her ear I didn't catch. Then to me:

'I'm sure she's perfectly all right. She's just forgotten to tell us about whatever it is she's doing, you know how thoughtless my sister can be, unlike me of course.' She spread out her palms and gave a fake-charming smile, miming a performer in search of applause.

'You haven't spoken to Ethel himself, I suppose?' I asked Jane.

'No, why should I? Did he say anything about Flo when you saw him?'

'No, but I had no reason to ask him about her. He sent his love to you all of course.' I don't know why I said this, because he hadn't, being too preoccupied with burying the African connection.

'I don't see why we need to get him mixed up in this,' Jane said, unable or not even trying to keep the dislike out of her voice.

'Well,' I said, 'he is her sort of employer, and he might have some plan for her which he hadn't told the rest of the office about.'

'I suppose so, but I don't want him taking it all over.'

'What you want is Flo back,' I said, firmly for once. 'I'll call him.' I headed out into the garden for some air and tried his mobile.

But Ethel didn't pick up. I tried the office. He was out at a meeting with some big American players, Gloria said, not without a hint of irony. When I came back into the sitting room, the police liaison officer was already sitting beside Jane on the sofa. Carole with an e was a strongly built woman, not plump but muscular with a frizzy bun and what I thought was too much make-up for someone in a comforter role, suggesting that she was giving too much thought to her own appearance. But she did have a lot of soothing things to say, such as that in nine cases out of ten the missing person gets in touch herself after a few days, although that of course immediately makes you think of the tenth case. Anyway, she held Jane's hand, not a thing most people did easily, and we looked at the photo of Flo in her ballet skirt which was all we had to hand, though it didn't seem entirely suitable, and Carole said what a lovely girl she was and they would stream the photo on their regional database, but as she said in most cases the missing person came back of her own accord without the police being involved at all.

I was glad that Carole had come but relieved when she left after half an hour. I could see that Jane was glad to have had someone to talk to outside the family, though she broke down again when the phone rang and it was her old assistant from the hospital saying that they hadn't heard anything there yet but she was sure that Flo would be back in two ticks, she was such a lovely reliable girl.

I don't know how we got through the next few hours – well, it was with the aid of a bottle and a half of Pinot Grigio and a Charlie Bigham fish pie from Ocado which is as near as Jane gets to haute cuisine. In these draggy hours of intense distress, I have to confess that I became more rather than less aware of Jane's faults – her sharpness, her awkwardness, her impatience with the unsupported theory – but at the same time this somehow made me feel more deeply sympathetic towards her, closer even, and I wondered whether she was feeling the same about me, but then in the same thought I realised how ridiculous it was to imagine that she would be thinking about me at all. Together anyway we drowned in a sea of alcohol and Nytol and knew no more.

The next day dawned so bright that the sun slipped in round the edges of our interlined bedroom curtains. Jane was still asleep and I couldn't bear to stay in bed a minute longer, though there was nothing in particular I could think of doing. Nytol always gave me a hangover worse than any wine, leaving me desolate even at times when there was nothing obviously wrong. Now was not such a time. I crept out of the bedroom and downstairs and out into the garden, the dew on the forget-me-nots brushing the hem of my dressing gown.

Jane's borders had never looked lovelier and I thought of other lovely mornings when terrible things had happened – I remembered the sun streaming into the kitchen at home when the news came that my mother had died in her sleep in the hospital. But then, oddly, as I wandered across the lawn, my mind turned to the pretentious game that Jane and I used to play, though we hadn't played it recently: she would point to a plant and if I knew its name, I would say 'Black-eyed Susan' and she would respond with '*Rudbeckia fulgida*'. Then I would point to another one, and she would say '*Edgeworthia chrysantha*' and I would retort 'Paperbush', and so on through honey spurge and bog sage and Juneberry to the end of the garden, a point being lost when either of us couldn't remember the right English or Latin name. The game seemed even ghastlier in retrospect, but just now it distracted me a little. I moved along the beds muttering to myself both halves of the rubric, '*Rudbeckia fulgida*, black-eyed Susan, *Coronilla glauca*, scorpion vetch' and so on, as though trying to recall the words of a song you used to sing when you fancied you were happy. At the far end of the garden I bent down to pick a sprig from a plant I couldn't remember the name of, to take it back to Jane to refresh my memory.

As I turned back to the house with the sprig in my hand, I saw Jane coming through the French windows. The sunlight was very bright, so that I could hardly make her out against the dazzling panes of glass. In fact, the first thing I recognised was the oatmeal jacket and skirt she was wearing which she used to put on for interviews with hospital boards. That, and the sunlight on her shiny black hair.

Then as she came nearer towards me and away from the windows and I could see her better, I realised that it wasn't Jane, it was Flo. And in the same instant I remembered, rather brilliantly considering the state I was in, that Flo had borrowed the suit to do some interviews with businesswomen for one of Ethel's projects – they were the same height now, she and Jane, the last time they had stood back to back in the kitchen in their stockinged feet.

She ran the last few yards and then fell into my arms and I have never been happier in my life, how could I ever hope to be? An unforgettable moment.

Then at that exact same moment my phone rang and it was Ethel.

'Dickie, they tell me you called. I can't apologise enough for what I've put you through, and I really want to make it up to you. As they say on *Monty Python*, and now for something completely different. Africa was always going to be a no-no, and I should have seen it straight away.'

'I wasn't calling about work. I was calling about Flo.'

'Your lovely daughter? What about her?'

'She disappeared, but –'

'Disappeared?' He broke in with a gasp, more of a gulp really. 'No, no, oh God, you'll never forgive me. I can't, I really can't –' He seemed lost for words, while continuing to talk in a hectic rush, giving me no chance to interrupt. 'You see, it was a last-minute thing. There was this hydro, in the Peak District, just reopening after refurb, and they offered us a slot, and Flo had to jump on the train, and she wasn't sure how to get hold of you in Africa, so I said I'd call you and explain where she was. But I was utterly focused on this American thing, and to my shame it completely slipped my mind. Oh God, how ghastly. But no worries, no worries at all. She'll be coming down this morning, she'll be with you in no time.'

He paused for breath, and I managed to get a word in. 'Yes, she's here now, I've seen her just this minute.'

'Oh, that's wonderful. What an awful time you and Jane –'

'Jane's just coming now,' I said.

There really was Jane coming down the steps in her short nightdress that didn't quite come down to her knees, the one with little cornflowers round the scalloped neck, like a child's nightie. I could have mistaken her for Flo, as I had just mistaken Flo for her. I stood motionless as they ran towards each other across the grass.

'I'll ring off now.' Ethel was still on the line. 'You won't ever forgive me, and I don't blame you. But I'm going to try to make it up to you, sooner than you can guess. Give my very best love to Jane, and tell her how desperately sorry I am.'

I could see Flo properly now, both of them in fact, because they were standing in the shade of the big *Ceanothus* (buckbrush, or California lilac). Her face was pearly pale, she looked tired from the journey but at the same time oddly confident.

'How was the Peak District?'

'Oh, Ethel did tell you then. The Peak District was fantastic,' she said. 'But the hotel was a dump. Eth says we shouldn't give it a write-up at all, because it would damage our reputation.'

'Ollie's office didn't seem to know where you were.'

'Didn't they? It was a last-minute thing, probably didn't get logged. I think Ethel fixed it himself.'

'You could have let Mum know.'

'Oh, I know, I know. But first I couldn't find my phone and then there was this terrible storm and the broadband was down. Do you mind if I talk to Mum by myself first, because if I talk to you both together, you'll just interrupt each other and I won't get a word in?'

'Fine by me,' I said, smiling and spreading my hands in a go-right-ahead gesture. What she said was not untrue, and I was pleased to hear the old impudence in her voice. They went back indoors holding hands. I turned back down the garden and to lower my pulse rate I restarted the naming game – elderberry, *Sambucus nigra*, *Cistus purpureus*, rock rose, etc. It was the last time I ever played that stupid game, the memory of this occasion was too plangent.

'Well?'

'She wouldn't tell me anything. She's gone upstairs to catch up on her sleep. Do you believe it?'

'The story, no, not really, but …'

'I suppose these things do come up at the last minute,' Jane said.

'Should I say something to Ethel?'

'You've already heard his story. What could you say which wouldn't be accusing him, accusing both of them, of making it all up?'

'I can't think.'

'All you can do is watch out for her. I can see she's not going to confide in me. But at least you're working in the same office.'

8

Jerrybuilt

I stood for a moment in the sunlight after she had gone indoors, then followed her, automatically tramping up to my room at the top of the house like a dog to its basket. I sat down and looked at the numb dark screen and logged on, expecting to see nothing much more than the stuff you always get overnight: invitations to Noble Caledonia cruises to Iceland or Patagonia, the neighbourhood website asking if anyone can lend them a pressure hose for their patio, how to lose 50lbs in 61 days. To my surprise, though:

BREAKING NEWS: Making Nice makes it in the States. We are delighted to announce our first major American contract. We have been exclusively hired as Lead Data Manager to the campaign of Senator Jerry Faldo for the presidential nomination. We already have our technical team working with Sen. Faldo's advisers in Chicago. They will shortly be joined in the Windy City by our Principal Political Strategist Dickie K. Pentecost.

MAKING NICE! GOING PLACES! WIN-WIN-WIN SITUATIONS!

Christ, I said aloud, though I was alone in the little room, *No.*

And then, this not at all to my surprise, the phone call, maybe forty seconds later.

'You've seen the statement we put out. Isn't it fantastic news? We had to get it out fast, so we could control the narrative.'

'Ethel, I can't possibly. Africa was bad enough, and in any case –'

'Listen, Dickie, I know I've jumped it on you, but the States are your old stamping ground, you know how their minds work. A British campaign team needs a true Brit to head it up, you're ideal.'

Ethel was no longer in apology mode. Now he had his easy wheedling voice on, the one suggesting infinite patience and any number of arguments up his sleeve.

'But you saw how out of my depth I was in Africa, this would be far –'

'Come on, Dickie, Africa was yesterday, it didn't happen. We weren't there, not in any real sense. And' – a touch of asperity here – 'we certainly won't be mentioning it in Chicago. You just have to go. We've got a great team out there, but they need a wise old head to front up the operation.'

'But I'm totally out of touch with American politics, and anyway isn't Faldo a Republican?'

'Dickie, Dickie, I didn't know you were such an old bigot. Yes, Jerry's a Republican, but he's wingman for the new Republican Party, he's also a former marine who worked for the Peace Corps, and he's a lay preacher on the South Side, and he made a fortune in medical supplies. What more do you want? Besides, all the Democrats in the race have their software teams in place already. I'm afraid the GOP came late to the IT party, but their misfortune is our golden opportunity to take the big stage. There's a business-class ticket on the morning flight waiting for you at the BA desk.'

I nearly, or only quite nearly, said all the things that were exploding in my head – about his unforgivable high-handed behaviour, his totally cynical attitude, and how he wouldn't know the truth if it hit him with a sledgehammer, and was this Peak District story really true anyway? – but I couldn't say the last bit, in fact I couldn't say any of it, because I knew that Flo would never forgive me, whatever the truth turned out to be.

So all I said was, 'Look, Ethel, this is terribly short notice, I've only just got my breath back, couldn't I take a couple of days to decide, at least to get up to speed on the American scene?'

'There's a briefing pack waiting at the BA desk too. You can read up the background on the flight. I'm relying on you, Dickie, time is desperately short, because Campbell Segal pulled out at the last minute. If we bring this one off, there'll be treats all round. The down payment is two million dollars with another two mil on completion, plus a success fee if Jerry makes it. This is serious money, Dickie, don't throw away your share. I'll give you half an hour to talk to Jane and confirm.'

At least it was an old-style phone call and not FaceTime. I couldn't have borne the sight of his pleading cockerel face and those chilling grey basalt eyes contradicting that oddly seductive smile.

'Yes, you're going,' Jane said to my amazement, when I complained about having to jump to Ethel's every change of tune. 'We need the money, and whatever's happening or not happening, this isn't the moment for you to throw a tantrum. Anyway, I know that basically you really like swanning around the world. After all, you've spent half your life doing it.'

'But that was reporting.'

'Well, perhaps it's time you started taking part a little. I hope you've got enough clean shirts left.' She laid a hand on my arm with a smile, as though conferring a blessing, and I surrendered, I wouldn't say gracefully, but I surrendered. The truth is, I take quite kindly to being boxed in. If I had been a prisoner of war, I would never have joined the escape committee. Anyway, I liked Chicago.

The next morning I had to leave the house long before the girls were up. They had spent most of the day in their rooms, Lucy still tired from the small fit she'd had after Flo's return and Flo herself catching up on her sleep. I crept out of the shuttered house, thinking how absurd my latest mission was and how even more absurd it was to leave them all for who knows how long – even the duration of my stay had not been settled. Ethel liked others to live on the run, just as he did himself. Improv was the name of his game.

'Mr Pentecost, why, this is a real pleasure, though I can't say it's entirely unexpected – they told me we'd be on the same flight. I'm not surprised you don't recognise me. We met in rather different circumstances. Dr Amos Musa.'

It was true, I hadn't recognised him without his spectacles and without his anxious look. He was smiling now, as he stood over me in the gangway, twinkling in fact. I couldn't disguise my surprise at seeing him, as well as my failure to recognise him. Ethel describing him as Musa the Loser suggested that he would be ruthlessly written out of the script. It occurred to me only then that we might be something of a stage army, with myself as platoon commander, marched to and fro at pace to give the impression of vast resources of manpower, the real point being that after the IT Revolution you didn't need all those boots on the ground to be master of the terrain.

'Ah, Dr Musa, hi, great to see you. It's a long way for you to come,' I said feebly.

'Oh, I'm just coming home. I'm a Chicago boy, raised on the South Side, graduated from La Salle High, did my PhD at Northwestern.'

'So you're not …'

'Never been in Africa in my whole damn life before.' He smiled at my ridiculously failing to spot him as an American. Through the window we could see the great shimmer of Lake Michigan and the skyscrapers along Lake Shore Drive shining silver and grey in the misty sun. I could see how moved Dr Musa was by the sight of it all.

I had hardly wheeled my trolley into Arrivals when I was seized by a high-breasted blonde woman in her thirties. She grabbed hold of my free hand as though to prevent me running off.

'Oh, Mr Pentecost, your picture doesn't do you a bit of justice. Welcome to Chicago.'

She was wearing a swirly pleated sky-blue skirt which made her slightest movement look like a football cheerleader limbering up.

'I'm Betsy Broadlee, Analytics Director for the campaign. I'll be working with you and Dr Musa. Amos, hi, it's so wonderful to see you again.' Her smile was so broad you wondered how she could manage to speak at the same time. Her accent was a deeper Southern accent than Amos's.

'You're from the South, I guess.'

'Why, you guess absolutely right, Mr Pentecost, Dickie, I may call you Dickie? You've got quite an ear. Yup, I'm an Alabama girl, never been this far north before, though I did do my master's at Johns Hopkins.'

'My folks were originally from Alabama,' Dr Musa volunteered, 'came up north in the forties. My pa worked in Gary, Indiana, in the steel mills.'

'Well now, isn't that something?' Betsy said.

Perhaps I was just tired after the flight, but I detected a certain something hovering behind her response, not quite a *froideur* but the after-flick of some earlier spat. At the same time, though, I felt the old restless excitement of being in America begin to stir a little.

'How do you come to be working for Senator Faldo?'

'Oh, Jerry and I go way back. We met on a yacht in New York Harbor at a Young Republicans party. He was an intern then, summer-crewing for a guy called Hank Kraus who was a very big lawyer at the time. And Hank asked Jerry to say a few words, and he gave such a great speech about reclaiming America, in his white ducks with the sun setting behind the Chrysler Building. I'll never forget it. He's only a little guy, but he's all heart. No, forget I said that, actually he's not so little, five foot seven, an inch taller than Winston Churchill. No, driver –' she rapped on the glass – 'you want to take Columbus and then double back up Walton. I already had my own company when I was twenty-one, Sunrise Domestic Services, basically finding Latinos who didn't have a green card to clean for employers who weren't too fussy. We had a ball, but the pointy-heads closed us down. So then I went digital, because I could see that's where the future was. I waved my master's in data technology around the place, but none of us had an idea in hell what we were doing. My ex used to say I went down the data mine without a safety helmet. *No*, you wanna take a left here and then travel the Loop. And I want you back out front at six o'clock punctualissimo. We're going to the Art Institute, it's on your schedule. The Chards are giving a fundraiser at the El Greco, and they insisted you absolutely must come along. Have you met Norfie and Eliza? – they're such darling people and they've been so generous to us.'

Ethel's briefing sheet had told me quite a bit about the Chard Foundation, which was paying most of our wages. Winthrop Chard, an engineer from Maine, had gone south when the black gold first gushed and devised an ingenious pumpjack that pumped twice as fast as the other nodding donkeys. His children and grandchildren had diverted the resulting billions into philanthropy, where they were now gushing impressive quantities into political causes and the arts. One thing everyone agreed on was that Norfolk Chard and his sister Elizabeth were amazingly modest considering.

I had barely time to wash before I was due back down in the gilded lobby. Betsy was already there, changed into a glittery black cocktail dress which I complimented her on and she said was just an old thing she threw on whenever she couldn't think what to wear. I noticed only then how beautiful she was. The high-piled tumble of daffodil-gold curls and the unnerving white teeth, that white which European dentists could only dream of, her impasto make-up – the whole public front seemed almost intended to distract attention from her fine, almost delicate features and the unusual green of her eyes. As an escort, I felt irremediably suboptimal.

The posters outside the Art Institute said *El Greco: The Agony of Ecstasy*, with the picture of some saint being flayed and looking back towards the viewer with an expression of total terror. His contorted attitude reminded me of that final poster of Julius which had been so cruelly defaced.

You could see how modest the Chards were from twenty yards away. There was a little respectful throng around them which managed to be distanced without ceasing to be a throng.

'Norfolk Chard. So glad you could come.' Tall and slightly stooped, he could have been a curator at the museum. He gave off a powerful air of not wanting to have a fuss made about him, being extremely attentive to the company, but in a rather unfulfilled way, as though expecting to hear something – a piece of valuable information, a practical instruction, not, I think, a joke – which he had not yet heard. His sister, six inches shorter, not quite dumpy, wholesome was perhaps the word, by contrast looked as if she wouldn't mind being amused. All around them, the guests in evening dress sashayed in a tactful minuet that paid homage to the presence of unimaginable wealth while pretending not to be ogling its possessors. On the walls, cadaverous saints writhed and cast their luminous eyes to the ceiling.

'I'm so sorry I didn't bring a dinner jacket.'

'My dear Mr Pentecost, don't give it a thought, this is the Midwest, we're just plain folks here.'

'We're so looking forward to sharing your expertise, Mr Pentecost,' her brother said. 'We're novices in data-driven campaigning. The Democrats really have the jump on us.'

'Well, I'm a bit of a novice myself too. I'm more of a political journalist.'

'Oh, your British modesty.' Eliza Chard gave a theatrical sigh and laid her plump hand on my arm, but I could tell that my disclaimer had not gone down well.

'Our foundation cannot of course make direct donations to political campaigns, though my sister and I do what we can to help in a strictly personal capacity. But the foundation does maintain a strong interest in political education, and that's where the new data science has, as I understand it, a significant role to play going forward.'

'Oh, very much so,' I said, striving to undo the look of disappointment that had crossed Norfolk Chard's face when I confessed my lack of expertise. 'We can use all sort of techniques to reach out to voters who've never voted before.'

'Voters … who've … never … voted … before.' Norfolk's speech, hitherto at a low cruising speed, now slowed to a crawl. 'Well, I guess you couldn't call them voters then, if they haven't ever voted. Are you by any chance talking about folks who aren't *registered*?' He gave the harmless word an almost sensuous stress, followed by something like a chuckle.

'Well, yes, I suppose I am, partly …'

'I want you to know, Mr Pentecost –'

'Dickie, please, Dickie.'

'Dickie, that in this state we pride ourselves on our robust system of registration –' again the sensuous emphasis. 'Nothing is more calculated, in my humble view that is, to destroy trust in the democratic system than voter fraud. In my young days, in Peekawa County, we had a system that was notoriously lax. "Vote early, vote often" was the name of the game. Some bums earned a week's pay going around the polling stations impersonating old folks who'd just died or were tucked up in a nursing home. We don't want to go back to those days. I dare say you'd agree with me on that, Dickie.'

'Well, yes of course, absolutely. I only wanted to say that we have had some success with mailshots explaining how to register, quite simple stuff really.'

'I shall be most interested to hear more,' Norfolk Chard said frostily. 'We are always eager to give opportunities to people who want to do the right thing.'

'You wouldn't believe what the Democrats get up to,' his sister put in. 'Registering folks who are just visiting and don't even live in the state, getting proxy votes for old ladies with dementia who don't know what day it is.'

'In California,' Betsy said, 'there's a bunch of Democrats pestering the governor to mail voting forms to every citizen.'

'Isn't that just the worst thing, Betsy?' Eliza clutched her hands in despair at the thought.

I was rescued by the museum director who wanted to show the Chards their latest acquisition.

'The one we bought off the Onassis estate, *The Martyrdom of St Jerome*, right?'

'Absolutely right, Mr Chard. It's an early piece, once attributed to Titian, can you believe?'

Norfolk gave a wintry chuckle at the implausibility of this.

'But as you know, Florsheim is one hundred per cent convinced that the picture's right.'

'You can trust Florsheim,' Norfolk said with some authority, as if to double the value of Florsheim's imprimatur.

'Let's go look at some pictures.' Betsy grabbed my hand and led me away from the exhibition to another part of the gallery which was quite empty.

'Never,' she said, 'but never get Norfolk T. Chard on the subject of voting rights. He thinks the whole thing's a conspiracy by the Dems.'

'And is it?'

'You cannot be serious. Of course it is. Campbell Segal reckons that unregistered voters would break 70–30 for the Dems, maybe more. We'd be lucky to carry more than three flyover states in the whole Union. No, what Norfolk Chard means by political education is stuff about how the government wastes your tax dollars and how illegal immigration has changed the face of the USA. As it happens, we've got some hot research in the can on those very topics. Oh look, what's happening to that poor lady?'

'That must be St Agatha. She's having her breasts sliced off for refusing to marry the Roman governor.'

'My, these days they only do that to you if you've got breast cancer.'

'St Agatha is, I believe, the patron saint of breast cancer patients.'

'Oh, that's so nice – I mean them having a patron saint. You do know a lot of stuff, Dickie.'

'Not the right stuff for this operation, I'm afraid.'

'Oh, don't worry, my dear. We'll muddle through, as you Brits say. I think we've done our duty here. How about we grab some ribs and go listen to some good old Chicago jazz music?'

She held my hand again as we walked out into the cool night air of Michigan Avenue. I didn't flatter myself that I was being singled out, I could see she was a touchy-feely person. All the same, I could not repress a faint throbbing of noontide. In the companionable dark of Bud's Place, she used her napkin to wipe the sauce off my chin.

'Bud Freeman, greatest tenor sax ever to come out of Chicago. You see, I know stuff too.'

'I never doubted it.'

The elderly jazzmen shuffled onto the little horseshoe stage, wrinkled tortoises joshing each other as they settled their instruments over their bent shoulders for the opening number, which Betsy told me was 'Tillie's Downtown Now', one of Bud's legendary riffs. As the lead sax settled into its mellow saunter, she beat time on my knee, not flirtatiously, more the way you beat out the rhythm of a nursery rhyme to soothe a fractious child.

Then they struck up an easy sentimental air which sounded familiar but I couldn't place until the ancient trumpet player put down his horn and sang in a gravel-landslide of a voice: 'S'posin' I should fall in love with you, / Do you think that you could love me too?'

And we sang along, rocking gently in the velvet dark of our booth.

In the cab back to the hotel she clutched me round the ribs and planted a long sweet kiss on my lips – well, I did as much of the planting as she did.

'Do you like my perfume?'

'I'm sure I'd love it, but I lost my sense of smell in a skiing accident.'

Why did I say that? It didn't begin to be true, in fact it was the sort of lie Ethel would make up. Perhaps mendacity was catching. Every lie you told loosened your hold on the truth. Or perhaps adventures always started off with a lie or several.

'How romantic,' she said, 'I never heard of that happening to anyone before.' And she kissed me again as a reward for having such an interesting thing happen to me. I moved my hand onto the upper slope of her right breast in a tender exploring.

'St Agatha never knew what she was missing,' she said.

'Poor Aggie,' I said, moving my hand a fraction lower.

Brrngg, brrngg. On a whim, I had selected the ringtone for my new iPhone because it reminded me of the electric bell which summoned us to the classroom at the end of break at my first school, a shrill double vibration repeated at short insistent intervals. My jacket had ridden up in our embrace and so the phone was ringing at about the level of our thumping hearts and it called time on this occasion too in no uncertain fashion.

'Wow, that's a loud one,' Betsy panted, as she pulled away to her corner of the cab.

'Oh God, sorry, I'll turn it off,' I said, but not for the first time pressed the loudspeaker button instead.

'Is that you, Dickie?'

'Yes, yes. Sorry I didn't call from the hotel, but we had to go out to this El Greco exhibition.'

'El Greco? Are you on an art tour all of a sudden?'

'There was a party given by the people who are paying for our services.'

'Well, it's three in the morning here and Flo's only just come in, refusing to speak to me.'

I crammed the phone as close to my ear as possible, vainly trying to concentrate the sound away from Betsy, who was huddled up in her corner looking intently at her own phone.

'Look,' I said, 'I'm in a sort of meeting. Can I call you back?'

'Don't bother – at least I know you're in the land of the living,' Jane said and hung up, or whatever you do with iPhones.

'Wife, huh?' Betsy enquired, without taking her eyes off her phone.

'Yes.'

'It happens,' she said.

'I probably shouldn't but can I ask what you're looking at on yours?'

'You shouldn't but I'll tell you for free. It's my therapist's emergency app, she calls it her online Little Book of Calm. I use it whenever I'm stressed. I'll let you download it too if you like. Sounds like you could use it.'

'I probably could.'

'Strange what El Greco can do to you.'

'Or St Agatha.'

'Yes, or Aggie. At least we're still in one piece. We're nearly at the St Clair. Driver,' she said, rapping the window, 'we want the Lobby, not the Ballroom.'

As we got out, to my surprise she kissed me just as warmly, but with an unmistakable feeling of farewell. She stood for a moment on the forecourt, looking at me.

'Yes, you do have nice eyes,' she said.

'I could say the same about you,' I said.

'You should. A girl needs all the encouragement she can get. Remember, we've got the breakfast meeting with Jerry in the Dirksen Suite, 8.15 sharp.'

She got back in the cab and I waved goodbye and turned back to the hotel, overwhelmed by a flurry of thoughts: guilt of course, that came flooding, but along with the guilt and not easily confessed, elation too, a sense of not having quite lived all the life there was to live, and then after that, a more sober sense of a narrow escape. If the phone hadn't rung, who knew what would have happened, or failed to happen? The ringtone was probably a blessed caesura, sent to save me from forgetting myself – that is, the self that was short on panache and long on self-preservation.

After three or four hours' sleep, I rang Jane back at her breakfast time, and said I'd come home as soon as I could. She had no fresh news about Flo who was still asleep. In fact, she had nothing really to say to me, except that she never cared for El Greco. Somehow she made it sting.

The Dirksen Suite was packed with interns, the boys in button-down shirts and the girls in crisp shirtwaisters. Betsy was already there already in her twirly sky-blue skirt, looking as fresh as a leaping salmon. The fragrance of the eggs Benedict and the brewing coffee added to the hyped-up feel of the whole thing.

'Hey, Dr Pentecost, come look at this. We got a surprise for the Senator.' Up on the screen behind the buffet flashed an image of what I thought were sailors, but the guy next to me murmured 'Marines', marching along a quayside. Then the clip switched to a boxing ring surrounded by cheering marines and in the middle holding his gloves above his head was a skinny but muscly young man, and underneath, the caption 'Jerry S. Faldo, US Marines Boxing Champion, 1997'.

'Isn't that great, Dickie? We just tack on a few simple slogans: He's Your Champion Now, that kinda thing. Strength, patriotism, all in one simple image. The Senator just loved it when we showed him a rush. It'll go down a bundle with the target audience. Everyone loves a fighter.'

Mapping out the scenario, Betsy seemed somehow to bulk larger, as though she was herself about to step into the ring. The soft yielding creature of the night before, well, she was gone.

'That's great,' I said. 'Tell me, what weight did he fight at?'

'Lightweight,' Betsy said, turning to the tall, bespectacled man beside her with an earphone. 'Isn't that right, Bill, he was a lightweight?'

'Yeah, that's right, Betsy, he fought at lightweight – 130 to 135 pounds, like Benny Leonard and Roberto Duran.'

'Lightweight,' I repeated in a musing sort of way.

'Lightweight,' Betsy repeated after me, as though mesmerised.

'You don't think …'

'Oh my God. I can see it now: little Jerry, he was a lightweight then, he's a lightweight now, always was, always will be. No, it's a definite no-no.'

'You don't think he could be the Little Guy Who Stands Up for the Little Guy?'

'Def not. The Senator has made it very clear that he does not want to run as the Little Guy in this or any other contest.'

'He's coming right now,' Bill said, listening to his earphone, 'you gonna break the news or shall I?'

'Oh, it's such a pity. He loved that clip to bits.'

'So it's not really a surprise then?'

'Not as such, no, but that's how we've programmed it.'

'So,' Bill said, 'we play him in with it just the same?'

'Yeah, that's what he's expecting.'

The glass double doors to the Dirksen Suite were flung open and the Senator strode in, with a couple of heavies and a gaggle of PAs trotting behind him. As he saw us all mustered, he spread his hands in a gesture of amazement and delight and unleashed his trademark grin, that small boy's rueful aw-shucks, only-kidding type of grin, which had done such a lot for him. Then came the blare of the marine band playing 'The Star-Spangled Banner' and we cleared a pathway for the Senator to get a proper view of the screen.

As he caught sight of his younger self prancing round the ring, Faldo threw up his hands and clasped them above his head in the same attitude, then slapped his knee with pleasure.

'Wow, I haven't seen that film in twenty years. I was in pretty good shape then. Where in heaven's name did you guys dig that one out from?'

'His PA sent it to us,' Betsy giggled into my ear.

As he skipped away from his minders to be introduced to the new guys, viz. Amos and me, I could see for the first time how astonishingly slight and lithe he was, not merely light on his feet but superbly at ease, making the rest of us seem lumpish and overgrown. It was as if he were modelling some new subspecies purpose-bred for an age of miniaturisation.

Amos said he was from the South Side, and Jerry lightly punched his upper arm and said, 'Is that right? We need more of your people. How are you folks getting along down there?'

'I'm a data scientist, sir, for my sins, not a district organiser.'

'Well, there's a thing. I'm pretty big on data myself. That's the new way to get up close and personal with the voters. You can't just wave to them from some godforsaken whistle-stop any more, you need to dig deep into their bank balances, how's it with their mortgage, their health insurance, find out where it's really hurting.'

Amos nodded vigorously and took Faldo through a few of the voter micrographs he had prepped, and the Senator nodded sagely.

'Uh, Jerry,' Betsy coughed politely,' I don't like to butt in, but we're doing the set-up for the rally backdrop and we wondered about using the boxing clip for the warm-up sequence.'

'Great idea, let's go for it.'

'There is just one thing.'

'Shoot, Betsy.'

'You boxed lightweight, right?'

'Sure I did. Greatest division in the whole damn game. Bobby Duran, Benny, all the best pound-for-pound fighters there ever were, barring Sugar Ray of course, all of them lightweights.'

'You don't think, lightweight, I mean –'

'Don't you fret, Betsy, you go right ahead with that film.' He patted her arm reassuringly. All the same, a soupçon of puzzlement had crossed his neat dark features. He was said to have quite a temper on him, and already I could see a certain mean intensity gathering in his whole body, like a storm just visible out at sea, and not that far out either. I noticed now that when his face wasn't smiling, the expression it settled into had a hint of grievance about it.

'Now then, Mr Data Scientist, you need to talk me through those voters some more. Tell me their hopes, their fears, their girlfriends' telephone numbers.'

'Well, Senator,' said Amos, 'we ran a couple of Senate campaigns, in Arkansas and Michigan, and we had some pretty fair results.'

'It was certainly a surprise when Tommy Schulz got back. We all thought he didn't have a prayer. Just how do you sprinkle your magic dust?'

'Well, first of all we take what we call the Persuadables, folks who say they might vote for us if … then we subdivide them into Worried Patriots, Carers and Individualists, and we target our digital ads accordingly. "Keep our borders safe. Don't mess with your family's future." That would be for the Carers. Then for the Patriots, we put gun control and national security into a hot mix: "Protect your country. Protect your family. Defend the Second Amendment."'

'And for the Individualists?'

'Quite simply: "You can take back your country." That worked nicely in South Carolina too.'

'How do you know which people are which?'

'Oh, a lot of it comes from this enormous data set we harvest from Facebook – church membership, PTAs, gun clubs, pro-life groups, that kind of thing.'

'Must cost a bomb to get that kind of material.'

'Oh no, Facebook let us have it pretty much for free. Their advertisers use our research, and we use their profiles. You can get, oh ten million profiles for a million bucks, less probably. Ten cents a voter.'

Amos Musa smiled benignly like one who has just given a guided tour of the Pearly Gates.

'Fantastic,' the Senator said, 'and tell me, how we gonna cope with this pesky voter registration campaign?'

'Well, Jerry,' Betsy jumped in, 'we have a series of digital ads which we target at the Worried Patriots: "Stop voter fraud. Defend your democracy. Lobby the Governor." But it's a rather harder sell, that one. We find it works better to discourage existing voters from going to the polls at all if they're likely to vote the wrong way. So – and this is the new departure – we target the Unpersuadables who are likely to vote Democrat to stay home.'

'Sounds dangerously like Voter Suppression to me.'

'It's what we call Deterrence Strategy, Jerry, not the same thing at all. There are no recorded cases of digital ads being prosecuted for VS. Physical intimidation, yes, if you send a bunch of heavies to block the way to the polling station, that's a crime, sure, but beseeching the voters not to waste any more of their tax dollars by voting for a Democrat, why, that's democracy in action.'

'Sure is, Betsy.' They beamed at each other. I could not believe that this magnificent figure and I had kissed the night before. She was like Boadicea or a Valkyrie, the Senator beside her merely a personable spear-carrier. Now he kissed her briefly by way of thanks for her advice, she gracefully dipping her knees to get level with him.

The younger staffers began to press towards the blueberry muffins and the eggs Benedict laid out on the long buffet. The briefing was over, and a sense of desolation overcame me.

'Don't overdo the eggs, we've got brunch at the Springfield Rotary at noon.' Betsy nudged me with her plate as she queued behind me. I wondered what, if anything, she thought about last night. To be filed under 'night, ships that pass in the', probably.

We drove out of the city down the expressway in a little convoy, led by the film crew truck with 'Jerry's the Berries' on the side, then a pickup carrying a pile of placards and a banner strung up proclaiming 'Jerry S. Faldo, Your Next President', then us in the black Cadillac and finally the security guys in an SUV convertible.

Soon we were out beyond the avenues of colonial clapboards and into flat rolling cornfields reaching to the horizon, relieved only by the occasional shining silo or sleepy gas station.

'Mm,' said the Senator, opening the window and taking a gulp of air, 'this is my kind of country.'

'Were you brought up on a farm?'

'Sakes no,' he said with a laugh. 'The only log cabin we ever saw as kids was the one my dad ordered from Sears Roebuck for us to play in. He was regional manager for Chase till they fired him after twenty-five years. That was a bad day, I can tell you. Say, you got the new draft, Betsy?'

She handed him a yellow legal pad with big handwriting all over it.

'You still do your speeches in longhand then?'

'Well, actually no, there's a cute little machine you talk into and it prints out in your own handwriting. I believe in the personal touch. Of course most guys these days go for those autocue things, but I reckon they give you a weird stary look, so I keep my notes in my hand, and brandish them like Winston used to, though I reckon to have the words pretty much by heart just like he did.' He waved the yellow pad, swatting me lightly on the cheek, I'm not sure whether on purpose.

We glided into a fair-sized town – I missed the sign with the name of it – and we came into the main square where there was a crowd gathered, seventy or eighty people perhaps, on the shallow steps of the town hall.

Jerry – after sitting beside him for an hour in the back of the Caddy, we were definitely Jerry and Dickie – jumped out and, well, I had heard about politicians who could switch it on, but even so, I was dazzled. There was an electrical charge about his exit from the limo, an explosive quality about his high fives to the crowd, and as for the smile, it was as wide as the Caddy's rear bumper.

'He's got it, you know, Dickie, he's really got it,' Betsy murmured ecstatically as the Senator shook hands and fist-bumped his way through the crowd lickety-split up the shallow steps until he stood on the esplanade and they swivelled to listen to him as the chorus in a Verdi opera swivels towards the heroic tenor.

'Those steps are just perfect. He only needs to be a couple of feet above them,' Betsy cooed, clasping her hands in delight at the success of the prep work.

I felt a tug at my sleeve. There was Dr Amos Musa, his shades glinting in the morning sun.

'Hi,' he said. 'Jerry said I should come along and see what it felt like at the sharp end.'

As I was about to answer, he in turn had his sleeve tugged by Bill the media manager.

'Hey, Dr Musa, we need you out front, to mix the crowd up a bit.'

'I'm a data scientist, not a cheerleader,' Amos said, but he consented amiably enough to be led up to the front row of the little throng which had gained a few more curious strollers. It was a delicious morning.

'Well, *hullo*, Lafayette! Who'd want to be anywhere else in the world on a morning like this?'

An answering rumble of greeting. Someone in the crowd held up a home-made placard saying 'Laffies for Jerry' — I say home-made, but the night before I had seen Bill and his team on their knees in the suite running up half a dozen of these homely boards with only the place name changed on each, and there was now a stack of them nestling in the pickup.

'I was raised in a small town just like this, Garfield, Michigan. We left town when I was twelve years old, but the values I learned there have stayed with me all my life — trust your neighbour, do the right thing, a fair day's work for a fair day's pay ...'

Out of the corner of my eye, I watched Bill crouched behind the monitor. On his little screen, I could just make out the beaming countenance of Amos in the front row next to a hefty fellow in a baseball cap.

'We had to leave Garfield because my daddy lost his job. And what he did he do when that catastrophe overtook our little family? He didn't sit on his butt and wait for the welfare cheque. No, he got up and took us off in our beat-up Chevy and drove up and down the state until he found another pay cheque. And that's what made me a Republican. Let me tell you something, folks, if you're expecting a traditional country-club type of Republican, you come to the wrong place. I'm a Republican because I'm with the folks who haven't had all the breaks, the folks who've had to pick themselves up and start all over again. Only a few miles down the road from here there was a skinny kid called Abe. He and his family had come from two states away where they hadn't had much luck and they had to build their own house out here from scratch with the timber offcuts they could beg from the local farmers. Well, you all know …'

My attention began to wander and I noticed that Betsy was surreptitiously catching up on her texts. What was it about the speech? The Senator's delivery wasn't exactly monotonous. More that the text seemed programmed too neatly to meet the expectations of the audience, to tickle their supposed resentments. Looking around the ruddy shirtsleeved crowd, they looked to me as if they weren't doing too badly. But what did I know?

This was what Betsy called his seven-minute rouser, timed to the second she said, and it seemed to do the business nicely. There were cries of 'Go, Jerry, go', and a couple of 'Faldo for President' banners waggled aloft which looked quite authentic to me.

At the side of the steps, where the crowd was thinner, I saw a scarecrow of a man with a grey straggle of a beard, waving a placard with some violence. 'Justice for Victims of Fent—' – the writing was wavery and I couldn't make out the ending of the last word.

'What's that one about?' I said to Betsy.

'Oh, it's a non-story,' she said, turning to put her phone in her tote bag.

'Non-story about what?' I persisted.

'Well, there was this painkiller and one of Jerry's companies – but it was a long time ago and anyway they were only share options and he put all his stuff in a QBT…qualified blind trust,' she added, seeing my baffled look. 'I expect you have them in the UK too.' I said I thought we did.

'Great, Jerry, just perfect. Seven minutes flat,' she said as the candidate trotted down the steps past us, his jacket hooked over his shoulder Jack Kennedy-style. He hadn't been wearing the jacket in the car, but put it on just before we got to Lafayette, so he could take it off and roll up his sleeves as he was saying Hi to the crowd.

On we went, through the chequerboard flatlands smiling now in the summer sun. Deeper into the country, the odd chipmunk scampered across the road, and there was an occasional stand of old oaks or cottonwoods by the roadside, where people were taking the shade. If there were enough of them, Bill in the lead car would signal the cavalcade to stop, and Jerry would hop out and say 'Hi, I'm Jerry Faldo and I'm running for President, how are you guys doing?' and the people would smile and say 'Great to have you with us, Senator, we're all good Republicans here', or, if they weren't, 'I'm afraid we're all Democrats but the best of luck anyway.' These encounters were brief, but they had to be genuine and so they were touching and made you think better of the whole business – and of course they made great pictures. The Senator himself seemed happier after them, as though these unforced blessings made up for the rest. After it was all over, Betsy sent me a bunch of the pictures, and these shots of the little shirtsleeved figure shaking hands in the dappled shade moved me all over again.

At the brunch, he gave the seven-minute rouser again, exactly the same, with all the pauses to seek for the right word, and the little catch in the throat when he talked about his father.

'By the way,' I said to Betsy when we were tucking into our second eggs Benedict of the day, 'what actually became of the father?'

'Well,' she said, 'he did get another job, in Colorado selling mortgages for the bank he'd always worked for, oddly enough, but he couldn't handle life on the road, and he took to the bottle. They found the car in a ditch just outside one of those old silver-mining towns, I forget its name, he'd been there for days probably because of it being a ghost town, and nobody quite knew whether it was an accident or not. The mother remarried, and, well, you know what stepfathers can be like. Still, it all helped to make the man.' She nodded not without affection at the Senator, who was mock-pacifying a cluster of smiling matrons.

The big evening rally was back in the city, at a convention hall which they chose because it was small and it was early days, and they were quite right because they had trouble getting the place even half full, but with ingenious use of screens and curtains there was a bright enough buzz to the scene when

Jerry's Barbershop Quartet scampered onto the stage and bounced into his campaign anthem, which was a rewrite of 'Life is Just a Bowl of Cherries', delivered with the raucous oomph of the Ethel Merman version rather than the wistful rendering of Doris Day (which I remembered as coming closer to the underlying melancholy that the composer intended). The point was, though, when the quartet got to the line 'So keep repeating, it's the berries', for the whole audience to join in 'So keep repeating, it's the Jerries', which they did fortissimo.

Then we had the biopic flashed up on the big screen: Jerry aged about eight in Garfield, a dark-eyed marmoset in short pants, then with his parents and sister standing beside the Chevy, father not looking too cheerful, then the skinny graduate in gown and mortarboard, followed by the smiling marine in uniform, and, the climax and really the point of the whole film, the lean lightweight champion with his gloves clasped above his head and underneath, a last-minute caption tweak by Bill apparently, YOUR CHAMPION. Then on came the candidate himself, mock-boxing on twinkletoes, before he stood to attention, gave the marine salute and threw his arms out to the audience. Wow, I said to Betsy who was clapping in a frenzy.

The full-length speech went well enough too, so far as I could judge. It contained all the material from the seven-minute rouser, with a whole lot more policy stuff thrown in – tax breaks for small businesses, crackdowns on illegal immigrants, better mental health treatment for veterans suffering from PTSD – and then a peroration about reclaiming America, from whom or what not specified.

'It was absolutely fine,' I said afterwards, 'but just a little bit predictable perhaps.'

'The Senator only does predictable,' Betsy said, with the nearest approach to glum she was capable of. 'I have tried to feed him a few off-beat gags, but he said, no, that's not me, Betsy. So instead I gave him a couple of Reagan funnies which he was OK with, because the sainted Ron had uttered them. That's the rarest quality in a candidate, you know, Dickie, genuine SOH. It's so precious and you just can't fake it. Fantastic, Jerry, fantastic,' she yelled, still applauding as the Senator passed by on his way to the green room, glistening with sweat under his pancake.

As we walked round the back of the convention hall to the parking lot, I caught sight of the man with the straggly beard, who seemed to be following us around. He was being hustled away by security guards, still trying to wave his placard, and the guards were whacking it with their nightsticks to make him put it down.

I said a chaste goodnight to Betsy. It had been a gruelling day, but I felt too restless to go to bed just yet, so I switched on the TV at random and found myself watching another campaign rally, this one in Minneapolis I think. And there was the big guy haranguing an audience of two maybe three thousand, at least twice the size of our little show anyway.

'Then there's Little Jerry Faldo. You know something about Little Jerry? He used to be a boxer. Fact. No, don't laugh. You thought he was a retired circus midget. But no, he boxed a little when he was a kid. He boxed Lightweight. Fact. He's a Lightweight, always was, always will be. A Lightweight, and a Loser. He was a Loser then. And he's a Loser now. And you know something else about Little Jerry Lightweight? You ever hear of a drug called Fent-an-eel?'

He drew out the word with infinite delicacy and disdain. Not for the first time, I thought how much his act relied on a brilliant sort of high camp, giving his words an affected teeny-weeny exaggeration, making refined little pinching gestures with his hands – all the tricks of the gay comic but somehow rebooted for straights.

'Nasty stuff Fentaneel. Very nasty. Ruins the lives of millions of decent American families. And you know who used to make Fentaneel? Why, our old friend Little Jerry Lightweight, that's who. Owned the firm that had a monopoly on its manufacture. Total monopoly. Fact. Now of course when Little Jerry Lightweight hung up his little boxing gloves and put on those tall shoes, no, I didn't say Cuban heels because there's an embargo on Cuban heels, so unless he's breaking the embargo – oh sorry I forgot, that guy, I can't remember his name, he abolished the embargo, so they may be Cuban heels after all. Anyway, when Little Jerry Lightweight goes to his momma and says, Momma, I'm going to run for President of the United States, she says to him, Jerry, don't you even think about it until you've got rid of all that Fentaneel, so he goes away and hires a fancy lawyer, and the lawyer says to him, don't you worry, you just put it all in a blind trust, and nobody will ever know a thing about it. So there you have it, folks. Put your blind trust in Little Jerry Lightweight, and everything will be fine and dandy.'

On and on it went, merciless, looping and zooming off at a tangent, and then coming back to the main subject again, in an apparently aimless freewheeling which was in reality a deadly calculated trussing-up. Mesmerised, I watched it out until the whole rally was over. The experience of it was so disturbing yet so entertaining that I didn't expect to get to sleep at all. But I dozed off before midnight into a deepish sleep.

It must have been an hour or more before the click of the door opening woke me and I poked my head over the bedsheet to see who it was. She came towards me on tiptoe, wanted to surprise me, I suppose, but I threw out my arms to her and swept the sheet aside. In the dusky light I could see her eyes shining as she tumbled down on top of me and threw up her swirly skirt and the rest was a glorious salty bliss. She bucked when I rode her, and said Dickie, Dickie, you are amazing, and I amazed myself, I have to say. Then almost as quickly she was gone, shaking her tousled locks and straightening her skirt as she went, and blowing me a kiss as she closed the door.

I woke at seven, perhaps half past, and remembered the dream in every detail. Could you be ashamed of a dream if it was your unconscious at the controls?

There she was anyway, fiddling with the coffee machine at the breakfast buffet and blowing me a kiss in real life.

I rather hoped she hadn't watched the other rally, but of course she had, it was part of her job.

'Yeah,' she said, 'between you and me we're toast. The funny thing is, though, that actually the polls have been shifting towards us in the past two days and we've been steadily moving ahead of the other candidates. But no, toast.'

When the polls closed five days later, we finished in second place, six points behind Jerry's tormentor but just ahead of the rest. I wasn't there when the Senator announced that he was pulling out, but Betsy texted me that they were all in tears, even the guys who had already decided to make the jump, which didn't include her because she'd rather boil in hell than work for that man. Among those transferring their allegiance and their billions were Norfolk and Eliza Chard, who announced that there was only one man left in the race who was capable of reclaiming America.

I called Ethel, but as usual he was way ahead of me. 'Fantastic news, Dickie, I heard amazing reports of what you achieved for the Senator. We couldn't have asked for better – a respectable second place and a speedy pull-out with no fuss. It has been tricky trying to ride two horses at the same time, but now we can see our way clear to an exclusive data management contract. The great thing is of course that the Chards pay on the nail. The bank transfer arrived yesterday for the full two mil.'

'You mean,' I said dozily, 'that you're going to work for –'

'*We* are going to work for the Big Man, yes. We had to prove ourselves on the nursery slopes first, and apparently his people were most impressed by our operation. As I say, Betsy could not speak highly enough of what you personally brought to the party. You and Amos between you – what a fantastic data analyst that guy is. Happy days are here again, Dickie, happy days.'

I couldn't think what to say, so I just said I supposed I'd see him back at Smothers.

'No you won't actually, not just yet anyway. I'm flying over today to make my number with the Man. So we can wave to each other in mid-air. I rely on you and the Glow Worm to mind the shop.'

If there was a cloud higher than nine, he was sailing on it. His voice trembled with an insufferable exultation.

9

Ghosting

'If there was any doubt about it before, there certainly isn't now,' Jane burst straight out, her voice severe but trembling. I still had my face buried in her neck, too overjoyed at seeing her to grasp immediately how near the edge she was.

'How do you mean? Has she said?'

'You don't sob all day just because your dad's boss who has given you a holiday job has gone to America if that's all he is. She cried most of yesterday too after he called her.'

'You're sure it was him?'

'Definitely. I could hear her on the upstairs landing. She started off all bright and excited, then went quiet as he babbled on, then she got excited again, only this time sounding anguished and protesting and then just sad, resigned, or at least that's what I thought. She wouldn't speak to me afterwards, just went back to her room and stayed there. How I loathe that man.'

'So what do you think's happened?'

'He's dumped her obviously. Waited till he was safely three thousand miles away to tell her.'

'You think she had no idea?'

'I *don't know*,' Jane shouted, shaking with anger as much at my questions as at the situation.

'Oh God,' I said.

'Oh God – is that all you can say?'

'And Lucy?' I asked, trying to deflect her fury. 'How is Lucy?'

'Oh, you know … the usual thing, one's down, the other's up.' Jane made a see-saw with her hands. 'The new medication seems to be working, fingers crossed. She hasn't had a fit since you went away. Says she's thinking of taking up martial arts. Couldn't be better.'

We stood there in the hall. How fine she looked in her misery, or perhaps it was her contempt for the whole shoddy business that gave her that look, the look of a hawk planing over a scrubby bit of country and not liking what it sees.

Then without warning the door upstairs opened and there she was at the top of stairs, Flo, in her rainbow-nation jumper, appearing utterly composed and quite pleased to see me.

'I've been so silly, Dad,' she said, after we had kissed. 'What on earth was the point of pretending? You both knew straight away about me and Ethel, it was so totally obvious. He even wanted me to go to the States with him, but of course I couldn't with ballet school coming up, and anyway the last thing on earth I'd want would be to have anything to do with that terrible man, I mean not Ethel, *him*. Well, I did think of it at first, then I thought, No, Florence, it's just not you' – this was a quote from a Young Adult novel which had become a catchphrase with the girls, this phoney way of talking to themselves as Florence and Lucinda. 'And of course I wasn't going to drop out of the Royal whatever else I did.'

'So what was all that yesterday?' Jane said sharply.

'All what yesterday?'

'That long phone call.'

'I don't remember giving you permission to listen in to my phone calls, Mum.'

'I didn't, but I couldn't help –'

'Don't worry, Mum, it was just a row. He called me later and it's all OK. Don't look so sad. I'm fine.'

'So things are still all right at Smothers?'

'Oh, it's all such fun' – another quote, I assumed, perhaps from the same Young Adult novel. 'One of the Brothers has been arrested for dealing, and Esmeralda and I are off for a girls' freebie at the Hoarwithy Arms which is legendary for its cassoulet and venison en croûte, according to the brochure. Oh, and you'll never guess what the Glow Worm has got up her sleeve for you.'

'Something nice?'

'Something unbelievable, but I'm not going to spoil the surprise.' She let out the gurgly laugh which she and Lucy had inherited from their mother, a wicked knowing Welsh laugh which sounded odd when it came, rather occasionally, from Jane who wasn't at all knowing but quite natural coming from the girls who in their different ways both were.

'Oh, come on, do tell me.'

'No, you'll know soon enough,' and she let out the gurgly laugh again, for the pleasure of keeping me in suspense.

'Must fly. I'm meeting Es at Euston.'

She darted off with her bag slung over her shoulder, covering our white panicky faces with flying kisses.

By luck not design, I had arrived back in time for the next meeting of the Demetrios Academy of

Dance Trust, which I was glad not to miss, not for the meeting itself but for the little display that Madame insisted should precede it, as a chance to show work in progress and get the pupils used to dancing before an audience – not that most of them seemed to need much encouragement – and as a *bonne bouche* for the trustees. The way she said *bonne bouche* stuck in my mind, it had such a savour of old Paris, of patisseries which smelled of icing sugar and fresh brioche. With all her severity of expression, not unlike Jane's I thought, no one knew better how to convey and create pleasure.

The other trustees were already trooping into the little cafe beside the dance floor, now all brasserie chic with bamboo chairs and a brass rail.

Biddy Tootal Ross bounced up and gave me a smacking kiss and said how smashing it all was. Our patron, the great Demetrios, gave me a big hug too, as though we had known each other ever since we had been boys together in Piraeus.

'You see, Pentecostas my friend, what fucking great things we have done.' He waved his hand at the Parisian cafe, the leather-clad barre and the great velvet curtain which now covered the back brick wall, midnight blue, to remind her of the Mariinsky, Madame told us.

'The very man.'

Bryce Wincott was only to be expected, but the force of his arriving was somehow even more obnoxious than I remembered, perhaps because he was so obviously blooming, bursting out of his houndstooth jacket, regimental bow tie twirling over his striped shirt.

'Just back from the States, I understand,' he said in that respectful way people like him speak to returned travellers.

'Yes,' I said.

'Well, it's bloody marvellous to see you. I can't tell you how pleased I am.'

I looked puzzled, but before I had time to ask why he was so pleased, he charged on.

'I asked for you especially, I want you to know that. I could see that you were just the right man for the job. On the same wavelength, you see.'

'Um, what job?'

'Oh, we don't need to keep it under the carpet any longer. The contract's all done and dusted. These good people will know about it soon enough.'

He waved at our colleagues who were now settling into their bamboo chairs.

'The thing is,' he went on, 'we need to get cracking. We have to get the book out as near as possible to the date of the reshuffle. What I can tell you, and this really is *entre nous*, is that I've had the nod from the PM. There's a couple of possibilities and I've told him that I'm up for either of them, but of course it depends on slotting everyone in.'

'The book?' I queried hazily.

'Oh, you are a joker, I like that. We want plenty of humour in the book. I don't want it to be a conventional autobiography, more of a personal journey. The original working title was "My Struggle", but the publishing chap pointed out the bad vibrations. That does give the flavour, though. I'd be very much guided by you of course. You're the wordsmith, after all.'

'You mean,' I said, the fog lifting, 'that you're expecting me to write your autobiography.'

'Help with, help with, old boy. What is this?' He drew up short, his good humour decidedly blunted. 'I mean, I know the contract is with Making Nice, not you personally, but I took it for granted that you were on board.'

At that moment, Madame clapped her hands and called us to order. 'We shall start this afternoon's little entertainment with a *bourrée*, which as you know is a sprightly sort of minuet, probably of folk origin. It used to be called the French clog dance, but I hope our version will be a little more *raffiné*. The music that Miss Baverstock will be playing is the "Bourrée fantasque" by Chabrier.'

Four girls in peasant costume skipped onto the floor, as Miss Baverstock hit the keys. She was a pretty redhead with a slightly melancholy air who had apparently been at the school herself but had grown too tall to go on dancing and Madame had swept her back up, seeing how bright and biddable she was.

As Miss Baverstock's pale fingers rippled up and down, her auburn ponytail flouncing in time, my mind began to explore this weird proposal. For a start, what on earth had given Bryce Wincott the idea that he and I were soulmates or ever likely to be? I thought I had conveyed my lack of sympathy pretty clearly, only a touch short of rudeness in fact. But equally clearly, he hadn't noticed – if anything, took pride in not having noticed. Was it that people like him were simply incapable of decoding other people's words, gestures, facial expressions, or were they deliberately indifferent to what other people thought of them? Perhaps, disquietingly, both. That is, Bryce might know he had no talent for unlocking other minds, but choose to regard this incapacity as a plus.

Ethel's assumption that I would jump at the opportunity was scarcely more sensitive. Or perhaps not so much insensitive as merely brutal. He knew I wouldn't care for the assignment, which was why he hadn't raised the subject when I was the other side of the Atlantic, fearing rightly that the distance would embolden me to say No. When I got back to Osmotherley House, he and Gloria could work on my better or at any rate weaker nature. Then of course – I was beginning to get the hang of how his mind worked – he knew that I would be reluctant to oppose his plans if I wanted to help Flo in any way possible. If she was shackled to him – and she certainly seemed to wish to stay shackled – then so was I. He had clearly forgotten that I would be seeing Bryce at the trustees' meeting, a rare lapse which only showed how excited he was about his own new assignment.

The music moved into a slower, caressing melody and the girls twirled with their arms round each other's waists in a dreamy serpentine pattern. A sleepy sort of acceptance overcame me, brought on by jet lag no doubt, but also by a certain amusement at the prospect of ghosting. What a strange line of business it must be. I once knew a man on the *Daily Mail* who had ghosted all sorts – a goalkeeper with a drink problem, a gay missionary who had been held hostage for five years, innumerable hell-raising pop stars. When I asked which of his clients he liked and which he didn't, he stared at me in total incomprehension. To him they were all just subjects, some easier to extract material from than others, but he thought no more about them than a hairdresser thinks about the clients in his chair, apart from how difficult their hair is.

'That was a joke, wasn't it, when you pretended not to know?' Bryce was still fretting when the dancing was finished.

'I was just observing top security,' I said with what I hope looked like an impish grin.

'You're absolutely right, Dickie. People have got to understand that it's all my own work. Authentic, that's what I want the reviewers to say, the kind of book that shows us that not every politician is in it for what he can get out of it.'

The little display ended with a solo from Darren, his last performance at the Beau, aka Demetrios – he was just starting at the Royal too. He'd now decided to keep his name, thought Darren had some street cred to it. How supple and easy he was, like a squirrel springing from branch to branch. In fact, now that I looked at the programme, this was a *pas seul* from another ballet I hadn't heard of called *Les Ecureuils*, and I meant to get hold of Darren afterwards to tell him that I knew he was being a squirrel without looking at the programme, which must be a unique experience in ballet-going. But the truth was that it wasn't the same without Flo, and I began to wish I hadn't come. It had been so heart-stopping to see the child you knew so well fly into this magical other world of which you knew nothing.

When I got home, there was Jane on the doorstep. She could hardly wait till we got indoors to bring me up to speed.

'She didn't tell us the half of it – she said because she didn't want to startle you. But she's just called me from the Whatever Arms to fill in the picture. Apparently they had been having a rough patch, scarcely spoke at first when he got to America. But then she doesn't know what exactly, perhaps he was lonely over there or perhaps realised how fond of her he was. Anyway, he started calling her every evening, as though he had just met her, or that's what she said, and he said that they must get engaged, but it must be kept secret, because it would put such a lot of pressure on her otherwise. I didn't quite follow that bit, and she didn't either, but anyway she agreed, and so there it is. They still have their rows – I must have caught the tail end of one – but most of the time they get on really well. In fact, they're secretly engaged, she's not to tell anyone, not even you and me, which of course was too much to ask, but she did insist that I wasn't to tell you under any circumstances because you would be so upset. It's all such a nightmare.'

'She's right, I am very upset, and I'm not sure I can go through with it.'

'Dickie, she's the one who is having to go through with it.'

'No, I can't deal with this secret engagement business which I'm not supposed to know about.'

'Well, how do you think I feel?'

'I don't think I can carry on at Making Nice – which I'm really only doing for her sake – while all this is going on.'

'Well, I must say I do think that is a rather selfish reaction.'

So I told her about my new assignment, which I was going to anyway, but I hoped it might stir her sympathy. To my surprise, she gave one of her rare gurgly chuckles.

'Ghostwriter! Well, they say you should try everything once. In fact you might be rather good at it. I always thought you were better thinking yourself into other people's shoes than filling your own. No, sorry, that came out nastier than I intended.'

'It did,' I said, but I could see what she meant. 'On the other hand,' I persisted, 'you haven't met Bryce Wincott.'

'But, darling, that's the whole point. Much more fun to be ghosting a monster than ploughing through all the great achievements of some famous goody-goody. Robert Maxwell or David Attenborough? No contest surely.'

'When you put it like that …'

I was taken aback by her enthusiastic embrace of the project. But then I had always suspected that she regarded all forms of journalism as in pretty much the same position on the sleaze meter, making little if any distinction between reporting on nuclear disarmament talks and writing the life story of Bryce Wincott.

All the same, I was not going to go quietly, or not entirely.

'You might have warned me, Gloria, when I was in the States.'

'You would only have said No.'

'Exactly.'

'We wanted to talk you through it carefully when you got home. Pity you bumped into the Wingco first. Anyway you should think yourself lucky. I'm just starting work on the life and times of Cassie Carcrash, the stupidest pop star since they invented radio, makes the Spice Girls look like Nobel prizewinners.'

'I didn't realise this was a ghostwriting agency.'

'My dear Dickie –' the Glow Worm flashed one of her smiles which Ethel swore you could see in the pitch-dark – 'the backstory is the cornerstone of Reputation Management. Once a celeb has their Life on the bookstands he or she's made. Doesn't matter if nobody much actually reads the thing – though of course we hope they do because we're on 5 per cent. The ones I really love are the ones who actually boast of not having read the book themselves, though it's got their name on the cover. Cassie you wouldn't believe. At least I assume the Wingco can read and write.'

'I wouldn't bet on it.'

Still, I had to admit I enjoyed being back in the office bustle. One of the Smothers Brothers was blading round the floor with smoothies and vegan wraps for those who had ordered them. I recognised Kaylee and he came up and fist-bumped me.

'You see,' Gloria persisted, waving Kaylee away with a good-natured flip of her bejewelled hand, 'you may try to deny it, but you can't help feeling differently about someone who's had a book written about them, or supposedly by them. They seem somehow more solid, though you know perfectly well how utterly *fake* they are.'

I was struck by her using that word, which I thought might have been taboo in the office – I certainly never heard Ethel use it. But then she was more grounded. That was one of the things I liked about her, that and her huge smile and the beauty spot riding on the pommel of her cheek.

'But how do you get started? Even if I do do this thing, I simply wouldn't know where to begin.'

'You certainly are doing this thing, as you put it. I don't mean just because it's in the contract, but because you'll love it when you get going. It's so beautifully weird, like living someone else's life but without having to endure any of the ghastly consequences. The way you start off is you take an old-fashioned tape recorder along to Bryce's flat, the clunkiest you can find that's still on the market. Of course you could perfectly well record on your phone, but he'll like the official BBC look of the old machine. Then you ask him to tell his own story in his own words, like he would to his therapist.'

'I don't expect Bryce has a therapist.'

'The most surprising people have therapists. Anyway you sit back and listen as he takes you through his GCSE results, and his first trip abroad and his going camping with the Young Conservatives where he meets this amazing girl, and it will all take an unbelievably long time, and you'll wish you were dead, and of course you won't use a word of it, but you'll pick up a few leads here and there, names of old schoolmasters, useful addresses and so on, and that's where you can really start work.'

'Won't he notice if I don't put in any of the stuff he tells me?'

'You will rewrite the whole story in your own golden prose and he'll think he wrote every word of it. I didn't believe this myself the first time I tried it out, but it happens every time. For example, I did the autobio of that man who invented the Wogglebox, total nerd, he went around after it came out saying that the publishers had sent him a girl who turned out to be useless and he had to write the whole thing himself. The ego is blind, my dear Dickie, stone, stonking blind.'

She really cheered me up and I went straight out and bought a Roberts Retro G17 Cassette Recorder for £49.99. Then I made an appointment for the next morning to go round to Bryce's flat in Whitehall Court. I was beginning to warm to the idea of ghosting, its gleeful irresponsibility, the opportunities for moulding and manipulating the supposedly solid character of your subject, so that by the end you were the real person and he or she was only the shadow on the screen, the ectoplasm you had squirted out of your spray gun.

'… I was born in Camberley, Surrey, though in fact it's almost in Berkshire. My father was a staff sergeant at the Royal Military Academy. He was a military man through and through, quite a disciplinarian but I respected him for it. When he gave me a clip round the ear, I usually came to admit that there was a reason for it, though it hurt like the blazes at the time. My mother was a gentler soul, fond of music and the theatre, the trip to the Windsor Theatre Royal was a highlight of the Christmas holidays …'

My eye began to wander round Bryce's sitting room. I wasn't surprised by the wedding photos and the ones of Bryce in RAF Reserve uniform grinning with his cap under his arm, not to mention the picture of him with the previous prime minister and another one of him with the Duchess of Cornwall. But the pictures on the wall were rather attractive Victorian landscapes and the sofa and chairs had William Morris covers. I wondered if they had taken the flat furnished. But then his wife Helen came in. She was rather handsome with the face of a marmalade cat and tawny curls to match, slightly taller than her husband, older too probably, and with an ease about her which seemed to relax him too. There was none of 'this is my better half' or 'here's the power behind the throne'. He said simply, 'This is Helen,' and she said, 'Well, you've certainly taken on something, I don't know whether to congratulate you or commiserate.'

After she had gone into the kitchen to make us what she promised would be a light lunch, he leaned over to me on the sofa and said in quiet voice, 'She's the real story, you know. Orphaned at seven when her father knocked her mother downstairs and then killed himself in remorse because he hadn't meant it. She brought up her younger sister, put herself through college, qualified as an accountant before she met me and had Theo and the twins. Never a word of complaint, always bright and cheerful. Without her I'd be, well, I'd be nothing.' I suddenly noticed that he was near tears. In the kitchen, I could hear Helen singing softly, only just audible above the clattering dishes.

This was not going at all as Gloria had mapped it. Quite against my settled expectation, I found myself beginning to be moved by the thought of their lives. Bryce wasn't the sort of person who was supposed to have an inner life, let alone a wife like Helen, rather than a downtrodden creature regretting the moment she had ever met him.

'Do you object to garlic?' She put her head round the kitchen door.

'I love garlic,' I said, though I don't really.

'Only Bryce can't have it if he's going to the House, so it's all right today.'

'How thoughtful of him.'

'I know, it's surprising, isn't it?' she said with a smile, before disappearing again.

'I can see how lucky you are,' I said, 'but when you say that without Helen, you'd be –'

'Oh, absolutely. I was going through a very bad patch. I'd broken completely with my dad after he went off with the cashier at the RMA, and my mum was going into a clinic and I thought she's never going to come out of there. She wasn't really a drinker, although Dad insisted she was an alcoholic, it was just being married to him. Then there was this trouble at the bank. I'd never have got through it without Helen. You see, she was one of the investigating team from Ernst & Young and she was the only one who could see in a flash that I hadn't done anything wrong. It was simply an error of interpretation.'

'I think,' I said as gently as I could, 'that we had better take this in easy stages.'

'That's what my therapist always says. You won't tell anyone about her, will you? They're rather old-fashioned about that sort of thing in the constituency. I probably shouldn't have told you, but you'd find out sooner or later.'

At least Gloria had been right about that. And so began a strange vagabondage together through terrain that was mostly desolate. I'm not sure which of us was Don Quixote and which was Sancho Panza. But however ill-matched we were, an unwilling comradeship did begin to grow – unwilling on my part, that is. Just as Bryce seemed never to have entertained the slightest inkling of how much I had loathed him, so now, as far as I could see, he hadn't a clue that I was gradually coming to the conclusion that there might after all be something to be said for him, if only in the sense that there was something to be said for almost anyone if you looked hard enough. Which did not of course mean that he had ceased to be odious when he was out and about.

10

Spinland

Thank heaven for email. If it had been a letter, Jane would have been on to it the moment it slapped the doormat. There would have been no hope of concealment. But there it was on my Mac, 'For Your Lovely Eyes Only' in the subject box, and I could sip it at my leisure undisturbed in my little room at the top of the house which Jane seldom or never climbed the stairs to.

My dearest Ricky-Ticky – where had she spirited this nickname from? I had never been called that in my life before (my given name is Domenicos, the Dickie comes from the initials), and I had not thought of Betsy as a *Jungle Book* fan, but I'd realised by now that she always knew more than you thought she knew. The email was signed off, after all, *From the office of Dr Betsy Broadlee, PhD, data scientist and political analyst*, and the font chosen was a flowery cursive script which was meant to look like handwriting and did.

Greetings from Spinland where it never rains or snows and the flowers are always in full bloom. I bring you intelligence of the greatest triumph in these parts since Washington crossed the Delaware. Your boy has swept all before him.

He did have a sticky start, though. We were huddled in the Briefing Room and Himself came in and said straight off, 'Who's that guy with no pants on?', so we told him it was Ethel, your amazing new data analyst. Luckily he misheard — his hearing isn't great these days — and said Ethan, that's a fine old American name, otherwise he might have thought he was some sort of weirdo and he would have been out on his ear. 'You reckoning to go on to the beach, Ethan, or is it too hot for you in here?' 'No, I'm cool,' Ethel said in that cool way of his. 'Great,' he said, 'hold the air con, Ethan's cool.' But somehow this was one of those bad starts which is really a good start, like in those romcoms when they first meet and they hate each other, but it in fact it's really only because they've made such an impact on each other that it's bound to ripen into Something Deeper.

It was just the morning after that terrible shooting in Everett High and we were thinking how to respond and nobody had anything fresh to offer, and he says to Eth, 'So, Mr Data Man, what can you tell us in your wisdom?' And Eth already has the figures up on his phone. Apparently there had been exhaustive surveys after South Bend, and after the West Arkansas massacre, and they all showed the same thing: Do you think we need more effective gun control laws? Yes, 62% obediently chorused, because if you ask, Do we need more effective laws about anything, law-abiding folk will always say Yes. But when one bold bunch of pollsters asked, Does the news make you feel more inclined to go out and buy a gun? 73% said Yes to that. The clear implication is that people want to see plenty of guns around in our society, but guns in the right hands. So the best play is: if those teachers and janitors had been armed, you can bet the bad guys would never have thought about it. And of course he lapped it up.

Then there was some disquiet about his tweeting morning, noon and night. Shouldn't he be a tiny bit more sparing, more selective? Wasn't it all a little undignified? Wouldn't it make folks think he had nothing better to do? Well, Eth had that one doped out too. They'd trialed three target groups of persuadables – the work had actually been done for Jerry, but of course he didn't say so. One group was fed major policy tweets once a week, serious stuff – they called it the Slab Mode. Number 2s got punchy short tweets once a day – that was the Daily Dose. And the last lot got tweeted pretty much all day long, whenever the candidate felt like it – Continuous Fire they called it. The results were conclusive. After the Slab, only 3% of respondents felt more favorable toward the candidate. The Daily Dose put on 5 or 6%. But Continuous Fire produced a 15.6% improvement. You might not think it, but people really seem to appreciate being bombarded. So The Man was right, and we were all wrong. Oh you may well wonder what I'm doing here at all, when I swore to you that I'd never work for That Man in a million years. To be honest, I have no idea. He's so gross. Just as you're thinking, well, he's actually got something original to say, he starts talking about women's pussies and insulting somebody for being crippled. He seems to have no sense of who he's talking to. I really cringe, not just because lots of us are of the female persuasion but we have several equal-opportunities hires – Mona in hospitality is a double amputee.

But of course he knows perfectly well what we're all thinking, and he says to Eth, 'Some folks say my tweets are too full-on, you got any data on that, Mr Data Man?' Well, Eth says, it happens there was a fascinating piece of work done in Ohio. Not many people know about it, because it was a flagrant breach of FEC rules. You remember

Tommy Schulz, dull sort of guy, couldn't say an interesting thing to save his life? Well, he was solemnly tweeting away, routine stuff about low taxes and strong defense. And some people we work with decided to use his campaign as an experimental base. They started sending out fake tweets in Tommy's name to a tranche of persuadables out in the sticks, only these tweets were quite different, full of salty jokes, personal remarks about Tommy's rivals, outrageous suggestions – nuke North Korea, death penalty for illegal immigrants and so on. Well, Tommy's ratings with that tranche started shooting up, so they tried it again in a different part of the state, miles away to the north, almost in Canada, and the same thing happened. They were careful not to roll out the experiment to the big cities where it might get noticed by the FEC. But our view is that these guys had already done enough to make the difference and Tommy squeaked home. I can't tell you how delighted The Man was by all this, not just because it showed that once again he was doing the right thing, but because he loathed Tommy Schulz and couldn't figure out how he got elected.

So then, I hear you ask, how did I let myself get mixed up in all this? Well, if I'm honest, it's partly because of weird stuff like that. It's a kind of holiday from being respectable. Oh, I'll probably regret it all when it's finished and probably for all the wrong reasons. But meantime, I'm having a ball, and Ethan the Wise and Strong, which is apparently what Ethan means in the Bible, is king of all he surveys and he surveys everything. I can't resist him either, although if you were here, there would be no contest, because I miss your warm British cheek and of course those eyes.

With love from Betsy, who you've surely consigned to the back catalog by now.

A week is a long time in politics, or so people keep telling you, especially when they're running a campaign and are doing a huge flip-flop. Even so, I was startled by the speed of Ethan's rise. In no time, word had got round that the English geek was the hottest thing. If you wanted access and influence, he was indisputably the go-to guy. And in no time, too, work started flooding into Making Nice. In state after state, the campaign was clamouring for our expertise, via our US partners. Elliott in Colorado had his focus groups up and running, he just needed a cash float before he pressed the button. Miriam in Fort Lauderdale had a fantastic offer from Facebook: a million names, seven million bits of data, at 50 cents a name, but Facebook wanted the money up front. No problem at all. The cheques from the Chard Foundation rolled in – we scarcely had to whistle for them. Every cheque bore the neat little signature 'Elizabeth H. Chard, Trustee'.

'Oh how I love that dear little signature,' Gloria drooled, as she kissed the Chard Private Bank cheque. 'A million here, a million there ...'

'... and pretty soon you're talking real money,' I completed the old gag. 'Must dash. I'm off to interview the Wingco's old sergeant in the Catering Division.'

An unproductive source, as it turned out. Sergeant Askew had no amusing anecdote about Bryce's skill or lack of it in peeling potatoes or making a white sauce. All he would say, and he said it several times, was: 'Bryce Wincott – I'd never have guessed we'd see *his* name up in lights.'

I hoped for more, a lot more, from Helen. I had cleared a whole afternoon to talk to her while Bryce was down at the House. As we sat comfortably together on the William Morris sofa, munching Helen's fig biscuits still warm from the oven, I felt utterly at my ease and rather tingling with anticipation.

'Well,' she said when I asked her what first attracted her – I was getting quite good at cutting to the chase – 'he was so sweet. I mean, you might not think that when he goes all frowny and starts talking about the legacy of Winston Churchill, but he struck me as just amazingly sweet, not exactly like a little boy, more like a little boy who had refused to grow up.'

'Like Peter Pan?'

'A bit – yes.' She tossed her tawny curls and laughed. 'Though even then he was probably a bit too tubby to be able to fly.'

'And when you came in to look at the books – that was the first time you met him?'

'Yes, it was a special audit. We'd done the annual accounts a few months earlier and signed them off. *Alles in Ordnung*. Then we get a frantic call from the credit manager, saying there were some mysterious leakages on two of the overseas investment accounts, and would we come back in. So we had a look and it didn't take long before we narrowed it down to the guys who looked after the index-tracking punts – you know, the bets people make about whether this or that stock exchange index is going to go up or down. It's a very lucrative sideline. The trouble is that it's so easy to fabricate deals which never happened, you write down an imaginary loss and pocket the money you haven't actually lost. What complicates matters is that the staff in these banks are all encouraged to have their own personal investment accounts with the banks, to keep as much money as possible in-house. So it's a standing temptation to divert the funds, requiring only modest forgery skills. Anyway, soon enough we tracked it down to this one man, F. S. Simmons, known as Fizz, not a very bright specimen and an all-round nasty piece of work if you ask me. He'd left a ridiculous paper trail – it was still paper in those days although electronic transfer was just coming in. So we confronted Fizz with the evidence of these fake transactions – which came out at 300K, a lot of money then, well, quite a lot of money now, and he broke down and admitted the whole thing. The partners wanted to just sack and forget. Unfortunately we have this fiduciary duty to make a public report, so he had to be charged. He got three years. I don't know how long he actually served.'

'And Bryce?'

'Well, it was a four-man department, so we had to go through the dealings of each of them to make sure they weren't in it together. After all, they were sitting side by side all day. The other two were totally clean, but when we came to Bryce, well, there were irregularities, undoubted irregularities, though not on the same scale as Fizz's. Oh, I can remember the poor lamb when we told him, like a desperately anxious cherub.' She laughed again at the recollection. 'So I went through the records very carefully again. And it became absolutely clear to me, in about five minutes, that it was all a slip of the pen. The numerical code for the office account was only one digit different from the code for his personal account. And the money was still sitting there, he hadn't tried to siphon it off into his current account, let alone spend it. And it would never have happened if they had the sort of security procedures we have today. It was quite difficult at first to convince my colleagues, and the partners too, but in the end they all came round to my way of thinking. The last thing they wanted was to be shown up as incompetent at looking after other people's money.'

'So it was all a complete accident?'

'Oh, totally. All the same, I think it would be better if you didn't mention it in the book. I mean, he did move on from the bank quite soon afterwards, but only because he wanted to start up on his own as a fund manager. You know Bry, he's as honest as the day is long.'

I agreed without hesitation, thinking all the time how lucky he had been to have such a persuasive advocate. If he hadn't looked like an anxious cherub, he might well have finished up like the wretched Fizz. As she cleared away the tea things, I noticed how strained she looked suddenly and I saw that telling the story had taken a lot out of her.

'I'm sorry,' I said, 'I didn't realise what I was putting you through.'

'No, how could you? You had to ask, but, as I say, it would be best if we could just leave it there.'

She began looking at her phone, as though this might somehow calm her.

'*Yes*,' she cried out. 'Yes, I think this is it. He thought it might be today.'

She looked back at me, scarcely able to contain the bright, hard grin on her face.

'Bry's just going over to Number Ten now,' she said. 'He's just hoping it's not going to be Northern Ireland, because that's a backwater these days. But you can't pick and choose, can you? – not at the stage he's at.'

It was not Northern Ireland. It was a brand-new department, invented to show off how forward-looking the administration was, how much juice it still had in its tank: the Department for Science, Countryside, Agriculture and Regional Development – or SCARD for short (though it wasn't long before the ill-disposed were calling it DISCARD). It was a trailblazer, no other country in the world had a department quite like it, according to its first Secretary of State, for there he was when she switched on the TV, the beaming Bryce coming out through the famous door, waving at the cameras.

'You must stay to congratulate him,' Helen said, giving me a delicious hug.

Quite soon there was the beaming Bryce bursting through the door of the flat. If he looked like a cherub at all now, it was a very bumptious cherub.

'I dreamed of something like this, Dickie. To be honest with you, I did rather more than dream. I think I can tell you that the structure of the new department is very much on the lines I set out to the PM three weeks ago, but I'd be grateful if you kept that under your hat because he wants it to be thought that it was all his own idea. Anyway, I'm absolutely delighted. It's about time that we had a little joined-up government in this country.'

His merriment bubbled on as his sturdy thumbs popped the champagne cork and we toasted his brilliant success.

'I see my department very much as the engine room of the New Approach,' he said as he carefully wiped some vagrant bubbles off the octagonal mahogany table. Then he couldn't resist telling Helen how coming in to Number Ten he had met poor old Damian Dodds coming out. 'He looked as if he'd aged ten years overnight. Mind you, the Dodderer should have been put out to grass years ago.'

'Now then, young man, we have work to do,' he said, turning to me as if I had only just come into the room, which I noticed he quite often did, as if his attention had to be switched on all over again, or, rather, as if it automatically switched off as soon as he stopped talking.

'We do,' I said.

'And I don't just mean the Great Book, though we obviously need to get our skates on to hit that deadline. The thing is, I thought it would add an extra dimension to the story if you were alongside me while I was shaping the department.'

'Watch you at it, so to speak?'

'Yes,' he said, though I could see that he would have preferred me to put it more elegantly. 'In any case, I shall need a spare pair of hands, for speechwriting, background briefing and so on. It may take the public a little time to grasp the full scope of what we're about. That's where every minister needs his wordsmith.'

He paused, and almost consciously seemed to put aside the merriment and take on the solemn look of someone who has just entered a church.

'So what I would like to propose is that you become my Special Adviser in the department.'

For a moment, there was a weird hush in the Wincott sitting room. Helen, standing behind the sofa, had a reverent, almost blissful expression on her face, clasping her hands together, as though watching a consecration or marriage ceremony.

'Oh, Bryce, this is so sudden,' I said, surprising myself by my response, which was both skittish and slightly overcome, neither of which I had intended.

'Well, one has to move quickly in these situations,' Bryce said, sounding rather pleased, I thought. 'You'd be a temporary civil servant of course, Assistant Secretary level on the salary scale, I believe.'

'Ah yes,' I said, not knowing what this meant, but thinking it vulgar to enquire at this moment.

'We could make a great team, with your diplomatic experience and my background in the services.'

'Thank you very much, it's a very flattering offer. I'll need to talk to Making Nice first of course.'

'Let me know by lunchtime tomorrow. We do need to hit the ground running.'

I didn't say that I had always thought this a dangerous ambition. All the same, despite myself, I was touched to be asked. As I left, Helen embraced me again as though I were already a member of the family, and whispered, 'You will say Yes, won't you?'

If I had thought of saying No, it soon became clear that I would face some reproachful opposition. Everyone was convinced I should take the job.

'But you know how ghastly he can be,' I whimpered to Jane.

'Well, you can't expect someone in his position to be *nice*, can you? In any case, you're always saying how much you'd like to see politics from the inside to see how it really works.'

Gloria was even more emphatic.

'How utterly brilliant. It's really frabjous news.'

'What about my work at Making Nice, though?'

'It's frabjous news for Making Nice too.'

'To see the back of me, you mean?'

'Oh, you don't get it, Dickie. You'll still be working with us in a very real sense. Think how many fantastic focus groups and data analysis contracts you'll be able to steer our way. The Home Office spent 73 mil on research contracts last year. We'll probably have to take back the top floor at Smothers from those hedgies.'

'But don't those contracts have to be put out to competitive tender?'

'Tender is the night, baby. There's only one person who decides the winner in these competitions and that'll be you. I mean, theoretically it's the Wingco, but he'll be busy-busy. You call Ethel and see if I'm not right.'

Ethel confirmed. He was just boarding a plane to St Louis, so he couldn't talk for long, but, yes, this was not just fantastic news for me personally but for the whole company, and I would of course be merely on leave from Making Nice while I was in post. As for his own gig, well, they were creaming down the home straight now, ten points ahead in Michigan, Florida sewn up, and he was just off to put Missouri to bed. All the same, I detected a certain holding back, a wistfulness even, in his congratulations. But then is anyone ever genuinely pleased to hear of a friend getting a desirable job, which this was if you could close your eyes and not think of Bryce too much?

So anyway I said Yes, and for the next few days I was swept up in the whole induction process. There was a one-to-one with the Perm Sec to the new department. He was clearly revelling in the novelty of it all as much as his minister. He had a light-bulb head, and a greeny-grey face with a letter-box mouth. Bryce told me they called him 'the Mekon'. Spot on, I said after my meeting with him. According to Ethel, all civil servants come from Outer Space. The Mekon must have given the lecture on the Civil Service code of conduct and the ethical responsibilities to a dozen other late-life recruits to the service, but he did it with an owlish relish which appealed to me. For the time I was in his cavernous office I almost felt a tinge of regret that I had not spent my whole career in this monkish profession which might have suited me better than the rackety world I had fallen into. He passed me on to Security, who was a squinny little man with a thin moustache which didn't look comfortable on his upper lip. Apparently they're not allowed any more to ask whether you've ever had any homosexual experiences, but I could assure him that I had never felt the remotest urge to join the IRA or the Workers Revolutionary Party, so apart from an early dalliance with the Liberal Democrats I was clean.

I walked along the Victoria Embankment in the early-autumn sunshine with a strange feeling of belonging, which I hadn't expected to feel and couldn't remember having had for a long time, if ever. The jangle of my mobile dispersed my reverie.

'This is Helen Wincott.'

At least I thought that's what she said, though it was a bad line, and so I said, 'Oh, hullo, Helen, I've just been interviewed by Security.'

'No, not Helen, this is Thelma, her mother-in-law.' Now that I heard her more clearly, it obviously wasn't Helen. The voice was harsher, with a faint northern accent, Yorkshire perhaps.

'Oh, sorry, hullo, did you get my number from Helen?'

'No I did not,' she said with some vim, 'I got it from the useless girl in Bry's office who told me you were writing his life story. Can't do it himself of course. He never was much good at that sort of thing.'

I sensed an abrasive presence at the other end of the line and paused for a moment to regroup.

'Well, do you want to come and see me or not? Isn't it usual to interview the poor old mother? Or is that old hat?'

'I'd be delighted to, only Bryce hasn't actually –'

'No of course he hasn't. Ever since he married Her, I've been kept out of the picture. Now she won't let me see the boys at all. I'm a complete back number.'

'Oh, I'm sorry to hear that.'

'It's perfectly simple to get here. There's a train every half-hour from Charing Cross. I'm only ten minutes' walk from the station.'

I made a fast calculation. Thelma had not made herself sound alluring, but she didn't sound dull, and she certainly sounded capable of making trouble. If I failed to go and see her, when the book was published she might advertise the fact that she had not been consulted and point out all the things we had left out or got wrong. From what she was saying, Bryce and Helen, especially Helen, might discourage me from going to see her, but even a ghost has to use his own initiative, and anyway I was intrigued. So, yes, I'd be very pleased to go down to see her.

An unfriendly salty breeze hit me as I got out of the train. I had been absorbed in the new Hilary Mantel and hadn't given much thought to the whole excursion, which was after all a mixture of caprice and curiosity. Nothing useful might come out of it. If Bryce wanted to leave his mother more or less out of the picture, except perhaps for a brief, possibly rather formulaic description at the beginning, then that was his decision. He was, after all, supposed to be writing the book.

But the truth was that once again I found myself slipping out of my impersonal ghostliness and into a more flesh-and-blood engagement. Why had Bryce and/or Helen apparently been so keen to cut off contact?

Thelma lived in a little close of brick cottages away from the sea, in fact a little further along the railway line I had just travelled on, because I could hear the rattle of another train passing as I reached her front door. Admiral Blake Close it was called. I wondered whether it was some sort of sheltered accommodation. Perhaps not, because the front patches were overgrown and the salt-bitten window frames needed painting, so nobody seemed to be looking after the estate.

She came briskly to the door and told me I was on time, but not in a welcoming way. She was short and square like her son, and had an abrupt way of turning her head to look at you as though she would rather be looking somewhere else, and that too had a touch of Bryce.

'Would you like a whisky?'

I said it was a bit early for me, and looked at my watch, which said 4.15.

'You are a journalist, aren't you? In my day journalists never refused a drink.'

I said we were all reformed characters these days.

'So am I. Bryce doesn't believe it, but then he never believes a thing I say now.'

'Did you use to get on better?'

'Oh, for years after the Sergeant left, there was just him and me. Well, the Sergeant never left completely, he kept on coming back and trying to put me in the clinic and take Bryce away from me. But we fought him off, the two of us. He was always a fighter, Bry, you have to give him that. Every time I went to the school gates, there was some other mum complaining he'd bashed her boy. So I gave up going to pick him up, left him to make his own way home, which meant he got into more fights.'

Her eyes shone at the recollection of his pugnacity, almost as though he had been fighting these battles on her behalf.

'He didn't have girlfriends as such. I mean, there were a couple of silly girls at the tennis club, but he didn't get anywhere with them. Never learned how to pay them attention.'

I could see that living as a twosome with Thelma might not be the best training in courtship. Whenever she stopped talking, she gave a sort of challenging glare, as if to say, there now, what do you make of that?

'So Helen might have been more or less his first real girlfriend?'

'Huh, you could put it like that. She helped him out and he was grateful.'

'You don't think there was more to it than that? She told me how attractive she found him, almost immediately I think.'

'Well, she would say that. Truth is, she was getting on a bit, and there was this man who owed her.'

'For having understood that it was all a slip of the pen?'

'Slip of the pen?' She raised her wiry eyebrows as though there was no need to say more.

'The two bank codes being so similar, I mean, and him muddling them up.'

'I can see she did a good job on you. She looks so nice people don't realise how hard she can be. Mind you, she's had to be if half the things she said about her background are true.'

'You don't believe her?'

'Didn't you think she was a bit too well spoken, as if butter wouldn't melt in her mouth? – though that's an odd sort of phrase when you come to think about it, because her mouth would have to be freezing cold, wouldn't it?' She gave a surprisingly merry laugh, and although she was so disagreeable, I found myself taking to her free way of talking, and to her clearly wishing to push the conversation further than it ought to go. I also liked the way she was seeking to convince me that Helen was better born than she pretended, the reverse of the usual insinuation.

'So,' I said, knowing that this in particular was the question I ought not to be asking because I might not know what to do with the answer, 'just to be clear, you really don't believe her interpretation?'

'Interpretation! Made-up story, more like. But it shows you what a smart operator she is that she got all those men to believe her. Anyway, I have good reason to know that it didn't happen like that.'

'What sort of reason?' I was in too deep now to hold back, but this was the moment Thelma realised she had gone too far.

'I am not at liberty to say. And I would rather you didn't say anything about it to either of them.'

'I won't. In any case, they don't want the incident to be mentioned in the book.'

'I'm not a bit surprised.' Though she had now closed down the topic, she did not seem much disconcerted by having got in as deep as she had. As she put the kettle on and took some fairy cakes out of a battered Silver Jubilee tin, I thought I heard her humming.

'They're shop cakes. I don't bake,' she said with wintry pleasure.

As I left, she gripped my wrist with her bony hand.

'I don't suppose I'll see you again,' she said, 'but it was nice of you to come.' The words seemed wrenched out of her, and I was touched. Not for the first time, I wondered whether I was cut out to be a ghost. Perhaps I was interpreting my brief too freely. After all, this wasn't supposed to be a no-holds-barred probe into the depths of the soul of Bryce Wincott, assuming such a probe to be feasible; it was a standard-issue campaign bio, nothing more. It wasn't long before I was reminded just how true this was.

He was waiting in the hallway as I came through the outer door of the flat the next morning. 'Dickie,' he said, 'is it true what Susan tells me, that my mother winkled your phone number out of her?'

'That's what your mother told me.'

'You mean you've actually spoken to Thelma? I don't remember giving you permission to talk to her.'

'Well, she called me, and I thought it only civil –'

'Listen, you are not to speak to my mother under any circumstances. She doesn't know what she's saying half the time. You haven't been to see her by any chance, have you?'

Of course I resented the interrogation, but he had a point and I responded mildly: 'I'm awfully sorry, Bry, but she asked me down there so I …'

'… thought it only civil,' he finished for me in a sarcastic parody of an effete voice. 'Well, what you must get into your head is that there is no point on earth in being civil to Thelma, because she's never been civil to anyone in her life. I don't want to know what she told you, because it wouldn't be worth repeating, a lot of evil nonsense about Helen, I expect.'

'Well, she did say they didn't get on.'

'That just shows you. Helen's the best thing that ever happened to me, and she did her very best to make a go of it with my mother. The truth is that Thelma's hopelessly jealous of her.'

'I'll forget everything she said.'

'Good. I have to say, Dickie, I'm disappointed in you, very disappointed. I had you down as a reliable sort. I certainly did not expect you to go off-piste at the first opportunity.'

He was red in the face and his upper body was tensed like someone about to jump off a diving platform. If it had been anyone else, you would have thought about calling an ambulance, but I had seen enough of him already to know that this posture was part of his repertoire. All I could do was take the rebuke lying down. My motives for going to see Thelma had not been exactly respectable, it had to be admitted. I had privately hoped to dig up a little something and I had not been disappointed.

11

In the Cockpit

Clang went Sir Anselm's steel-tipped heels on the stone flags. In his hands he jangled the keys that had let us in from the Downing Street back entrance to the Cabinet Office. Following him through the green baize door, I felt shades of the prison house closing in. Annie Arkwright, as he was known in the office (apparently only Ethel and Bryce called him the Mekon), said he had been parachuted in as Temp Perm Sec to the new department. 'Funny old ragbag, I thought when I first heard about it,' he flung over his shoulder, 'but in this game you go where they send you.' He spread out the festoon of keys on his slender white palm and picked one to try on the door at the end of the passage. 'Ah, right first time,' he said with amiable air of someone who was usually right first time. 'I'm afraid the cleaners haven't been in yet, the chap who was in charge of the Bishops only left last week. The Secretary of State's office is beyond that door.'

We sat down together in the dusty half-light. The room seemed to have no windows, though somewhere I could hear the hum of ventilation. On second thoughts, more like a monastery than a prison. In this crepuscular cell, the Mekon could have been an abbot in some intense order, grave, alert, ready to hear anyone's confession.

'You know where we are, don't you?' he said.

'No, not really, I've rather lost my bearings, I'm afraid.'

'This used to be the Cockpit, where Oliver Cromwell had his lodgings. When he seized the mace, this is where his guards brought it.'

'Take away that bauble?'

'Precisely. Not exactly according to the Ministerial Code.' He smiled his abbot's smile. 'I hope you won't treat that as a precedent. We are of course anxious to assist you in any way we can. I do hope that you and your team will think of yourselves as very much part of the Service, albeit a temporary and unestablished part. We welcome fresh input into our thinking, but I have to say that any proposals you may advance will have a better chance of success if you advance them through the usual channels. We have had some trouble in the past with special advisers who preferred the backstairs route, so to speak. I offer this in no way as a threat, simply as a piece of friendly advice.'

I took the threat in the spirit in which it was offered, and assured Sir Anselm that we would always work with and through him and his staff.

'I'm delighted to hear it. You'll find us a pretty relaxed bunch of guys. I understand that you and your minister have been doing impressive work with this ballet school. I am a lifelong balletomane myself – I first saw *Les Sylphides* when I was fourteen.'

I was about to disclaim any expert knowledge of the dance, but then I thought that it might be wise to bank any slight testimonial that came my way in this austere warren.

'Apparently your Mr Evers is having a *succès fou* in the States. The Prime Minister is most impressed. As you may imagine, Mr Evers's master is not exactly our preferred candidate, but if it comes to it we shall be glad to have a friend at court.'

'Yes, he does seem to be doing pretty well,' I said.

'We had rather expected to be seeing something of him here, but I can quite understand that he might wish to spread his wings on a larger stage.'

'Oh, he'll probably pop up at some point,' I said. 'He usually does.'

'Our Mr Zelig, you might say.'

'Oh, yes … precisely.'

There was something so arctic about his mien that even when he said something quite chummy, it took you by surprise and you found it hard to decipher, as though what he said needed to be passed through some process of decryption which you didn't have the key to. In any case, Ethel wasn't really a bit like Zelig, who was famous for being nondescript, which was one thing you couldn't accuse Ethel of.

'Well,' he said, 'I mustn't keep you. Katie will be in touch about some extra space for your team. At the moment, I gather that the only people in there are Broderick who's just off to Work and Pensions and a certain Dr Grogan whom I wot not of but who comes highly recommended by Evers. You'll find him second door on the right after the gents.'

'Thank you so much, Sir Anselm,' I said, as he pressed the relevant keys into my hand.

'Anselm, please, or Annie if you must. We're not all as stuffy as you think.'

My protestation that I didn't think that at all carried scant conviction, and I said goodbye to him feeling that this was an interview I had failed but which there was probably no way of passing.

As his steel-tipped footsteps faded away outside, an icy silence fell, making the ventilation sound weirdly loud, as though some watching operative had at that moment decided to turn it up. We were far too deep in the warren to hear any noise from the street, and there was not a squeak from the adjoining offices.

I riffled through my in-tray. There was a note from Establishment about my pay, which in my flustered state I had quite forgotten to enquire about, then something about enhanced fire precautions, and a copy of a note from Wrangham in Security to Sir Anselm, reporting that he had carried out a full security check on Mr D. K. Pentecost, and provisionally found no objection on security grounds to his employment as Special Adviser to the Department for Science, Countryside, Agriculture and Regional Development. Nothing else.

Suddenly I had a fancy that this was how it would always be. I would bustle in every morning and find nothing at all to do, nobody would come near me, but I would continue to tell everyone that the work was extremely interesting, although the hours were rather long. I would carry on like this for months, years even, until someone noticed and I would be gently eased out, probably on health grounds, to save embarrassment. Wasn't there a Russian short story about a man who spent years living like this? The fancy must touch a chord in lots of people who worked in offices and who secretly feared that this was their own story. The moment the management consultants came in, they would spot how surplus to requirements you were. No, superfluous, that was the word. 'A superfluous man' – that was the name of the story, or was it? I began to search for the title on my laptop, reflecting that this was my first significant action as a member, albeit temporary and unestablished, of Her Majesty's Civil Service.

Just then, the door was flung open with a violence of which it had not seemed capable under Sir Anselm's graceful opening and shutting. Before me stood at mock attention, offering a half salute, hand to the shoulder rather than the forehead, more like someone taking an oath, an enormous man, six foot six at least, with great hulking shoulders and a head carved out of some implacable hardwood. Although at this moment creased in a smile of greeting, his muscular lips looked more suited to the snarl–scowl end of the spectrum. If you met him outside on the pavement, your first instinct might be to take evasive action and jump into the path of the oncoming traffic.

'Standish Grogan, your servant, sir,' he said, in a surprisingly light, rather charming voice, dropping his saluting arm to his side and fishing out a card from his pocket.

The card said:

Dr Standish Grogan, DPhil, MSc
Astrophysicist, Political Strategist, Bard
Savile Club, London W1

'Great stuff,' I said weakly.
'Stan, by the way, everyone calls me Stan. I can see you weren't expecting me.'
'Well, Bryce didn't –'

'The poor wee man's been on the run, you can understand.'

'Absolutely, Stan,' I said.

'It was Ethel's idea. He thought our skill sets would complement each other nicely.'

'Great, well, welcome anyway,' I said, not immediately able to offer much in return, unsure even whether I could claim enough skills to make up a set.

'The way I see it is that together we can offer rigorous data analysis combined with an upskilled comms capacity, not just in terms of rapid rebuttal, though that comes with the rations these days, but so that we can dominate the narrative twenty-four/seven.'

'Mm, yes, quite ambitious.'

'Nothing venture, don't you think? I can see you're admiring my suit.'

He was right, I was. The suit was woven from a heavy cloth more suitable for a travel rug, in contrasting shades of sage green and a lightish mauve, plus a matching waistcoat with scalloped revers.

'It's the Connacht tartan, the heather on the moorland. Connacht is Grogan country, what they used to call the Congested Districts in the bad old days. Of course we came over years ago. My Scouser granny made proper Brits out of us.'

'Well, I'm an immigrant too, sort of.'

'Pentecostas – what a lovely name. Ethel told me something of your family history. And those two lovely girls, he says they're adorable.'

'I think so, but I'm biased,' I said, somewhat miffed that Stan appeared to be so well briefed about me. Far from leaving me to my own devices, Ethel seemed to be operating a remote dating service.

'How I envy you. I'm still waiting for the right Mrs Grogan to come along.'

'I'm sure they're queueing up,' I said, suddenly finding myself rather at ease with my huge ungainly new colleague. Not that he had altogether lost his miasma of menace, more that this too seemed part of the act, designed to divert, not to be taken too seriously.

'I've brought the document with me. It would be good to have your input as soon as poss, we need to hit the ground running – do forgive the cliché.' He smiled as he passed me a glossy folder in his huge hands.

'"Reboot UK",' I read the title on the bright blue cover.

'Somewhat catchpenny, I fear. It's only a first shot, but Bryce wanted to get it to the PM as soon as it was in any sort of shape.'

At that moment the door at the other end burst open and Bryce himself bombed in.

'Greetings, greetings. Wonderful to have you both with us.'

'Greetings, master,' Stan responded with a mock salaam.

'Dickie, hi. Are they looking after you properly?'

The little unpleasantness over my visit to Thelma seemed quite forgotten. At the same time, I had that sensation, experienced not for the first time in my life, that they both seemed to know me better than I knew them, possessing some fast track to intimacy with which I had not been equipped.

'I'm afraid I need to take Alexa away with me for a few minutes. I'm rather struggling with this artificial intelligence paper.'

'Alexa?' I queried.

'Oh, because he can give you the answer to anything.'

Standish Grogan grinned in his wooden way at this compliment. He was definitely growing on me. His ungainly effusive manner seemed to have a kind of awkward innocence, or so I thought.

The two of them disappeared into Bryce's office, leaving me alone with Reboot UK.

It wasn't such a fat file, forty-five pages long, but I soon saw that it set out to cover the waterfront, not to mention the harbour wall and the far horizon. On the first page, there was a lively colour sketch of a stream of buses painted all over with Union Jacks zooming into some great Victorian railway station: 'ROADRAIL – the only answer to congestion. Convert commuter rail tracks into busways and double the number of passengers per hour.' On the succeeding pages there were pictures of the same buses zooming on high tracks through some Scottish moorland past herds of startled deer. The general effect was rather like the old 'That's Shell, that was!' adverts. 'Bring the UK back together with the Union Jack rail buses and save billions!' The sketches certainly had pizzazz. I suddenly noticed that they were signed S.G. – was there no end to Stan's talents?

Flicking through the next pages, I found myself splat in the middle of the next section: 'Bring Winston's dream to life. With his unique imagination, Churchill saw that the answer to Home Rule was to revive the heptarchy, that dynamic group of principalities which made the Anglo-Saxon nation great, bringing good government and the rule of law to every corner of the kingdom. The modern version would include Scotland, Wales and Northern Ireland. In due course, the Republic of Ireland might well apply to join, and so unite the Islands of the North Atlantic once again.'

I was still blinking at this prospect when I found myself ankle-deep in a new chapter. 'BIRTHRIGHT: new choices for the underclass. Modern genetics for the first time gives every family the chance to make its own destiny. Under Birthright, any mum whose kids qualified for free school meals would be offered screening in pregnancy for Down's syndrome, Huntington's disease and all other genetic defects and an entirely free choice of pathways. Old-style eugenics called for compulsory sterilisation and abortion of the lower classes. New Birthright would improve the national breeding stock on a purely voluntary basis.'

The presentation of each scheme had been so brief that I was still only on page 13, but I'd already had enough, and I flipped on to the end to see if there was any general conclusion. Page 44 signed off: 'These proposals are intended as building blocks towards a rebooting of British society for a healthy and sustainable future.'

Then to my horror, the signatures: Bryce Wincott, Secretary of State, D. K. Pentecost and Standish P. Grogan, Special Advisers, and yesterday's date.

It was another ten minutes before Stan came out of Bryce's office, time enough for me to work up a serious lather.

'What the hell does this mean? This is the first I've seen of this fucking rubbish.'

'I know, I know, it's absolutely unpardonable, Dickie, totally out of order. But speed was of the essence, and we needed to have the imprimatur of the senior Spad to carry the full weight of the department. We thought, well, we desperately hoped that you wouldn't mind. We really did want to allow space for your input, but the timing was just too tight.'

'We? Who the hell are we?'

'Bryce and myself, and Ethel of course.'

'Ethel? What on earth has he got to do with any of this?'

'Well, we knew you would be pretty much in tune with his thinking, because of your close association with him.'

'*His* thinking? You mean these are Ethel's crazy ideas?'

'Well, we've refined them quite a bit, Bryce and myself, but in essence, yes, Ethel is the *fons et origo* of the governing concepts.'

'In that case, why the hell isn't *his* name on the paper?'

'I'm surprised you feel the need to ask that question, Dickie.' Stan sounded a little surer of his ground here. 'You will recall that Ethel is currently employed in a senior capacity by a leading candidate for the US presidency. If it got out that these proposals were in any sense the work of what could only be described as the agent of a foreign power, it would be curtains for the whole project. And although Bryce does have reservations about some of the detail, he is totally on board with the general approach.'

'Detail? There isn't any bloody detail. It's all back-of-a-fag-packet stuff.'

'There are also some supporting papers if you'd care to see them.'

'No, I would not care to see them. All I want is for you to take my name off that document this minute.'

'I'm afraid that won't be possible. Bryce was eager to press on, so we popped it in the PM's box last night.'

'Then send a note saying that I had nothing to do with it.'

'It would completely undermine the authority of the document, if it became known that one of the signatories had withdrawn.'

'I don't care.'

'I think Bryce would care.'

We stood there glaring at each other in the dusty neon light. Then my mobile rang.

It was Flo.

'Hi, Dad, I think I'm going mad here.'

'Join the club,' I said. 'Where's here?'

'I'm in this terrible place, it's called the Hostelry at Hook Bryan, and it's really awful. The bathroom smells of drains and the mattress is so lumpy, and the food is absolutely disgusting. They said I had to try the kedgeree at breakfast, and I hate kedgeree anyway, and I threw up in the toilet, the fish must have been a hundred years old. And the man at Reception, he just glares at me as though I was a shoplifter or something.'

'Oh poor you. Have you asked the office what to do?'

'I called Eth, but he was on a plane to Florida, so I talked to Ollie, but he said it was above his pay grade and I'd better talk to Gloria. I had to go to the bottom of the horrid little hotel garden, because I thought I might be bugged, I was getting so paranoid, Dad, and Gloria wasn't a bit helpful. She said, look, Flo, we're trying to run a business here and the way things are at the moment the customers who come to us aren't going to be your impeccable five-star places. They come to us because they've got teething problems and we try to help them through the pain barrier. So I said to Gloria, you mean I've got to go on saying, come and stay at this lovely hotel, though it's obviously vile, hoping that if they get more customers they'll clean up their act? Darling, you are sooo quick, Gloria says in that husky voice which is meant to sound all warm but it's really sarcastic.'

'So what did you say to that?'

'Well, I said, I didn't think I could go on telling lies and she said, why don't you talk to Ethel when he gets to Tampa, I'm sure he'll explain things so much better, so I said I would, but, Dad, I really can't go on doing this.'

'No, I entirely agree. But it's ballet school in a couple of weeks, isn't it? Couldn't you just fudge this one and then take a fortnight off, you know, to get back in shape?'

'That's brilliant, Dad. Then I needn't go back to astroturfing ever.'

The sound of her sweet, eager voice knocked me off balance. I could so vividly see her hunched up on the lumpy bed with the mobile nestling against her ear under the dark flop of her hair, gesturing with her free hand in that flung-out way that she must have picked up from Madame. I couldn't bear her to be unhappy and felt so responsible.

The silence fell again in the Cockpit. I could feel the dusty reverbs of the ventilator brushing faintly across my cheek. Perhaps it was always quiet at the heart of things. I imagined the panting soldiers clumping in with the heavy mace, all full of themselves, the clamour of the outraged MPs still ringing in their ears, and Oliver sitting round the table with his closest aides, the Spads of the day, all of them exhausted by the whole crazy business, and then silence falling, as even the Protector began to wonder whether he had done the right thing, and what the hell they were to do with the bloody great mace. The silence probably felt like an eternity to those who were caught up in it.

Then the door from the S of S's suite opened, and in came a cheerful-looking woman, in her thirties probably, with bouncy fair hair. She said she was Katie and she was so sorry that she hadn't been there to greet me, but it had been a bit of a morning. 'I hope you'll enjoy being with us. It's a lovely office to work in, even if we are all a bit mad here,' she added with a laugh.

'I expect you're really the only sane ones in the asylum.'

'Of course we are, but don't tell anyone,' she said, grinning as she dumped a pile of papers in my in-tray, with the hearty thump of a stable girl filling a hay manger. 'There's plenty more where that came from,' she said. 'Tea or coffee? We've managed to get an espresso machine at last.'

From that moment on, for the first time in my life I was blissfully consumed with paperwork. From all over Whitehall, from every department and half a dozen quangos: this month's economic and employment stats, briefing papers for Cabinet and Cabinet committees, comments on the briefing papers, comments on the comments, invitations to meetings, cancellations of meetings, cries for help from other Spads whose ministers were besieged by complaints from MPs or members of the public, the flow never stopped. My first inclination was just to initial the ones I hadn't a clue about, to show that I had read them, and dump them straight in the out-tray.

'No, no,' Stan explained, 'always respond. That's the only way to make your presence felt.'

'Even if it's on a subject I know absolutely nothing about, this memo on recalibrating energy prices, for example?'

'Especially then. You just minute in the margin "regional breakdown needed", or "what about solar power?" Then they have to come back to you, and after a bit of toing and froing, you'll begin to get the hang of whatever it is.'

'You've got a strange gleam in your eye,' Jane said. 'Almost as if you were actually enjoying yourself.'

'Oh dear,' I said. 'I'm afraid you may be right. Did Flo call you?'

'She did,' Jane said. 'And I have to say, she made me feel so guilty.'

'What about?'

'All those places we went to together and you wrote such glowing reports about, were they really just as ghastly as this place?'

'No, I think those places were as nice as we thought they were, they just needed a helping hand to get their message out. But those places are probably self-supporting now, they don't need astroturfing any more, they've got genuine punters enthusing about them on TripAdvisor.'

'So Making Nice is reduced to scraping the bottom of the barrel.'

'That's rather the way it looks.'

'Well, I'm not having any daughter of mine mixed up in that sort of nonsense.'

'She won't be for much longer.' Jane's righteous indignation reminded me so much of Flo's when she was fired up that I almost began to feel sorry for the Hostelry at Hook Bryan.

'Fantastic news,' Stan said, as I was hanging up my coat the next morning, the first chill of autumn and the Cockpit passage as chilly as it had been outside. 'The PM's scheduled Reboot UK for a brainstormer at Policy this afternoon, kick-off six thirty. I don't know how many of the boys over the way have actually read it yet, but they all say that P is desperate for new ideas. We're both invited along with Bryce to explain ourselves.'

There was a pause.

'No,' I said, 'I don't think I'll be able to make it.'

'I know you're upset about not having had much input, but the PM will be leading the discussion. You'll never have a better chance to make your number.'

'No,' I said with a mixture of firmness and panic, not such opposites as they might seem, 'I would be coming under false pretences, claiming a share in something I had nothing to do with.'

'Suit yourself. You may come to regret it. I'll give you a full debrief, of course.'

I went home early to avoid being swept up in any last-minute summons to this dubious conclave. Jane filled me in on the latest twists in the Hook Bryan saga.

'She checked out after she spoke to us, then called Gloria on the way back, saying she wasn't going to file a report. Gloria said that was unprofessional conduct and anyway the report was part of the deal, so they'd have to refund the Hostelry and the money would have to come out of her wages. So Flo said she didn't see why she should have to pay and it was only a holiday job anyway, and she was going to speak to Ethel who of course was still in the air. Once she got home, I told her to calm down and do her exercises. For once she seems to be taking my advice.'

She paused to allow me to hear the comforting thumps from upstairs. An unromantic noise, but it always makes me think of Flo at the barre, her face furrowed in concentration, her long dark hair bound up in a swishing ponytail, oblivious to everything except getting the steps right.

When she came down to supper, her face faintly pink after the exercises, I managed, not quite to forget whatever was happening or had happened in P committee, but to shuffle it off to the side of my mind.

All the same, the next morning I was dreading the day to come. I hadn't even got to the office, was only just coming through the ticket barrier at Victoria, when my mobile rang.

'Ah, thank Christ' – for the first time I noticed a faint Irishness in Stan's breathless greeting – 'I apologise for this unceremonious buttonholing, but I think we need a brief word before we meet in the office.'

'You mean, somewhere outside?'

'Indeed. You are familiar with *The Burghers of Calais*?'

'In that garden beyond the House of Lords?'

'That's the ticket.'

'I'll be behind the third burgher from the left. I'll be the only one without a halter round his neck.'

'See you there in ten minutes.' Stan was too flustered to react to the pleasantry.

As I squelched across the grass, the dew lay heavy on the flowing bronze figures, barely visible in the morning mist still rising from the river beyond. Low tide, I noticed, old cans and driftwood exposed on the grimy shingle, human remains too, probably.

Stan plunged straight in, without further greeting.

'It was a catastrophe, an unmitigated catastrophe. Annie said he'd never known a Cabinet committee go so badly. Bryce took most of the flak – after all, he'd insisted the paper be brought to P – but God, the vitriolic looks they gave those of us crouching in the cheaper seats. Of course most of them hadn't read the thing properly, if at all, so they were desperately trying to keep up as Bryce did his overview, but they were taking in enough to know that they hated it. It was when Bryce got to the end of the Birthright section that the PM stopped him in his tracks. "Please forgive me for interrupting, my dear Bryce, but I rather think that I am interpreting the sense of this meeting correctly in saying that our inclination is to proceed no further with these proposals –" general burble of Hear, hears and Quite rights from the assembled toadies – "Moreover, it would, I fear, prove deeply damaging if it were to become public knowledge that we were even considering plans of this nature. I think therefore I must insist that this paper goes no further than this room, and that all copies of it must be destroyed forthwith. And I must also insist that no word of this discussion should leak. Sir Anselm, I would be most grateful if you could gather up all the copies from around this table." So Annie gets up and starts pouching the papers. And of course the Blither can't resist stirring it. There's no situation so bad that the Rt Hon. Rodney Blythe-Roe can't make it worse: "Are we sure, Prime Minister, that it is wise to dismiss this paper so hastily? There may be some fruitful suggestions in it, wheat among the chaff, so to speak. Personally, I rather warm to the idea of reviving the heptarchy. And this section about how to prepare for the next pandemic –" But the PM jumped on him, hard, which went down well because the Blither gets everyone's goat, and they moved on to that dreary paper about energy prices.'

Out here, shivering in the misty morning, disdaining any overcoat, Standish did not seem so overwhelmingly huge, possibly because even he was dwarfed by the gaunt Burghers of Calais. In the foggy air, even his Connacht tartan faded into just another suit. But the anguish in his voice resonated across the sodden green.

'Can they really do that, destroy all the copies, physically I mean?' I asked.

'Of course they can't. Most departments will have run off their own copies, and even if they haven't, some of the brighter sparks will have the gist of it in their heads. And of course the news that they've suppressed the paper will only add to the hoo-ha. You know the old saying, it's not the crime, it's the cover-up that does the damage.'

'So?'

'We keep our heads down and say sorry, and hope to hang on somehow. I've already drafted a formal apology to Bryce which I don't expect you to associate yourself with.'

'That's decent of you,' I said, thinking it was the least he could do.

We crept across Parliament Square and into the office the back way. Katie gave us a particularly bright smile which only revealed how aware she was of the depth of our humiliation. As she leaned over my desk with the coffee, I felt like a shell-shocked subaltern being cosseted by a splendid VAD nurse.

Mercifully, Bryce himself was away visiting an epidemiology lab in Cheshire. I filled the anguished hours by reading Reboot UK right through. Some of the stuff was even more horrific than I had thought, though I did find myself agreeing with the Blither that the section about how to prepare for the next pandemic made a lot of sense, but who cared about that now?

We crouched in our offices for the rest of the day, pretending to work on this and that, but really just waiting for the fallout. Which wasn't slow in falling. You had to take your hat off to Fleet Street's finest. They might not be much interested in the finer details of policy, but give them a whiff of a punch-up in Cabinet or an embarrassing leak, and they pounced.

'GOVERNMENT TO BRING IRELAND BACK INTO THE UNION'. 'SCOTTISH PARLIAMENT TO BE SIDELINED'. 'RAILWAYS TO BE TORN UP AND TURNED INTO COMMUTER RAT-RUNS'. And – most pungent of all – 'POOR TO BE STERILISED – GOVERNMENT PLANS TO IMPROVE NATIONAL BREEDING STOCK'. By lunchtime the next day, the Irish Ambassador had requested clarification of the plans, the Cardinal Archbishop had denounced the inhumane eugenics, and the rail unions were threatening national industrial action. The Number Ten press office began by denying that the government had any such plans whatever, then had to fall back on the line that an irresponsible policy paper had somehow found its way into the system but that it was never seriously considered and had been instantly rejected.

But the paper had been floating around, so perhaps there was a secret plan, one which really did represent the government's deepest, most unholy hankerings.

'I'm sorry that our collaboration has turned out to be so brief,' said Stan, as he was gathering his belongings together at around teatime.

'Me too,' I said quite genuinely. I did not want to say too much, because I could see he was on the edge of tears.

'I told Bryce that I would continue to act as a flying buttress to this great edifice, offering support and advice from outside. He begged me not to go, but I could see he was relieved when I insisted.'

'He's still hanging on himself, though?'

'The PM's very fond of him, and if he got the push too, it would look as if the government really had been taking Reboot seriously at the highest level.'

'I see,' I said, not quite seeing. How strange it was, the etiquette of when you had to go and when you didn't have to, and they said the Court of Louis Quatorze was complicated.

Stan shook my hand vigorously and effortlessly picked up the large cardboard box that Katie had found for his files. In a few minutes I could hear the flip-flop of his giant brogues trudging along the stone flags and up the steps leading out to Whitehall. According to Sir Anselm, exactly the route taken by many another adviser whose advice had been found inconvenient. At least Stan didn't have a halter round his neck.

12

The Golden Jacket

That flowery cursive script brought Betsy straight back to me in all her wonderful ebullience before I had read a word.

Howdy Partner.

Excuse my frontierspeak, but we're all dressed as cowgirls for the Houston rally and my leather bolero is a tad tight around the chest. I am writing to let you know that there is one cowboy who won't be riding this particular range any more. Like everything The Man does, it comes out of left field. There you are, the Numero Uno favorite at court, the Svengali's Svengali, then suddenly you're an unperson, whirling in outer space for ever more.

    It happened in Monterey, no it really did. We were prepping for the Gail White show, and there was Ethan looking gorgeous in a golden jacket with a high collar and not a lot on underneath – think Elvis in Vegas – and he was pumping out some fantastic stats, about how all the grape pickers and construction workers were rooting for us and it was only the pointy-heads in Berkeley who hated us. And I was standing right behind the Candidate and I noticed that he had stopped nodding and he'd gone into that weird frozen posture he does sometimes. Then he turned round and muttered to Calvin, the new chief of staff, 'That guy looking like a daffodil.' 'Oh, you mean Ethan,' says Calvin, chuckling dutifully. 'Get him outta here, I don't want my campaign run by fags.' 'I really don't think —' 'I don't care what you think, get him out of here now, and don't let him have a red cent in comp.' So Calvin sidles round the room and whispers in Ethan's ear that he needs to have a word with him in private and they shuffle out of the room together and Amos takes over the presentation. And that was the last we saw of him. In this campaign, when you're gone, you're really gone. Calvin was as mystified as I was. Tried to get an explanation, but The Man just said, 'I don't want that English fag lousing up a great American campaign, probably the greatest campaign in our history,' which of course Calvin couldn't say to the press. So he just put out a statement that Ethan's temporary assignment to the campaign had come to an end and how grateful they all were for his outstanding contribution.

I tried to work it out for myself and I went back over the scene frame by frame, and pretty soon I clicked. We had been in a conference room at the Fairmont and it had a little stage with a screen for the presenter. And Eth had been standing there, a couple of feet higher than the rest of us, with his snappy little conductor's baton, talking us through his slides. And I suddenly realized that he had become the Sorcerer when he was only hired to be the Sorcerer's Apprentice. The gold jacket, which was kind of glittery too — wasn't it too much like the jacket The Man himself had worn two nights earlier in that amazing rally in the Bowl? And his pitches — well, they were so compelling — way beyond mere slices of data. Already that night in Monterey he had actually spoon-fed the Candidate a couple of tweet lines,

not just the thought but the sassy way of expressing it.
And those tweets are supposed to come fresh out of The
Man's giant genius brain. It would be curtains if word got
round that he had a bunch of staffers feeding them to him.
No, in retro it was all painfully obvious. Dear, dear Eth
had simply got too big for his cowboy boots – yes, he was
wearing those too, with gold stars all over them. So adios,
amigo, but we had such a ball while it lasted.

So now I'm just a lonesome cowgirl who, unlike her
boss, is yearning to have her Brit back in her arms, and no
I don't mean Eth. Come by and lasso me sometime.

Your own Betsy

Like Betsy, I was startled by what had happened,
though when I thought about it, I ought to have seen
it coming. The prudent adviser always had to be aware
of the danger of becoming the story, instead of merely
concocting it. Step over that line, and you were toast.
See Standish Grogan, his rise and fall.

But how vividly I could picture Ethel there in
his moment of glory, data flowing from him like an
unstoppable lava stream, wisecracks and insights
bobbing along with the flow. How irresistible and yet
how insufferable for any rival planet in the same solar
system. I couldn't wait to see him back, to see how he
had taken it, or more precisely to hear his take on the
whole giddy experience.

I didn't have to wait long. I was bracing myself for
another grim day at the Cockpit, and I was trying to
spruce myself in the grubby gilt mirror in the hall – the
midnight-blue suit, seldom worn after Jane said it made
me look like a loss adjuster bringing bad news, with a

rather pretty tie of strangled forget-me-nots – and was startled by the moany jangle of the front door bell.

'Ethel,' I said, 'you must have just got off the plane.'

'Yes, I have,' he said rather severely, as if I wasn't supposed to know that, which of course I wasn't. 'I thought it best to come straight here rather than call you.'

'Oh, fine,' I said. 'Great to see you. Did you have a –'

'We've had trouble with phone security. There's an epidemic of hacking which we've only just got wind of, and we haven't had time to get our systems re-encrypted.'

'Oh,' I said, 'that's very –'

'The thing is, we need to have a private word.'

'I'm due at the Cockpit at 8.15, but I'm sure –'

'That's just it, Dickie. I needed to head you off at the pass. Now this is going to be hard, but I have to say it to you as someone who is by now a pretty old friend and I want to be entirely upfront about it. What we have decided is that it's in the best interests of all concerned if you take this opportunity to move on. I know this must seem very sudden, but things move fast in this game, and Bryce has come to the conclusion, reluctantly, very reluctantly, that after the events of the past few days he really needs a Spad who's more data-focused. In fact, I can tell you that he had originally hoped all along that I might be able to do the job, but of course at that moment I wasn't available.'

He paused and looked out at the sunlit street as if to gather inspiration.

'To be honest, my work over there is just about done now. We're 5 to 10 per cent ahead in the polls in all the swing states except Michigan. The Man's a shoo-in. He'll continue to consult me informally, but he has agreed to release me from my contract. There's a non-compete clause naturally, but that won't apply to working for anyone in the UK.'

'You mean,' I said, putting on the surprise a little as though I was only just tumbling to his intention, though I had got his drift in a matter of nanoseconds (it was, I reflected later, remarkable how my uptake had sharpened over the past few months – perhaps this line of work might delay the onset of Alzheimer's), 'that you want to take over my job?'

'Fill the vacant slot, Dickie. I'm afraid that after Reboot, Bryce needs a fresh team which carries no baggage. I'm well aware that you were not the lead author of Reboot, but alas, your name is on it. What I envisage instead, and I really do hope that this will appeal to you, is that you should become a joint managing director at Making Nice, with oversight of the government contracts which we have every reason to expect as soon as Bryce has got his feet under the desk. Financially of course, I need hardly say that you'll be considerably better off in your new role than toiling for dear old HMG. The Glow Worm is delighted by the thought. She just loved working with you while I've been away.'

'Gloria knows already?'

'I called her last night. I want to emphasise that you'll still be very much part of Bryce's support team but working on the outside. A sort of flying buttress, as they say.'

I searched his face for any smidgen of remorse or shame. But then I reflected, staring into those grey basalt eyes, that I wouldn't really know what to look for. Nor could I see any sign that his recent experiences had deflated him at all. His parrot profile was as bright and alert as ever, not even a hint of jet lag.

'The Wingco will call you as soon as he's sorted, but I think he was quite relieved to leave the arrangements to me, since you and I are such partners in crime.'

'Jane will be disappointed,' I said, trying to think of a way of making light of my humiliation while making it plain that humiliation was what it was. 'She rather liked the idea of me being at the heart of the spider's web.'

'But you will be, Dickie, you'll just be spinning another part of the web. We have plans, great plans, and they're oven-ready. The PM's already agreed in principle and the department's just firming up a task force.'

'What sort of plans exactly?'

'Well, it's a bit early to circulate them to a wider audience. We don't want to alert the oppo and give them time to mobilise. The great thing is, the PM's already on board, so there'll be no trouble from Cabinet.'

We were still standing on the doorstep, brushed by the dew-damp chrysanths that spilled across the steps. I heard someone behind me coming down the stairs, rather slowly.

Flo opened the door wider, and looked out to see who I was talking to.

'Oh,' she said, tightening the belt of her rose-pink towelling robe. She looked quite rosy herself, fresh from her bed or from the bath. Every day the sight of her moved me more intensely.

'Darling,' Ethel said, 'you look so amazing.' Which sounds all right when written down, much what I was thinking myself in fact, but the way he said it, the greeting seemed to carry no special surge of affection, appeared no more passionately felt than a compliment tossed at a party to an old friend who expected that sort of treatment.

'Oh, Eth,' she said, 'it's so great to see you,' and she said it with all the feeling in the world, and I had to hold back the tears. Even in that moment I found myself remembering what Byron had said about love being a thing apart for men but a woman's whole existence, although that was obviously a hopelessly antiquated way to look at it and Byron might not be the most reliable role model. Anyway, you would never call Ethel the Byronic type. Being good-looking was not what he went in for, though you felt he could have managed it if required.

I went inside to make Ethel a cup of coffee and when I came back they seemed to be teasing each other in a relaxed way as though they had been seeing each other every day in the office, rather than being apart for weeks.

'Come in,' I said. 'Do come in. It's cold out here.'

'I so wish I could, it would be great to catch up with you guys, but Bryce's got a provisional slot with the PM at ten thirty and I have to prep him first. Devon's already making faces at me.'

I followed the direction of his outstretched arm to see for the first time the ministerial limo parked opposite and the chauffeur gesturing at his watch through the open window.

'See you all at Smothers,' he said, giving me a gentle rub in the ribs and them moving past me to embrace Flo.

'Laters, darling. Oh, you look so *well*,' he said, standing back with his arms lightly holding her waist.

Then he trotted off down the front steps, turning as he reached the pavement to give the two of us a dinky wave. I remembered how deftly he could manage a farewell.

A profound desolation overcame me as the limo eased off down the street, or not desolation so much as an almost physical sense of loss, as when you wake up to a scam or pat your hip pocket to find your wallet gone after a stranger bumps into you and apologises with the utmost courtesy.

'You see,' Flo said, 'he doesn't care about anybody.'

'Well, he's got this meeting.'

'You believe that, Dad? Oh, you mustn't go on making excuses for him. It wouldn't be so bad if I didn't still …'

I could hear her sobbing as she went up the stairs. The first thing, the only thing in fact, was to bring Jane up to date, which I was dreading.

'Was that Ethel I heard at the door? What on earth was that horrible man doing here at this unearthly hour?'

I told her, trying to put a positive spin on events. The upside of the whole thing, I said, was that I now had an upgrade at Making Nice and quite soon when the book was finished I wouldn't have to see so much of Bryce Wincott, perhaps never have to see him again.

'I don't believe it.'

'What don't you believe?'

'That you're going to lie down and carry on as if nothing's happened. You have to sue for wrongful dismissal. Dermot does these sorts of cases all the time. Anyway, what's Ethel doing back in London? We weren't expecting him until after their election.'

'He says his work is done over there.'

'You mean he's got the sack?'

'I suppose it must amount to that. That man does seem to get through his advisers at a rate of knots.' I knew enough not to determine how much I knew or what my source was.

'Well, all I can say is the sooner she gets shot of him the better. Anyway, I'm going to have it out with her and tell her exactly what I think of him, which is what I should have done months ago.'

Her anger was inspiring. I had always thought that righteous wrath was something you only read about and when people tried it on in real life it sounded like futile posturing. But Jane's anger was so strong and steady that you felt it really might achieve something.

She stumped off upstairs, and I sat perched on the edge of the sofa, waiting. She wasn't away long, ten minutes at the most.

'Well, it may not look that way, but she says in theory they're still engaged, in fact more engaged, because the latest news is, she's pregnant. Coming up for three months, the doctor thinks. That's why she threw up at that dreadful place.'

'Oh God, no. How ... oh, I don't know what to say. Did she not tell us sooner because she thought we —?'

'No, no, she was sure we wouldn't really be angry because she knew we loved her, she just wanted some space to think things through.'

'Do you mean, whether to —'

'No, no question of that,' Jane said sharply. 'You know how much she loves babies. The only thing she says she's sad about is missing a whole year of ballet school. I said it would probably be more than a year, and she said, yes, of course she knew perfectly well that really it was all over, and then she burst into tears again, and she shooed me away to bring you up to speed.'

'So he's ruined her whole bloody career, her whole life in fact if dancing really was going to be her life.'

'Well, when it comes to it, she might not be quite good enough,' Jane said.

'That's not what Madame says. No, it's a total catastrophe for her, and we know it and she knows it. Getting pregnant at her age is ghastly enough for any girl, but for a dancer it's curtains.' I was trying not to shout because Flo might be in earshot, so my words came out like a stifled snarl which I was immediately ashamed of.

'She could start again in a couple of years,' Jane said.

'Hardly. Besides, it's not just the dancing, he had a duty of care. Anyway, that settles it, I'm off. I can't go on working for a man like that.'

'No, it doesn't settle it at all. You have to carry on at Making Nice until either they finally split or they actually get married, which looks pretty unlikely the way she was talking about him just now.'

'But two minutes ago you were urging me to sue him.'

'That was two minutes ago. Now you have to stay in position to steady the ship, if that's the right phrase.'

'So it all depends on Flo?'

'Yes. You may think it strange at your age that your immediate future should depend on your pregnant daughter who isn't quite seventeen, but that's the situation you're in, and she's the one who matters.'

Which was true. And it did soften the humiliation to think that I was enduring it in Flo's interest and not just because I was too feeble to fight my way out of it.

In fact, as I was pedalling along the new Embankment cycleway, I became conscious of what can only be described as a change of character – my own, that is. A peculiar claim to make about yourself when you're middle-aged, peculiar perhaps to make at any age if you believe that a person's character is more or less fixed from the start.

But there it was, a definite midlife hardening in my resolve, a discovery that I was capable of doing things in defence of myself which I would formerly have shied away from. Was this fanciful, a mere comforting illusion? No, I thought to myself as I slowed at the lights, I had seen the same thing happen to other mild men who had been put upon once too often, even in newspaper offices: 'Wouldn't have thought he had it in him,' the villainous Tosh would mutter as some inoffensive leader writer launched a full-scale lawsuit after being sacked, and pursued it to the bitter end, usually doing himself no good at all. True, I had fallen in with Jane's second thoughts, but if Flo had not been involved, I was confident that I would have been on the phone to the rumbustious Dermot and fought the case all the way to the High Court. The outside observer might see no change, but it was at that moment that the iron entered my soul, the Araldite hardened and my backbone made a late entry on the scene. Which will explain what was to happen a little later on.

For the moment, though, all it meant was that I arrived at Bryce's dismal flat in Whitehall Court in a sunny mood which would have amazed me if I had been Bryce but didn't amaze Bryce at all, since the trade secret of people like him is never to admit surprise at getting away with anything.

'Good man, I knew you'd understand, and of course we'll still be working closely together, which is great.'

'Yes indeed.'

'We're fantastically lucky that Ethel can join us at such short notice. He's done great things over there, I hear, and even the Martians know it.'

'Martians?' I said, pretending ignorance.

'Ethel says you always have to remember that basically civil servants all come from Mars and don't have a clue about Planet Earth. But they do have some respect for success, and Ethel's track record precedes him, which is a major plus for us.'

'I'm sure it will be,' I said keenly. 'How did it go this morning?'

'With the PM? He's really excited about the new project. I wish I could share it with you, Dickie, but at the moment it's restricted to the two of us. Not even cleared for the top Martians.'

'But Ethel is in on it, naturally?'

'Ethel's been the greatest possible help drafting the whole scenario. I couldn't have got this far without him. It's going to be a real game-changer, you know, Dickie. The face of this nation will never be quite the same again.'

He stood there in his sitting room in front of the Morris sofa, legs wide apart, jacket off, twanging his regimental braces. I had never seen a man of forty-nine so happy. For myself, I did not feel as resentful as I might have expected. My new-found hardness was curiously comforting, like a pebble you've picked up from the beach and roll around in your pocket.

The Wingco parked me in the little snug where he kept his constituency papers. I sat there idly riffling through old folders, occasionally letting my gaze stray to the photos on the wall: RAF Logistics Corps 2nd XV, B. H. Wincott (Capt.), with the oval ball nestling between his boots, and so on.

'You won't believe it,' Jane broke in on my reverie. She was on her mobile, hospital noises in the background. She was full-time again now because Lucy was so much better. In fact, she was apparently already in line for promotion to senior consultant. 'He's got round her again.'

'How do you mean?'

'Rang her from work in floods of apologies. He knew how heartless he must have sounded on our doorstep, but he only did it to protect their secret, because he was totally confident that she wouldn't have told either of us. Which he can't really have believed if he knew a thing about human nature, which he must because he has to imitate it every day of his life. So yes, he's more in love with her than ever, and he couldn't bear being separated from her a moment longer, which was why he refused when they tried to make him stay with the campaign right through to polling day.'

'Did they really?'

'No, I don't believe it either. If you ask me, he only came back because he heard about your job and couldn't resist stealing it.'

'I expect you're right.'

'And what exactly is this top-secret project that he can't tell anyone about?'

'Search me,' I said, 'I haven't got clearance.'

At least I was invited to the grand unveiling of the project – I could hardly not be, as it was destined to be Bryce's comeback moment, his Finest Hour, the Battle of Britain after Dunkirk, and he needed to have his Boswell on hand. Nothing showed the huge significance of the occasion more strikingly than the launch being held in the garden at Number Ten, with the PM and senior ministers present, plus assorted movers and shakers, some of them with their partners and their children too, which made a cheerful throng but struck me as odd all the same.

It was a golden autumn afternoon. Instead of the usual Number Ten waiting staff, the champagne and superior canapés from Mr Mustard were being handed round by half a dozen of the more presentable Smothers Brothers, not dressed in their usual gear but got up in mob caps and Victorian ragamuffin costumes. I spotted Kaylee, who managed to fist-bump me while carrying his tray without spilling a drop.

'How's it going, Kaylee?'

'Mega, man, it's the most mega gig you ever saw.'

At that moment Bryce began to shoo us all down onto the lawn, while staying at the top of the steps himself.

'First, let me welcome you all to this little entertainment. I'm extremely grateful to the Prime Minister for allowing us to use his fantastic garden. And I'm grateful to someone else who's going to start off our proceedings, someone you may or may not immediately recognise, but who I am sure you will be as delighted as I am to have with us this afternoon. My lords, ladies and gentlemen, Mr Robert Browning.'

Through the French windows onto the balcony stepped a tall figure in a floppy frock coat, loosely tied cravat and black slouch hat. He had long black curly locks and a springy black beard, and a commanding, even merciless eye. As soon he started speaking in that harsh, dry-throated, high-drawn resonant voice – a voice that took me back far beyond his own glory days on the stage to the days of Olivier and Wolfit, even perhaps to the heyday of Sir Henry Irving – there could be no doubt of his true identity.

Hamelin Town's in Brunswick,
By famous Hanover city ...

The motley throng was instantly rapt.

But, when begins my ditty,
Almost five hundred years ago,
To see the townsfolk suffer so
From vermin, was a pity.

The opening lines were declaimed in a jovial, easy manner, but now the poet switched into a grim, blood-curdling snarl:

Rats!
They fought the dogs, and killed the cats,
And bit the babies in the cradles,
And ate the cheeses out of the vats,
And licked the soup from the cooks' own ladles,
Split open the kegs of salted sprats,
Made nests inside men's Sunday hats,
And even spoiled the women's chats
By drowning their speaking
With shrieking and squeaking
In fifty different sharps and flats.

The children in the crowd, pushed by their parents to the front to see better, dissolved in shivery giggles.

As the poet cantered on to describe the angry panic of the citizens of Hamelin and the fluttery hopelessness of the Mayor, he was jovial and sardonic again. At the end of this section, he paused, looked up as if hearing something, creating with his mastery an unnerving hush. After what seemed like an age, there came from somewhere, far off it seemed at first, the sound of a flute softly playing. Then from the French windows underneath the balcony, there stepped forth an undeniably weird figure in a golden coat and a scarlet-and-gold cap with a bell drooping from its tassel. Below the golden coat, he had on leggings but not his old mossy-green ones. These were patterned with psychedelic whirls of scarlet and azure. As he turned from side to side to spray the audience with his music, the parrot-profile was as unmistakable as the voice of the poet who had introduced him. This, I hazarded, must be the same golden coat that had caused him such trouble on the American campaign. The tune he was playing on his gleaming flute was familiar to me, but I could not place it any more than I could place the tune the same flautist had played that evening at St Dingle's. It was light-hearted, almost scherzando, yet somehow melancholy, but perhaps flute solos always have something sad about them.

He took the flute from his lips, and began to recite, but in such a relaxed conversational way you scarcely guessed he was speaking verse: 'I'm able, by means of a secret charm, to draw all creatures living under the sun, that creep or swim or fly or run, after me so as you never saw! And I chiefly use my charm on creatures that do people harm, the mole and toad and newt and viper, and people call me the Pied Piper.'

The children gazed open-mouthed, several of them squealing with pleasure as the Piper pursued his tale. And then from the same French windows he had come through, half a dozen creatures, in brown and grey and black rat costumes, ran out across the lawn, squeaking and growling and swishing their rubbery tails. These must have been the rest of the Smothers Brothers, no doubt not considered suave enough to do the waiting here but ideal for rat duty. As the rats scrabbled and pranced their way across the grass, the Piper danced ahead in his leggings, tootling the while, until he vanished through a little door in the wall which was opened by an unseen hand, with the rats following close behind.

The poet drew our attention back to the balcony, telling us how the bells of Hamelin rang out to celebrate this brilliant exercise in rodent control. Then, as he continued his tale, back through the door in the wall came the Piper, demanding in dumbshow his thousand guilders, to the consternation of the niggardly Mayor and Corporation, these roles now mimed with gusto by the Prime Minister and Bryce and other senior Cabinet ministers.

Then came the spine-chilling moment. The poet went on: 'And the Piper blew three notes, such sweet notes as yet musician's nerve never gave the enraptured air.' Sinister too the notes were, from this particular Piper, and as he blew them, the Brothers who were dressed as Victorian ragamuffins took the hands of the children at the front of the crowd and led them at a merry skip across the garden the same way the rats had gone, and they all followed the Piper through the little door in the wall, and in an instant they were gone, completely gone.

13

The Locator

The children's parents rushed forward, stricken with a sudden anxiety which had taken several seconds to gather, so mesmerising had the performance been. Anxiety grew into consternation as the little door in the wall banged shut. Several of the children can have been no more than six or seven years old.

The parents looked wildly back up to the balcony for comfort or information. But the poet had turned on his heel with a flounce of his frock coat and he too was gone. The parents turned round again to fret with one another, discussing what they could possibly do next. A junior minister at the Treasury ran towards the door in the wall, dragging his wife by the hand.

Another unnerving pause. Then the door to the balcony opened again, and Bryce stepped out. Not in my book the ideal person to reassure anxious parents, better cast as the Mayor of Hamelin, I thought. Even the calming way he spread out his hands seemed to me the kind of gesture that only riles up restless crowds.

'Ladies and gentlemen, there's absolutely no cause for alarm. Look, they're having a wonderful time.'

At the far end of the shrubbery that ran along the wall, two of the waiter-Brothers had slipped back into the garden and were hauling out a large screen on wheels. An unseen projector whirled into action and there on the screen was Horse Guards Parade, on the other side of the wall, where there was a little funfair set up, with a roundabout which the stream of children were already climbing onto. 'Oh look, there's Jago!' some mother cried and the audience broke out into relieved and prolonged applause, with a few whoops of delight from the back (possibly from Number Ten staffers).

'I'm sure you'd all like to join me in giving our warmest thanks to Sir Ian for his memorable performance here this afternoon.' Then, after these cheers had died down, 'And now I'd like to introduce you to my special adviser and best mate, Ethel Evers, alias the Pied Piper, who's going to put you in the picture.'

And there was Ethel again, with his jester's hat tucked under his arm now but still in his golden jacket and leggings, his parrot's crest sticky and spiky from his exertions.

'Thank you all so much for coming along and for lending your children to be part of our entertainment. As you can see, the story has a happy ending. What you may not know is that the tale of the Pied Piper was based on events which really happened in the little town of Hamelin, near Hanover, just over seven hundred years ago, when 130 children – actually they were teenagers or young adults – were led away by a mysterious piper in a brightly coloured costume, never to return. But they weren't swallowed up by a cave in the mountainside – there aren't many serious mountains near Hamelin – nor were they victims of the plague, as some later tellers of the tale suggested. No, they were led off to seek new economic opportunities in the unsettled wastelands to the east. These resettlement schemes were inspired by what they called "locators", young entrepreneurs who arrived with a pipe band in run-down towns like Hamelin with an attractive offer to make to the unemployed youth. So the locators were a mixture of estate agent and recruiting officer. They would turn up in their colourful gear and play a tune the lads could whistle to.'

Ethel paused to take up his flute and play a few bars of 'Colonel Bogey'. In no time, he had quite few in the crowd whistling along with him.

'And that, ladies and gentlemen,' Ethel continued, after putting the flute down and wiping his lips, 'is how Prussia was born, the mightiest industrial power ever seen on the Continent of Europe, a nation of in-migrants from the western parts of Germany to the sandy wastes and woods of Mecklenburg and Pomerania. They called it the Ostsiedlung, the Eastern Settlement, and it was the making of the nation. Note, I said "in-migrant", not "immigrant". These were people moving from one part of their own lands to another part in search of work. In-migration is the unique dynamic of economic growth. You saw it in the US in the nineteenth century. Industry only really took off when Americans on the Eastern Seaboard tramped over the Alleghany Mountains to settle round the Great Lakes and build the great Midwest industrial centres of Chicago and Detroit. Same thing in Britain when farm workers left the land after the repeal of the Corn Laws to work in the cotton mills of Manchester and the steel mills of Sheffield.

'The trouble with Britain today is that we are a stuck nation. We need to get moving again, in the most literal sense, from the towns and cities that have had their day to the places where the work of the future is going to be. We need a new breed of locators to pipe them aboard the Relocation Express. That is what my good friend Bryce and his amazing team are all about. In the coming weeks and months we shall be spelling out the timetable for the New Age of Mobility. But that's enough from me for the moment. If anyone has any questions …'

A thickset man with curly salt-and-pepper hair shot up his hand, in the same instant almost bellowing at a pitch too loud for this curious garden party. I recognised him as a presenter who read the news on off-peak bulletins.

'Why don't you move the work to the workers instead?'

It was this rough interjection that somehow broke the spell that Ethel had cast upon the party. People began talking among themselves. Several of the parents, their anxieties still unsatisfied, made for the little door in the wall to retrieve their children.

Ethel was unfazed, the smile spreading over his beaky features in a way familiar to me when he was about to explain what I was thinking and why I was thinking it.

'Yes, that is the question, isn't it? That approach sounds so much easier and so much *nicer*, which is why we've gone on trying it long after we should have realised that the market just doesn't work that way. Any private business that refused to learn from such a repeated experience of total failure would have gone under years ago. We go on calling it regional policy, when it ought to be called regional illusion. Any other questions?'

He had said all this in the mildest, most good-humoured way imaginable, almost as though he was agreeing with the curly-haired man. Perhaps it was the amiability of this putdown that deterred other questioners, or perhaps they were just too bowled over by the whole performance to keep the debate going.

The newspapers the next day had no such hesitation. They waded in like swimmers on the first hot day of summer. For the cartoonists, the image of Bryce as a portly puffing piper was too good a target to miss. Downing Street resorting in desperation to other nursery rhymes for policy ideas was another angle – the PM as Little Bo-Peep who lost her sheep, the Foreign Secretary as Georgy-Porgy who kissed the girls and made them cry, etc.

Ethel seemed not to mind this mockery one little bit. 'Always start by tickling their fancy,' he said when I congratulated him on his piping and said how unfair I thought the papers had been. 'Then they'll be broken in to the general idea when we get down to the real-time policy choices.'

Which turned out not to be true, not to start with at any rate. This may be because it was Bryce's task to do the explaining. He had chosen to confide in a long-time crony in the parliamentary lobby whom he thought could be trusted to put the most favourable spin on any briefing.

'Fuck McIntee, I did not say Abandon Burnley, or anything of the sort,' he blasted at me when I came in the morning after Craig McIntee had told his readers that the government proposed to run down some of the depressed former cotton towns in Lancashire and shift their inhabitants to new towns built on unproductive breckland and heathery waste in the south-east. High-flying 'locators' would be established on prime sites in towns designated for rundown. The future of Liverpool as a going concern was also said to be on the table.

The anger came in faster than a tsunami, knocking over innocent backbenchers who hadn't uttered a word, drenching in *merde* the entire profession of town planners and architects, and washing up at the doors of Downing Street before lunchtime. The PM's spokesman had protested that Liverpool was as safe as, well, houses, and in the afternoon the PM himself was wheeled on to protest his undying loyalty to Burnley and every last one of its inhabitants.

'Did you not expect this?' What *I* hadn't been expecting was a call from Ethel, I thought he would have better things to do. But since he was on the line, I could not resist asking the question that had spurted up as soon as I read the headlines.

'Yes of course, I'm not a complete thicko. You have to shock and awe, Dickie, before you can begin to change people's mindsets.'

'But doesn't it sound a bit too much like, well, the Highland Clearances?'

'What was wrong with the clearances was that the crofters didn't have a decent life to go on to. After the war, they made the opposite mistake, knocked down the slums, then rebuilt them in exactly the same places which didn't have a future. We're doing something entirely different.'

'But will they want to move?'

'Oh they'll move all right, when they see what we're offering. In fact, the reason I rang, Dickie, was to invite you to come with me on a trip to the north to take a look at what we have in mind. There's a whole lot more that you don't know yet and you have to be in there at the beginning if you're going to bring the book alive. This is going to be Bryce's Monument, remember.'

So there we were on a grey morning two days later walking down Gladstone Street in a town I'd never heard of called Gormley.

'Gormley's the pilot for rundown,' Ethel said. 'The place is dead on its feet, only kept going by the DSS and the council housing department.'

It was a melancholy prospect as we bumped over a weed-strewn canal and saw the main street steepling up the hill in front of us: a straggle of two-storey houses, all in the local dirty-honey stone which looked as if it was being rained on even when it wasn't. Half the shops were boarded up. There were still special offers advertised in the dusty windows of a defunct Dorothy Perkins, and rusty lettering saying Barclays over a shuttered bank. Two Nonconformist chapels conforming to no religion now: one selling motor parts, the other a junk shop crowded with brass lamps and battered fenders. The only bright spots were the premises of Joe Coral and William Hill, sandwiching the East Lancs Hospice shop – betting and dying the only businesses that were still viable in Gormley. Nowhere capable of sustaining its original purpose, not even the oversized Gothic town hall which was boarded up and had a huge sign saying FOR SALE OR RENT. Either side of the town hall, the street forked up to the moors, a dim and bleak panorama at the best of times but especially forbidding in this mid-morning autumn light which felt like five o'clock in the afternoon.

'There, you can just see Gormley Edge, which is where the coal seam runs out. They shut the pit thirty years ago. The town's been pretending not to be dead ever since. We really don't need to linger, but I did want you to see for yourself what it was like.'

As we walked back to the car, some of the few shoppers glared at us, suspicious of Ethel's open Merc and because we looked like cocky strangers. I don't think they could have guessed why we were there. Gormley was too insignificant to have been mentioned in the media as a possible target for the locators.

'So where are we going now?'

'To High Fell Manor, to meet Mr Christian Blankers. You won't have heard of his firm, because it's not one of your high-profile department store empires. Its critics say it makes Aldi look like Harrods, but it's as big as any of its rivals in the EU. Christian has been building up his landholdings round here for ten years now at least. When I last checked, he had 90,000 acres.'

We drove out of the brief suburbs of low granite villas until we were climbing into the bare moorland with wind-bitten alders and hawthorn along the brimming ditches. Ethel pointed out High Fell Manor when it was still four or five miles away, a turreted baronial affair in the same dirty-honey stone crouched in the lee of the crags with wooded parkland stretching back down to the valley. The usual belt of rhododendrons and azaleas protected the demesne from the harsh surrounding country, but the place was not exactly welcoming. You felt that nobody had ever had much fun at High Fell Manor.

As we glided over the immaculate gravel to the front door, a slender shortish man in a tweed gilet with spectacles dangling on a scarlet string trotted down the steps to greet us. Christian Blankers could not have been more friendly, yet there was an unmistakable tinge of melancholy about him, reminding me a little of our American benefactor Norfolk Chard. Hard to tell, really, whether this gloomy ambience came naturally to those burdened with great possessions or whether they felt obliged to put it on, so as not to seem to be revelling in them.

'What a wonderful view.'

'Yes, it is, isn't it? The estate now reaches down to the old turnpike, but we're in negotiation to buy the two farms between there and the town boundary. And after that, well, who knows?' He turned to Ethel with a shy enquiring smile.

'Most of this side of the town belongs either to Legal & General or to the council. Both are pretty eager to sell as many freeholds as they can. The council is particularly strapped after they made a series of bad bets on the futures market.'

'That is most encouraging news, Mr Evers. I do not wish to seem at all predatory.'

'Ethel, please. No question of that, Christian. I am confident that you will soon be seen as a liberator. It's only a question of changing perceptions.'

'I'm gratified to hear it. I've been more occupied in recent months with our plans for rewilding. The lynxes, as you know, came to us at the end of last year, and we've just finished the perimeter fencing for the wolves, who have been ordered from Poland and will come over as soon as we have the necessary permissions. There has been talk of ocelots too, but I'm not sure about the climate, although they do like rain.'

'Christian's dream is that the whole area from Gormley up to the Cumbrian border should eventually form a single wilderness, as large as anything in Scotland or anywhere else in Europe. We plan to retain and refurb a few of the better farmhouses as safari lodges.'

Another shy smile spread over Blankers's pale features as Ethel expounded the finer details of the grand design. A core of buildings in Gormley itself might also be retained as holiday homes for handicapped children, but public access remained a tricky question. What was clear, though, was that the whole huge expanse – it might eventually be as much as 200,000 acres, perhaps more, there was no set limit – was to belong solely and exclusively to Christian Blankers.

'I don't much care for the term "wildlife park" – it smacks too much of Disneyland. For myself, I prefer "sanctuary". What do you think, Mr Pentecost?'

'Oh, sanctuary is a lovely word,' I said, though actually I thought it rather creepy.

'I'm so glad you think so.' In his quiet way, he gave off a powerful expectation of being agreed with. 'I thought we might take our lunch on the run, so to speak, if that's agreeable to you.' He pointed to a sage-green buggy at the far end of the gravel sweep where a young man in a black coat was loading up a silver cool box. How quiet the whole place was, as though someone was dying upstairs in the Great House and everyone had been told to go about on tiptoe. The clanking of the bottles in the cool box sounded like pistol shots.

With Christian at the wheel in his chamois leather driving gloves, the buggy bounced over the moorland track that led behind the house and through a gap in the crags, its fat tyres cushioning the shock so well that we seemed to be almost floating across the ground. Beyond the crags, the country opened out into a vast shallow bowl. It was a wild and desolate place, streaked only by stuttering watercourses with a silvery fringe of low bushes and the odd rowan tree still showing a few red berries. For several miles coming down from the pass, there was no sign of cultivation, then I made out the rough rectangles of what had been pasture – half a dozen fields at most – but as we came closer, I saw that the fences to the fields had all been ripped up and were now neatly piled at the side of the road. Already rushes and pale green scrub were spreading out from the scant hedgerows. Below these fields was the farmhouse, or at least from a distance it looked like a farmhouse, but close up, it was just a heap of stones, these too arranged in neat piles. Beyond the stones, a young man in overalls was thrusting a can of petrol at a huge pile of sodden rafters and other debris.

'Upper Haggs Farm,' Christian said, pointing to the dismal scene and saluting the young man as we drove past him. 'Old Ayscough only went into hospital last month. It must have been the most unprofitable farm in the north, but he just wouldn't give up.'

'You have to admire his spirit,' Ethel said.

'Of course you do, but …' Christian spread his gloved left hand in a gesture of bewilderment at the cussedness of people.

I was glad when we had floated on beyond Upper Haggs and we stopped on a small bluff to admire the view and sample the chicken vol-au-vents and chilled rosé de Provence, which Christian unpacked from the cooler and spread out on a Mondrian-patterned rug as punctiliously as though laying for a state banquet. His obsessive neatness was somehow charming, yet at the same time unsettling. It seemed, paradoxically, that rewilding required the most exact organisation, would get nowhere without unremitting attention to detail. I was reminded of my old friend Harry Warre-Jones who was obsessed with the classical ideal of leisure or *scholé*: 'Think about it, Dickie, our word "school" only comes from the Greek word for frigging about. What we need to relearn is how to be idle.' Yet in some ways he was the most energetic man you ever met, always bobbing up with new ideas and planning fresh adventures, even if nothing much ever seemed to come of most of them.

As we rode along the floor of the valley, half a dozen deer came into view halfway up the slope above us and cantered along with us, as though detailed to provide an escort. Christian smiled and gave them his curious half-salute, the stiff waggle of the forearm favoured by public figures who have to do a lot of waving. The deer abruptly turned away from us up a gulley and vanished as though their task was done, and we were alone again in the great wilderness.

Christian turned to me, as though sensing something of my feelings. 'It may seem rather empty at the moment, but it won't be long before they're all back – the hares, the hawks, the butterflies, the rabbits. Modern agriculture has a lot to answer for.'

He spun the wheel to the right up through a clump of ash and sycamore on either side of the road, the nearest thing to a wood we had come across. As we came into the thick of the trees, he stopped, the squeak of the handbrake sounding like a squeak of pain in the soughing of the breeze off the moor. Ethel was about to say something, but Christian put a finger to his lips to call for silence.

Out from a bramble thicket trotted a little procession: two hairy umbrous hogs with long black snouts questing through the bracken, then four little ones trotting behind them in strict single file. They crossed the road without pausing to look at us and disappeared into the undergrowth the other side.

'We had them from the same place in Poland where we're getting the wolves from. They're very reliable, the boars. I've never been up here without them coming to say hullo.' Christian spoke tenderly, as if wild boar were worth keeping for this quality alone.

'And the lynxes?'

'Strictly night-time only, and you can't really see them properly without the infra-red.'

Perhaps I had been unfair. He seemed to be just as fond of the lynxes for being so elusive.

'Your children must love coming up here,' I said. From a newspaper interview I had gathered that he had a son and a daughter, 'a pigeon pair' as he called them, which is apparently an old-fashioned phrase for boy-and-girl twins, or a family consisting of a boy and girl only. I thought it was rather odd to use a term from the animal kingdom to describe his own children.

'Oh, they prefer waterskiing with their mother in Biarritz.' He spoke without bitterness, as far as I could see, as if this was only to be expected.

We were coming back towards the great ridge again, and I could see several falls of scree on the slopes, paw-shaped like giant rabbit scrapes.

'Old copper workings, from the days when the Duke's land reached this far. When we came here, there was a row of miners' cottages just below, but they were too tumbledown to be worth keeping. I'm rather proud of the way we've restored the land.'

I stared at the barren slope but could see no sign of former human habitation.

'Thank you,' he said when I told him this.

We had been driving for half an hour now and the only other human being we had seen was the young man chucking petrol at the pile of rafters. We drove on for another half-hour back up a different valley and never saw another soul. Sitting beside Christian Blankers, I could feel how satisfying this excursion into emptiness had been for him and how fulfilling he found his project, incomplete as it still was. I told him this too and he said 'thank you' again, in a way that was both clipped and heartfelt.

The sky was darkening by the time we said goodbye to him. After shaking hands, he gave us a little bow like an actor at the end of a show, which after all is what this had been. By the time we hit the A1, we had the headlights on, and it was raining hard. Ethel drove in silence, which was unnerving. I couldn't remember being in his company for any length of time without being on the receiving end of some effortless descant on this or that. Then I saw that he was peering anxiously into the dark.

'Lousy visibility,' I said soothingly.

'I need glasses for driving at night,' he said rather curtly. This confession of frailty was unlike him too, seeming to spring from a more general unease. We were breaking our journey at a Travelodge north of Grantham. He strode ahead of me across the car park at an impatient march, and I could see that his impatience was not just with the weather.

'Well, you certainly didn't bother to conceal your feelings,' he said almost the moment we sat down in the dining room.

'You couldn't not think it was an enormously impressive enterprise,' I said, nettled because hiding my feelings was exactly what I thought I had managed to do rather well.

'Couldn't not,' he repeated with mocking acidity. 'You hated every minute of it. And he could see you hated it. He may be a prim little Dutchman, but he's not stupid, you know.'

'How do you know that?'

'It was so fucking obvious. In any case, Christian murmured to me when he was showing me the way to the loo, "I hope we shall bring your friend round in time." Here we are launched on one of the biggest policy breakouts since World War II and my number one collaborator is walking about as if he had a permanent smell under his nose. Don't assume that just because you stay shtum most of the time, people can't see what you're thinking.'

This, I would have admitted if I hadn't been so wounded, was a rather acute critique of my underlying assumption in social life, which is that I am an invisible observer of events. I have noticed other low-key characters who appear to be making the same assumption, and I can also see them wondering why they are not more popular.

'I'm awfully sorry, I don't think you –'

'I really do not want to have to put it like this, Dickie, but we simply cannot afford to carry any reluctant passengers on this trip. I could see from the moment we launched the Piper show that you weren't fully on board. You thought it was all a stupid gimmick, didn't you?'

I had never seen him angry before, not genuinely angry. It was a sharp biting anger and I did not care for the lash of it. Perhaps he might have been less annoyed if I had openly and boldly queried the whole enterprise. It was my ineptly hidden disdain that really riled him.

'You thought I'd made it all up about the Piper, didn't you? I could see you there down on the lawn thinking this is just another one of Ethel's spiels. Well, I'll tell you again here and now, every word of it was gospel truth. On 26 June 1284, a locator deputed by the Teutonic Knights, and dressed pretty much like I was dressed, led a party of 130 youths out of the depressed, war-torn town of Hamelin in Lower Saxony to seek a better life in the east, in the forests of Mecklenburg and Pomerania. Their leaving was much mourned by their families who stayed behind. For several centuries thereafter, the city dated events as happening so many years after *die Jungen* left. That's all historical fact, and it's geographical fact that the names of Hamelin families and local towns are found to this day hundreds of miles to the east in the area of the new colonies. The Piper was not a myth, he was a human people-carrier, leading one of the great race migrations of the Middle Ages.'

'What about the rats?'

'Forget the rats, they were a later interpolation. There are folk legends all over the world about mysterious magicians who can enchant animals with their music. Think Orpheus for a start.'

'And how exactly –' I was trying to think of a softer angle to cool him down and steer me out of trouble – 'did you come to think of using the tale? Or, to go back to the beginning, how did you come upon it in the first place, the true historical facts I mean, not just the legend which we all learned as children?'

'Well now.' He put down his forkful of beetroot and feta salad and looked at me with his grey basaltic stare, not now in a contemptuous or unfriendly way, I thought, more as if calculating whether or not he really wished to go on with what he was about to say, or more particularly whether I was really the person he wished to say it to. 'We've been together quite a while now, you and I, and I'm so grateful for all the things you've done for Making Nice and for me personally, and I can think I can say that we've become fond of each other, though we're such very different types.'

I risked a faint smile to encourage him, though 'fond' was not exactly the word that came to me, 'mesmerised by' would still be more accurate.

'And we have family links too, which this is not the time to go into, because we promised to keep it secret for the moment, though I'm sure you're well aware what I am talking about, because those sort of secrets are hard to keep in a family which is really close.' He was speaking more softly now, almost hesitantly, and I just nodded in a stupefied way. It was such a creepy way for him to acknowledge what he hadn't hitherto shown the slightest sign of wishing to own up to. This, I suppose, would have been the moment to ask him what his intentions were towards Flo, but that was such a stilted phrase – did anyone in real life ever ask, 'and what are your intentions?' – and I couldn't. Just listening to him in a sympathetic way might get more out of him, for the moment anyway.

'You remember, I expect, when we first met, champing in Wales, and I said my name was Ethel short for Ethelbert and I'd got the name because my father was an Anglo-Saxon nut who'd been vicar at St Dingle's, and you all laughed, or the girls did.'

'Yes of course, how could I possibly forget?'

'Well, that wasn't entirely untrue. The bit about my father, yes, that was all made up, but my name being Ethelbert, Ethel for short, that was quite true, *is* quite true. Look, here's my driving licence.'

He flipped the mauve plastic out of his wallet and there it was: 'Ethelbert J. Evers', and at the same time I sneaked a look at his DOB: '25.06.1982', so twice Flo's age and more, which by now was no surprise.

'You didn't believe me, did you?' he said, putting the licence back in his wallet.

'Never doubted you for a moment.'

'But that's not what it says on my birth certificate.'

'It doesn't?'

'No, my infant self rejoiced in the name of Adelbert Johannes von Everstein.'

'So you're actually German.'

'Saxon to be precise, just not Anglo-Saxon. Adelbert is the German equivalent of Ethelbert, which means noble and shining, as I'm sure you must have guessed just by looking at me. Unfortunately when my poor old dad was making me into an English gentleman, he thought Ethelbert would be a brilliant name, the Anglo-Saxon king and so on. What he didn't realise was that after *1066 and All That* the name was just comic. I stuck with it, though. Retreating to plain Johnny Evers would be merely going with the crowd, and I always wanted to stand out a bit, but you may have guessed that too.'

He was certainly living up to his name at this moment. Leaning over our table at the Nunthorpe Travelodge, his grey eyes were really shining bright, for the first time since I had met him, with that intense warmth which some people display only when they're talking about themselves.

'But why ...'

'My dad always said you couldn't imagine how the anti-German prejudice lingered for years after the war. The people who didn't hate him for being German hated him because they thought he was Jewish, which he wasn't. He knew enough not to change his name to Everstone when he got to England, because the same people would hate him even more for being Jewish and pretending not to be. And they had had enough of being pushed around, my mum and dad, they just wanted a quiet life.'

'So where did they come from originally?'

'A little place called Naugard, it's in Poland now and they call it Nowogard with a w in the middle, but for centuries it was a German town in Pomerania, one of the towns that the Germans settled in the Piper's time. And the chap who led the settlers there from Hamelin was a local squire called Count Albert von Everstein. He was the locator for that patch.'

'And you ...'

'Direct descendant, or so my grandpa insisted. He was a curious mixture, my grandpa, very much a leftie. Organiser for the Social Democrats before the war, yet unbelievably proud of his ancestors. Neither of which did him much good. The Nazis chucked him out of university for his political views, so he had to work as a pharmacist's assistant, then when the Russians came he was driven out of the country along with millions of others simply for being German. Most of the *Vertriebenen* went to West Germany, but he liked the sound of the GDR though he had a lousy time there too because they sussed him out as a toff. They had to leave everything behind in Naugard, except my dad, little Rudi, who was eleven months old at the time, oh and their best pairs of skates, they had to take those with them.'

'Skates?

'There's not much to recommend Naugard nowadays. The magnificent Schloss Everstein was demolished by the Swedes in a war you've never heard of. Naugard's only sight is a huge lake in the middle of town which freezes in winter, and that's where my grandpa learned to skate and where he met my grandma, who was an even better skater than he was. And the first thing they taught little Rudi was how to skate. My dad told me he could skate backwards before he could walk properly. And when he got bigger and stronger, he was really good. By the time he qualified as a doctor, he was on the fringe of the East German ice hockey team, and the manager said why don't you come and be our team doctor? As you may know, the sporting federations were a law unto themselves in the GDR when they were winning medals for the Fatherland, so although Dad wasn't exactly *persona grata* with the regime because of his social origins, he was allowed to be their chief MO and my mum, who couldn't skate for toffee but was a brilliant physio, worked alongside him, which meant that almost uniquely they could travel abroad together as a couple to look after the team during international competitions. And so, well, I'm sure you can guess …'

'They defected?'

'In London, European championships 1980. I was born two years later.'

'What a story,' I said, and meaning it. 'Thank you for telling it to me. But …' I could not think quite how to put what I wanted to say, but Ethel was there before me. The blaze had gone out of his eyes, and he had that familiar one-jump-ahead look.

'You're going to say, why aren't you sick of all these mass migrations, in-migrations, emigrations, the whole painful process of upping sticks and starting a new life?'

'I wasn't going to put it so strongly, but you've rather got the gist.'

'Well, the short answer, my dear Dickie, is that there are times and places, lots of times and lots of places, where staying put is living death. You don't hear much about the economic background in the way they tell the legend, but Hamelin in the Piper's time was a ghastly hole, torn apart by the wars raging all over Germany, abysmal wages, slum tenements, brutal taxes on the young as well as forced labour. Any young person with any sense or enterprise would have wanted to get the hell out. Same with the GDR in my dad's day. And as for Gormley today, well, you've seen it.'

'Yes, I have.'

'Think of Gormley, and then think of New Malden where my parents finished up, nice semi with a big garden backing onto the local bowling green, Waitrose five minutes away with fully stocked shelves, not just black bread and jars of gherkins, which was all there was in Naugard at the end of the war. The question is, how do you get from Naugard, or from Gormley, to New Malden? That's what real politics is all about, Dickie, the only thing.'

He stopped talking to finish his steak and chips, which were getting cold. I looked round the Travelodge carvery. There were only half a dozen of us in the place. The lighting was as subdued as the clientele. I wondered how much the other diners had heard of Ethel's life story, which he had told with some flamboyance, and what they would think of it if they had.

I passed one of those troubled hotel nights when you aren't quite sure whether the angry cries, the dogs barking and the odd whistling noise are all part of some disordered dream or are really happening somewhere in the hotel. For a time, I was staggering on borrowed skates across an endless stretch of ice with Ethel shouting advice to me, and then I was tumbling somehow, not through the ice, but down a filthy slope with nothing to cling to anywhere, reeling through space with thorn bushes scratching my bare arms.

'It should take us about ninety minutes from here to Hadock End. Remember, it's spelled h–a–d–o–c–k, there's only one d and it's pronounced Haydock. Apparently the locals are very particular about that.'

I didn't feel much more at my ease as we drove on down the featureless plains of the A1. In a way, I had been more comfortable with Ethel when he was still a total mystery. It had even been comforting somehow that you couldn't believe a word he said. The possibility – likelihood even – that most of what he had just told me might be more or less true, that was unsettling, just as unsettling as Ethel's family background and his reinvention of himself as a crusader for human flourishing.

Almost exactly ninety minutes after Ethel had told me how to pronounce Hadock, we were driving along a bleak treeless lane and drawing up outside a stretch of chain-link fencing with a faded sign half hanging off the fence saying 'RAF Hadock'. Ethel was always accurate about things like times, dates and distances, as though to make up for his imprecision in other areas.

He hooted twice, clearly by prearrangement, and a burly man in a tweed cap standing the other side of the gates began to unlock them. The man was wearing a green tweed gilet much like Christian Blankers's, but in all other respects he could not have been more different, being a big sprawling fellow with an old check shirt half unbuttoned and a grumpy-roguish red face which gave off the general impression that he might not suffer fools or anyone else much except on his own terms. He twirled the hefty bunch of keys at us.

'The RAF gave us the run of the place when they left. Not just out of the kindness of their hearts. If stock got loose through a hole in the fence, they'd be liable. It's an enormous stretch, as you see. We've grazed a fair few sheep here in the past and the ruddy dog took all day to bring them in.' He waved at the great flat expanse of cracked tarmac and rough grass with a few huts and a radio mast in the middle distance.

'George Marchbanks, of this parish,' he said, turning back to us and shaking our hands. 'We've been farming in these parts since before they invented aeroplanes. In fact, the RAF took these fields off my grandfather in 1936. Remember Stanley Baldwin, "the bomber will always get through"? Well, it bloody didn't, not after Fighter Command set up shop at Hadock.'

He looked round the desolate scene with a proprietorial pride.

'Now my good sir,' he said to Ethel, 'what have you got to tell me?'

'Well,' Ethel said, 'as of yesterday we have the MoD's commitment that as soon as the Bill is presented, they'll set in motion the arrangements to release the 1,800 acres of RAF land for immediate sale to the Enterprise Town. That has to happen in sync with your commitment to sell the entire 3,500 acres of the Hadock estate to the ET at twice the going agricultural price, as agreed. Parliament will make trouble unless the landholdings are secure and transparent. With the other parcels we already hold in trust for the ET, that will make up an area roughly twice the size of present-day Gormley district. So there'll be room not only for the Technology Park but also for an amazing recreational facility that Gormley can only dream of. And, this is strictly confidential, but the PM has kindly agreed that the park might be named after him. And it's all only fifty minutes from Liverpool Street,' he said, finishing with a magician's flourish of his hand.

'As long as they don't name the bloody park after me, I'm in enough trouble as it is. Oh fuck, here they come.'

Marchbanks ran back to the gates and locked them again, leaving our car outside in the lane. He could run pretty swiftly for such a big clodhopper of a man.

At first I couldn't see what he was swearing at, then I saw a small crowd coming up the lane from the direction of Hadock Green, several carrying banners. Although they were still nearly half a mile away, I could already hear their cries on the raw morning wind.

'What the hell is this?' Ethel had to shout to make himself heard above the wind. 'We agreed on total blanket security.'

'I can't apologise enough.' Marchbanks sounded more aggrieved than sorry. 'I had to give my agent some idea of what we were up to, so that he could give me accurate up-to-date particulars for sale. Then we had a silly argument about money and I had to let him go, so I'm afraid he's a rather loose cannon now.'

'But he must be covered by a non-disclosure agreement.'

'My dear sir, he only has to drop two words in the pub, and the entire fucking village knows I'm selling up and has a pretty good idea who I'm selling up to. They'll really hit the roof when they find out that I'm buggering off to my wife's people in north Norfolk – there's a nice mixed arable set-up they used to own which they'd love to get back. I don't mind telling you, the sooner we're off, the better. The sugar beet's a goner now they're letting the Jamaican cane back in. Anyway, they're a ghastly lot round here, the worst sort of stuck-up commuters.'

He gazed with unrestrained loathing as the little crowd drew nearer. I could read some of the banners now: 'No New Town Here', 'Save Hadock', 'Essex Lives Matter'. The cries, the ones that I could make out, were more violent: 'Fuck off, Farmer George' was the most nearly printable. Two young women in dungarees at the head of the procession were carrying gleaming pitchforks, which didn't look as if they had yet touched dung.

'Let's hop in the Land Rover. There's a back gate they can't get round to because there's no bridge over the drain outside the fence. We'll come back for your car later when they've gone. You've no idea what these people are capable of when they're fired up.'

We sped off across the deserted aerodrome, rumbling noisily over the broken tarmac and bumping violently over the rough grass. Nothing could have been less like our floating over the moors in Christian's buggy.

The aerodrome seemed to go on forever. Finally we hit the main runway and were speeding along a better stretch. Just below the end of the runway, where the Spitfire pilots had once soared off to meet their fates, there was a rusty gate in the perimeter fence, and after some fumbling Marchbanks found the key. Just before the fence there was a broad drain full of algae with a rotten wooden bridge over it, which Marchbanks took at full tilt, cracking our heads against the roof. 'Haven't been this way for years,' he bellowed. 'We could go home for a bite, but they've probably got people there too. Best to go to the Fox at Burston, the landlord's a mate and he can hide us in the snug.'

As we sat in the back room at the deserted pub with cheese-and-pickle sandwiches, my companions' spirits seemed to perk up. 'Didn't fancy those harridans with the pitchforks.' 'Or that big fellow with the black beard.'

'The one who looks like a poacher? He's quite high up in the Inland Revenue, they tell me.'

They might have been hunting men back from the chase, rather than their quarry. Locators in the old days probably had similar hairy experiences.

Then the two of them quietened down and they began discussing the commercial prospects for New Hadock: securing the Amazon distribution centre had been the game-changer, several other big names were now planning to set up hubs, and there would be a branch facility for the DVLA. I began to lose track of the acronyms, and my mind strayed longingly to my overnight bag nestling in Ethel's boot.

For some reason, Hotspur's words to Glendower floated into my head and then onto my lips:

'But will they come when you do call for them?'

They looked at me as if I was mad.

'How do you mean, Dickie?'

'These people from Gormley, or wherever, will they really come all this way south to a new town that isn't even half built?'

'There'll be the firm offer of a job and guaranteed accommodation for two years. They'll come all right.'

'But what sort of reception will they get, from the locals, I mean?'

'Oh, that shower,' said Marchbanks. 'They'll simmer down, you wait, then they'll be the first in the queue for the jobs. They won't even remember the pitchforks.'

'Teething troubles, Dickie, with every new baby there are teething troubles.'

I at least was not destined to forget the morning's events. By the time we limped back to the front gate of

RAF Hadock, the demo had dispersed. Unfortunately Ethel had not had time to lock his car, and one demonstrator had opened the boot and poured the stuff they use to lay trails for drag hunts all over my overnight bag but missed Ethel's which was neatly stowed behind the front seat. Every time I pack to go away, I can still smell RAF Hadock.

14

Lost and Found

Looking back, I think it was better that I wasn't there when it happened. If you are going to be useless, you might as well be useless at a distance. But I still remember as if it were yesterday the shock of sadness when I heard.

Jane is not one for preambles. She has had to give too many people too much bad news over the years to be under the illusion that the slow build-up really softens the blow. The reverse, if anything. The heart's strings are strung even tighter by the wait.

'I'm afraid she's losing the baby.'

'Oh no. Are you sure?'

'Bleeding this heavy can only mean one thing, I remember that much from my GP days. I've rung Dr Spring. As you know, I'm a strong believer in getting an outsider in – well, that is the rule after all, when it's practical.'

I was not going to argue, though I thought Flo might have preferred her mother on her own.

'Yes, do come back if you can, but there's no need to rush. It will only upset you to see her in this state.'

I picked up my coat and put my head round Gloria's door to explain why I was leaving. I was sure her sympathy was genuine – she had such instinctive warmth – but her lips were so used to smiling that even when pursed in commiseration there was still a hint of merriment about them.

Getting born is never child's play, I knew that much. All the same, it had not occurred to me that this might happen to Flo. She was so robust, so sure in herself. I longed to see her now but dreaded it at the same time.

She was crying bitterly, her head almost lost in the pillow, but she flung out an arm and curled it round my neck as I stammered out my regrets. I sat on her bed and held her hand, and then wondered when or even if I should raise the question of letting Ethel know, but said nothing. We sat there like this for about five minutes. Then she raised her head and said in a drowsy, still weeping voice, 'You'd better tell him, Dad.'

I said I would, rather hurriedly, because at that moment I heard a knock at the front door and went down to answer it, expecting Dr Spring.

Standing on the doorstep was Kaylee holding an enormous bunch of autumn flowers, chrysanthemums and Michaelmas daisies mostly.

'For Flo, in deepest sympathy from Ethel and Gloria and all of us at Smothers,' he recited in solemn tones.

'You must have come like the wind, Kaylee.'

'Thirty-three minutes door to door, you can't beat the blades.'

Even in this gesture of sympathy, which touched me, there was an assertion of mastery. Ethel seemed to be on top of the script while it was still being written. Then he seemed to know the right moment to phone, half an hour later, when her grief had gone below the surface for the moment and she had agreed to a cup of tea and a Welsh cake.

They talked for quite a while, twelve minutes by my watch – I'm not sure why I timed the call, as though knowing the length might help. Even from downstairs I could hear her crying during part of the conversation, but then it all went quiet and I guessed she was being comforted. I went upstairs with the teapot but she only said, 'No thanks,' and when she saw my enquiring look, 'He was very kind, Dad, I really don't want to talk about it.'

My mooching about the house and watching her every move was obviously going to do her no good at all, so I went back to what passed for my normal schedule, while Jane took Flo shopping and in the evenings she and Lucy played piquet again as they had in the old days. In their usual see-saw relationship, Lucy blossomed in her role as her sister's comforter. If you had met Lucy then for the first time, you would have been amazed to hear that Jane and I had ever worried about her. She was so thoughtful and so cheerful, without jarring at all on Flo's sadness. With fingers crossed, we even dared to hope that she might be growing out of the fits too. But Flo was still so sad.

'How is she?' Ethel rang me five days later. 'She's so brave and it's such a ghastly thing.'

'Oh it is,' I said. 'We like to think she's coming through, but then I expect parents always try to think that.'

'That's great to hear, Dickie. You must give her all my love. While I'm on the line, I'd just like to say a couple of things on the other subject, if you don't mind.'

'Say away.'

'As I think I made clear at the time, our little trip to the north was strictly under cover. Negotiations on all fronts were at a delicate stage then and they still aren't firmed up.'

'Understood, totally.'

'I would be especially grateful if you said nothing about Gormley to anyone.'

'Gormley? I didn't know there was trouble up there too.'

'I wouldn't call it trouble exactly –' said Ethel, nettled by my rather breezy tone – 'but we do have intelligence that there is a so-called Gormley Defence League being formed, with several rather disquieting figures behind it. You remember Jason Brotherton?'

'Wasn't he …?'

'Britain First originally, then the English Defence League. Turns out he was born in Gormley, and he's chummed up with the last person you'd expect him to have anything in common with, Todd O'Hara of the Lancashire Workers Party. They were on opposite sides in the Burnley race riots, but now they're in total solidarity. Just the usual suspects, you may say, but you wouldn't want to give them anything they can get their teeth into. Christian B is utterly discreet, but he can't help leaving a paper trail behind him.'

Ethel sounded confident enough that the project could weather these early squalls. As a measure of his confidence, he was busy recruiting locators for other run-down towns, and Making Nice was being commissioned to set up focus groups in some of these benighted spots which would prove how eager people were to move to pastures new if they were given the chance. The place was humming in fact, and so I was taken aback when an email popped up on my screen saying that Osmotherley House would be closed for refurbishment during the following week.

'I didn't hear anything about a refurb.'

'Oh, just a couple of things that need fixing, darling, and this seems like a convenient time,' Gloria said, scarcely bothering to look up from her screen.

The break was fine by me. I was eager to spend more time with Flo, now that she seemed to be through the worst. We went for gentle walks in the park, the same park where Ethel had picked me up and inveigled me into this whole malarkey.

It was a peaceful autumn interlude and as the weeks went by I began to feel more hopeful about things, about Flo most of all. Then in a flash everything changed. Overnight, Flo was racked by sobs again, wouldn't speak, wouldn't eat, wouldn't leave her room. Jane told me that sometimes the grief could come back several weeks after the actual miscarriage, and worse than before as the irretrievable loss finally sank in, but she did not sound convinced.

In these racking days, the last thing I expected to see was that cursive flowery script blooming all over my inbox again. But there it was:

From the Boudoir of Betsy, Marquise de Broadlee:

Remember me? The Data Doll from Dullsville, Alabama? You'll never guess where I have landed up. In the Madame de Maintenon Suite at the Château de Fontenelle, that's where, and my personal chambermaid is just bringing me my hot chocolate in the dearest little Sèvres cup and saucer with a heap of those madeleines that Marcel raved about. After I have made my leisurely toilette, I shall saunter down to the pool where the Clooneys are expected presently and Mick (Jagger – need you ask?) may well pop over later from his château which is only a few kilometres over the colline. And what brings me to this abode of luxe et volupté? (You didn't know I majored in French lit at George Wallace High?) Well, you certainly ought to know the answer, because the question that hovers on my lips after I have wiped them with the delicate lace napkin provided – oh, that chocolate was so delicious – is: why the hell aren't you here, Dickie dearest? It's the wedding party of the year, and the ravishing groom is your closest colleague and buddy – he's still wearing that golden jacket, it really ought to go to the cleaner's – and I understand that you've been pretty much hot-desking with his lovely bride. Of course I asked Ethan when you were arriving – we Alabama girls never hold back – and he just said you couldn't make it, leaving me with the distinct impression that you turned it down. What a pity if so, because we could have had a ball together, a bal masqué to be precise, which is what is on the tapis for this evening's entertainment with music provided by the Hot Pickles who they've flown over from LA for the gig.

But underneath the razz, they're really such a homey couple. Gloria tells me that in fact they've been together for ten years now, but they've never found the time to have a proper wedding. So you managed an improper one, I shrilled! And she gave that gorgeous laugh she has and said, yes, we did go through a ceremony of sorts, but we didn't make much noise about it because I wasn't properly divorced from my ex at the time. Oh bigamy, I said, I just love it. And we became the bestest friends.

It was her idea apparently to have the messenger boys from your office dress up as eighteenth-century pages. They *look so cute and them being mostly coloured makes them just like those blackamoor torchères when they carry the candles out to the pool.*

But hey, hold the front page, I fear that I may have given the wrong impression, not for the first time — Betsy Broadlee Inc., Wrong Impressions a Specialty. From the warm temper of this missive, you may be thinking that there exists a vacancy beside me in this handsome Louis XV four-poster. This is not the case, for I Am Not Alone.

You'll never guess who my beau du jour is. Well, I suppose you might, for you are a man of fertile imagination. I am in fact being squired on this trip by none other than Senator Jerry S. Faldo — whom you may remember better as Little Jerry Lightweight, although as I have frequently pointed out, he is an inch taller than Winston Churchill was. But of course we do not refer back to such matters, any more than we recall any of the disobliging remarks I may have made about the Senator in the heat of the campaign, and I would be obliged if you didn't either. He's a dear really, and I knew it the moment we met on Hank Kraus's yacht in New York Harbor all those years ago, it being Hank Kraus's yacht being another thing we do not mention, owing to him still being in the cooler. Who knows where this romance will end, but if we reach anchorage, I do hope you will come by some day and tie up your sloop alongside.

Ever your old copain

Betsy

PS Did you really turn down the invite? I just cannot believe it.

'Oh, Flo knows about Gloria. Well, she knows now,' Jane said. 'He told her before he left for France. That's why she's like she is.'

'But before, did she have any idea before?'

'Not a clue. She thought they were old friends, who might perhaps have had a thing years ago. But the depth of it, that it was still going on, no, she had no idea. And you?'

I thought back to the first time I had seen them together, driving away from our local park in the old scarlet Merc convertible, and I shook my head. 'I suppose I should have guessed something. But they seemed so casual together, not intimate, so, no I didn't.'

'Casual is what Ethel does, so nobody ever thinks he's serious because he isn't. That's how he gets away with such terrible things.'

She paused for a moment, then cleared her throat in an odd formal way.

'I suppose this is the moment to tell you,' she said. 'I promised myself I never would because it would upset you too much, probably more than it upset me at the time, which was quite a lot. But I might as well get it out and be done with it.'

'What are you talking about?'

So she told me. Curiously, even now, I find it hard to write down in direct speech, it's still surprisingly raw. What she said in essence was this: she reminded me that once Ethel had said that he would love to come and talk to her about the genetic causes of cancer, which was her special subject and which he had an amateurish interest in, as he had in all sorts of scientific topics, usually the ones you read about in newspapers. And I said, yes, I did remember him saying this and thought no more about it, assuming that it was one of those things that had caught his fancy but which he hadn't followed up.

But he had. They had exchanged several emails on the subject, and he turned out to have read a couple of the leading authorities quite carefully, which impressed her. And then he referred, again quite knowledgeably, obviously having read it, to the paper she had published in the *Lancet* a few years ago on possible hereditary influences in colon cancer, and she was flattered. She hadn't really had the time to publish much, what with her clinical duties and bringing up the girls. So then he said, could he come and have a talk with her, and she couldn't see any harm in it, because his interest was so clearly genuine. So he came round to our house when I was away in West Africa and Flo was off on an astroturf assignment and Lucy was at school.

'He didn't?' I broke out.

She nodded.

'Not just come round, I mean?'

She nodded again. She couldn't believe at first that he was putting his arm round her, or thought that perhaps this was the way he behaved to everyone. But then he started kissing her, and she really had to fight him off, because he obviously thought at first that she was just being flirtatious, and so she had to hit him as hard as she could to make him stop, somewhere on the neck she thought, and then he did stop and he got up and said he had better be going, and she said he better had. By the time he got to the door, though, he was more or less back on top of things, and he said he was sorry he had misread her signals and she said there were no signals – no bloody signals, in fact she said – and slammed the door on him.

'So was this before or after he and Flo –'

'I can't believe you're asking that. During of course — that was the whole point of it, you can see what pleasure it would give him, mother and daughter at the same time.'

I was ashamed of having asked the question, and I now want to move on briskly to what happened next, which was simple and imperative. No, not what happened next, what I did next. There was exhilaration as well as anger in my programme: resignation first, then revenge.

Within the hour, I had made the formal arrangements: a letter of resignation from Making Nice, addressed to the MD, Ms Gloria Wormsley; then another letter of resignation to the Rt Hon. Bryce Wincott MP. I emailed the Wingco, intending to warn him and explain that in the circumstances I felt I could no longer carry on with the book, but got an out-of-office about him being in France.

'But what will you do instead?' Jane was calm again now, her usual self, outwardly at least.

'I'll train as a teacher and live off your earnings until I'm qualified.' It was the first thing that came into my head.

'You're too old,' she said. Definitely her usual self.

'Thank you,' I said and went to get my coat.

'Where are you going?'

'To make a phone call and then catch a train. You'll see, everything will be fine.'

'Even Flo?'

'Flo will be fine. And we'll be fine.'

The next thing I did in what I afterwards thought of as my Hour of Decision was to ring Thelma Wincott. I had carefully kept her details, somehow divining that she and I were not yet done with each other.

Thelma greeted my proposal that I should pop down for a quick visit with an unseemly cackle. 'I knew you'd be back,' she said. 'I'll be ready for you.'

She meant more by that than I could have hoped.

Two hours later when I knocked on her door in the little not-quite-seaside close, she had the tea things and the cake she hadn't baked out on the table, and sitting on her sofa was a skinny, weathered-looking man in jeans, aged about fifty, who got up awkwardly as Thelma led me into the room.

'This,' she said with the air of one showing off a hidden treasure, 'is my friend Fizzy Simmons.'

'Thelma's always been very good to me,' he said after we had shaken hands, 'from the days when Bry and I used to come down from the office for a seaside jaunt, and then she stuck by me all through my trouble. And when I came out, she set me up in the gardening business.'

'Fizzy's a first-rate gardener,' Thelma said, 'he's got the touch, you can always tell.'

'So I come and do a bit in her backyard now and then, and when she said you were coming round I really wanted to meet you. Old Bry having a whole book written about him, who'd have thought it?'

He must once have been handsome in a gaunt and sallow way, but his face was too lined now to be anything but sad.

'Oh yes,' he said, 'we were in it together, you couldn't not be. What that woman didn't realise, the one he married, Helen, or pretended not to anyway, was that we worked in pairs because the contracts all had to be countersigned. If you were faking them, you had to fake two invoices. When the shit hit the fan, we agreed to stick together, but Bryce didn't, because he could see a way out for him but not for me. He still had the money sitting in his account at the bank, because he hadn't yet summoned up the courage to wash it through, so he could pretend it was all a clerical error, and that's what saved him, that and Helen turning a blind eye because she fancied him.'

'That's really fascinating, Fizzy, and would you be prepared to –'

'Of course, it's all water under the bridge now, isn't it?'

'Sometimes it may be possible to make water flow backwards, Fizzy.'

'I like that idea, Dickie, I like that very much.'

Helen, I thought, had not been wrong in describing Fizzy as a nasty piece of work, which was just what I needed, as I was joining the club myself. Thelma looked on benignly. It was still a shock to realise quite how much she disliked her son.

I thought that my old friend Simon Redditch would be the best man to handle the story. He jumped at it. 'Leave it with me, dear boy,' he murmured in his inimitable Balkan brogue. Within a couple of days he had all the names, dates and figures from Fizzy, who was delighted to receive what I thought was a rather modest fee for his help, but which Si insisted was the going rate in these straitened times.

'And, Si,' I said when I had fed him a few extra useful pieces of information, 'there's something else I would be really grateful for your help with in return.'

'Anything, dear boy. This is such wonderful material.'

'Would it be possible, do you think, to find out anything about a couple who defected from the GDR in the 1980s? I believe they came over with the East German ice hockey team to some tournament in London.'

'I think I vaguely remember the case, though I must have been at school at the time. Should be a piece of cake. That's the wonderful thing about the Stasi. Like the British Raj, they wrote everything down.'

As soon as the Wincott story broke, Bryce instructed his solicitors to issue a writ against the paper, but he never stood a chance. The documentation was too overwhelming. Fizzy had kept hard copies of all the dockets and internal memos involving Bryce which Helen had managed to have excluded from Fizzy's trial. Worse still, the only possible witness for the defence was the woman Bryce had subsequently married. There were already several cases of sleaze hanging over the government, and the Whips were not prepared to let this one fester a minute longer than necessary. Bryce was dragged out, protesting his innocence but obediently repeating the formula that he did not wish to be a distraction for the government at such a crucial stage in its groundbreaking programme of reform, or he may have said world-beating.

'I can't thank you enough,' Si cooed over the phone. 'I've never had an easier scoop to bring in. Oh, and that other matter you asked me about, that looks rather like buried treasure too.'

'I thought there might be more to it,' I said gleefully.

'The way the story was presented in the media at the time, and there wasn't that much coverage really, was that Rudi and Maria Everstein had simply seen the light about the GDR, and had manoeuvred themselves into positions of trust which gave them the chance to defect. But it wasn't like that, according to the East German files, and I'm sure the MI6 dossier would confirm it if we were allowed access. What really happened was that the Eversteins were deliberately placed with the ice hockey team so they could keep an eye on the players during their travels. They were accredited Stasi operatives, not political innocents.'

'Aha,' I said. It's not a word I'm accustomed to using, but this did seem like an Aha moment.

'But that's not the end of it. What we don't know for sure, what the files don't tell us, is whether their defection represented a genuine change of heart or whether they were in reality being deployed as bait for our own Secret Service, with instructions to carry on as double agents. They were a curious couple in any case. Apart from ice skating, which he really was a whizz at, Rudi was obsessed with the idea that he was descended from this ancient noble family in Pomerania, so much so that the Stasi took the trouble to look into it, thinking that he might perhaps be working for some deluded counter-revolutionary group of monarchists, but they found that Rudi's family was of really quite modest origins, farm managers and bailiffs, that sort of thing, and they had just taken the name of their feudal overlord, which apparently quite a lot of people did at the time when this law came in saying you had to have a surname for the records. The truth is that the Eversteins remain a bit of mystery and I need to do a bit more digging. But what I could do in the meantime, if it would help, would be to mark the card of a bright chap I know in the Cabinet Office who would know what to do with the thought.'

'I like the sound of that,' I said.

Si, as brisk as ever, was back to me within ten days.

'Apparently my chap managed to get a word with the Permanent Secretary, the one they call the Mekon, and I understand that partly as a result of their conversation your friend will shortly be leaving the Civil Service and taking up a senior position in California, with Breaking – apparently it's the new rival to Google. The difficulty was not of course that Mr Everstein was found to have acted improperly in any way, but now that his minister had departed, it would be difficult to find another Special Adviser slot for him, particularly with this security clearance problem which might take some time to resolve.'

'Thank you,' I said.

In any case, the whole Locator project had run into terminal trouble. The property deal with George Marchbanks sounded decidedly iffy when the details were disclosed, enough to provoke the headline 'THIS HADOCK SMELLS FISHY' in the *Daily Mail*. Meanwhile, up in Lancashire, Christian Blankers was alleged to have resorted to some complicated sort of tax fraud, in order to stave off the ever-growing threat that the Internet was now posing to his stores, and he had started to sell off his landholdings. The wolves never left Poland. Besides, the government had reached that stage which most governments reach, when its brightest ambitions have faded and mere survival is as much as can be hoped for. So old Gormley was left to moulder on, and New Hadock remained a mournful wasteland of cracked tarmac and decayed scraps of sugar beet.

But Ethel was long gone, flown back to the ethereal realm which was his natural habitat, a globe-girdling Puck who never belonged with us earthlings. I don't believe that bit at the end of the play when Puck comes forward to the audience and says the whole thing was just a dream and he never meant any of the bad stuff. To be fair to Ethel, though he always explained, he never apologised, except when he was trying to get something out of you.

I looked out of the window of my little room at the top of the house, and saw Jane deadheading at the end of the garden in her baseball cap, while Flo was practising her ballet stretches on the lawn, with Lucy behind her mimicking her movements. The Royal said she could start with them next term if she felt ready. She was going back once more to the Demetrios, to dance at the gala to celebrate Sir Giorgios's well-deserved knighthood. Unfortunately, to his great annoyance, the honours list in which Giorgios appeared was elbowed out of the headlines by the first prosecutions in the scandal of sex trafficking in the big international charities. Among the high-profile officials indicted was William de Lillo Jr, now of the World Health Organization.

I turned back to *Basic Teaching Materials for Graduate Students: No. 17 – The English Novel*, and resumed reading the passage about the Unreliable Narrator. No, I thought, that's not me, I've moved on to the next stage: the Unpleasant Narrator. But nobody seemed to have written about him. Revenge really is so sweet, though it's not supposed to be. What they don't tell you is that you are never quite the same after you've had it.

It was a month or two since I'd heard from Si Redditch, and I was quite surprised when I heard his memorable hiss over the phone.

'Correction,' he said, 'in fact, major correction. You remember that ice hockey couple you asked me about?'

'Of course I do.'

'Well, a spook I know, or used to know, he's semi-retired now, not that they ever retire completely, not the one I talked to first, this one's rather higher up or used to be, and he tells me that they were ours all along. Apparently the Stasi had fixed it for them to come over with the ice hockey team, on the understanding that they would act as double agents after they defected, which was all prearranged.'

'Wasn't that more or less what the other chap told you?'

'Except that the control in the Stasi was a mole, and the Everses were only going to feed them back stuff we wanted them to have.'

'So in fact they were triple agents?'

'You are quick, Dickie. Have you ever thought about a career in SIS? The only thing is why would Tweetie, Terence always known as Tweetie, why exactly would he be telling me all this? Volunteering it, in fact. We had been talking about something quite different when he came out with it, as though it was a message he had to deliver.'

'To set the record straight? Make our spies look better than theirs?'

'But how did he know the record was crooked? I should add that Tweetie never told me a thing I could use before. Strange, but there you are. I'll keep you posted if I hear anything more.'

Later, much later, eighteen months or more, I was sitting on this little pretend terrace outside the staffroom, just a square of scuffed Astroturf which made me think of Making Nice, cradling my coffee and watching Year Ten mucking about in their break. When I had finished my coffee, I went inside to return the cup to Sadie. Someone had turned on the little TV in the corner for the midday news and I lingered idly to see what was happening.

And there he was, striding along Downing Street with a pretty girl scurrying along behind him half buried under a bundle of folders. He was wearing a powder-blue t'ai chi tunic, and powder-blue leggings to match, but the parrot's quiff was the same as ever. '… former CEO of Breaking jets in from LA to take over as Chief of Communications at Number Ten.' As he passed the cameras, he stopped and turned to face the photographers and gave a vigorous karate chop in their direction. Then he stalked on in a rather resentful way as if it was the photographers' fault for making him late. The pretty girl laughed and scurried on after him, still laughing.

The End

Thanks

I am especially grateful to Mary Mount for her brilliantly perceptive comments and to Katherine Fry for her acute and rigorous copyediting. I am also delighted to thank everyone at Bloomsbury for getting this book airborne, in particular to Robin Baird-Smith, Jamie Birkett and Nigel Newton.

In exploring the data minefields, I have learned a great deal from Tom Baldwin's *Ctrl Alt Delete*, from Brittany Kaiser's *Targeted* and from Christopher Wylie's *Mindf*ck*.

For the true history of the Pied Piper and his descendants, I have relied on Professor Radu Florescu's *In Search of the Pied Piper*, on Franz Kössler's *Die Nachfahren des Lokators* and on the numerous publications of Hans Dobbertin, especially *Der Auszug der Hamelschen Kinder*.

This book is dedicated to my fellow Wonks and Spads, who have so diverted me over the years.

Note on the Author

Ferdinand Mount is a novelist, essayist and former editor of the *Times Literary Supplement* between 1991 and 2002. He was previously head of the Number Ten Policy Unit under Margaret Thatcher. As a journalist, he has contributed regular columns to *The Spectator*, *Daily Telegraph* and *Sunday Times*. His previous books include *Of Love and Asthma*, winner of the 1992 Hawthornden Prize, and two bestselling memoirs published by Bloomsbury, *Cold Cream* and *Kiss Myself Goodbye*.